Entwined Publishing books by Zoe Normandie

Unbreakable Heroes
Under Control
Under Pressure
Under Fire

Secret Service
His American Oath

Secret Service

HIS AMERICAN OATH

ZOE NORMANDIE

ENTWINED PUBLISHING

His American Oath
ISBN # 978-1-80250-240-4
©Copyright Zoe Normandie 2025
Cover Art by Artist ©Copyright January 2025
Interior text design by Entwined Publishing
Published by Entice, an Entwined Publishing imprint

Published in 2025 by Entwined Publishing, United Kingdom.

Entwined Publishing is a division of Totally Entwined Group Limited.

HIS AMERICAN OATH

Chapter One

Washington, DC

The Oval Office was unnervingly quiet, the weight of history pressing down on Caleb Knight as he stood at rigid attention. The words of the oath fell from his lips with practiced precision, each syllable as steady and unyielding as he was.

"...to protect the President of the United States, against all threats, foreign and domestic..."

Caleb's voice was low and even, carrying a conviction honed over years of military discipline. This was his purpose now — protecting not just the person but the institution itself. The duty felt heavier than any mission he'd taken as an Army Ranger, and that was saying something.

When the final word left his mouth, the room seemed to hold its breath for a moment before the agent administering the oath nodded in approval. "Welcome to the detail, Agent Knight."

Caleb simply returned the nod, maintaining his unreadable expression.

The door to the Oval Office opened just as Caleb stepped back, and in walked a woman who carried the kind of energy that made everyone else seem like background noise. Grace Williams, the president's lead strategist.

She was tall and poised, her navy blazer sharp and tailored, her brown hair pulled back into a sleek ponytail that screamed control. Her heels clicked against the polished floor as she strode in, respectfully greeting the president. Then her gaze flicked to Caleb as if she were assessing him in a single glance.

"Is this the new bodyguard?" Grace's voice was calm but laced with the faintest edge of impatience. She didn't waste time on pleasantries.

"Yes, ma'am," the agent beside Caleb answered. "Agent Caleb Knight, newly assigned to Presidential detail."

Her almond-shaped eyes narrowed as her gaze swept over him, lingering just a moment longer than polite. Caleb met her gaze, his expression giving away nothing. He'd never met a woman with those ice blue husky eyes before — intense and stunning.

"Right," she said, before turning her attention to the Chief of Staff waiting behind her.

Caleb's jaw tightened. He didn't need her approval, and the brusque dismissal rubbed him the wrong way. But he was here to do a job, not make friends.

As Grace spoke to the Chief of Staff about the upcoming campaign strategy meeting, Caleb allowed himself a moment to study her. Her movements were precise, her tone commanding but not overbearing. She was someone who expected things done her way and had little patience for anything — or anyone — that got in the way.

She reminded him of the officers he used to work with, the ones who prioritized results above all else. The ones who thought they were invincible until the bullets started flying.

Grace caught him watching and raised a perfectly arched brow. "Something wrong, Agent Knight?"

"No, ma'am," Caleb replied, his expression neutral. "Just getting familiar with the team."

"Good," she said, her tone clipped. "Because things move fast around here, and we don't have time for slow learners."

With that, she turned on her heel and walked toward the Resolute Desk, already diving into a stack of briefing documents.

"This afternoon — meeting with Senator Chalney at the House. We need to go over the immigration plan again. This is key for the election."

Caleb exhaled quietly through his nose, his frustration buried beneath layers of discipline. He'd faced far worse than an overbearing strategist. But as he watched her command the room, part of him couldn't shake the feeling that Grace Williams would be a complication he hadn't anticipated.

And he hated complications.

"I wouldn't just walk over," Wyatt interrupted. "Unfortunately, there's a protest being staged. They'd love a piece of meat to sink into."

"Agent Knight," the president said, breaking Caleb's focus, "get Williams to the House. We have one month left in this election. I don't want to find a new strategist."

Caleb's gaze flickered back to Grace. She didn't even look up from her conversation. He could feel the tension between them already. She didn't need protection. She didn't want protection. She probably thought she could handle herself just fine. And from the look of it, she didn't give a damn about what Caleb was there to do.

"I'll make sure she gets there," Caleb replied, his voice flat, eyes already scanning the exits.

"Good," the president added, as if reading Caleb's mind.

Caleb didn't need a second explanation. He understood his job, loud and clear. He didn't need to make friends. He didn't need to like anyone. He just needed to protect them. That was his job. Simple.

But as he caught Grace's eyes for a split second across the room, he saw the calculation there. She wasn't looking at him the way people looked at a protector. She was sizing him up — assessing the threat. Assessing whether he would slow her down.

He had no doubt in his mind. She didn't need him. She didn't want him.

"Ms. Williams," Caleb said, stepping closer to her after the meeting broke up.

She didn't respond right away. She was busy giving instructions to her team, her voice firm, unwavering. The way she spoke, the way she carried herself — everything about her screamed power. The whole room was drawn to her. But Caleb wasn't looking for power. He was looking for something else.

"I'll be your detail," Caleb said, his tone matter-of-fact, watching her reaction.

Grace didn't even acknowledge the seriousness of his words at first. Instead, she just raised an eyebrow. "Got it," she said flatly. "Just stay far back."

She wasn't hostile, but there was a cool dismissal in her words. She didn't have time for him. She didn't have time for anyone who wasn't helping her push forward. And Caleb could tell, she wasn't going to make this easy.

"I'm here to make sure you stay safe," Caleb said, not backing down.

"I'm more than capable of handling myself," Grace replied, barely sparing him a second glance. She adjusted her blazer and turned back to her strategists.

Caleb stood there for a beat longer, frustrated. It wasn't the first time he had dealt with people who thought they could do it all without help. But Grace Williams wasn't just anyone. She was smart, driven, and ruthless in her ambition. She didn't want him there, but that didn't matter. It wasn't about what she wanted. It was about duty.

"You don't get it," Caleb muttered under his breath.

"What was that?" Grace asked, turning back to him for the first time. She'd heard him, and now she was looking at him. Really looking at him.

"I said, it's not about what you want. I'm here to protect you. That's my job. Deal with it."

Her lips twitched into a barely there smile, but it wasn't one of appreciation. It was a smile of someone who knew she was in control.

"Fine. But don't expect me to slow down because of you." Grace's eyes flickered over him one last time before she turned her attention back to her team. "We have little time left. Let's go."

And with that, she was gone—leaving Caleb standing there, feeling the weight of the disconnect between them. It sure as hell didn't feel good to be written off before he'd even had a chance to do his job.

Caleb kept his distance, following her to the parkade, doing his job the only way he knew how—quietly, efficiently, without unnecessary interaction.

Caleb had been through wars. He had seen things that would make most people crack. But he saw pretty damn quickly that Grace Williams was a different kind of battlefield. She wasn't afraid of the dangers. She wasn't afraid of the threats.

But she should be.

Caleb's boots thudded against the pavement as he followed Grace through the underground to the armored SUV, his patience wearing thinner with every second. She was like a storm, relentless and unyielding. Every step she took screamed defiance, every glance she shot his way daring him to push back.

But this wasn't a fight Caleb was willing to lose.

He opened the door for her without a word, his jaw set, his eyes scanning their surroundings. The evening air was thick with the lingering energy of the rally, and though most of the crowd had dispersed, Caleb didn't like the feel of the city tonight. Too many blind spots, too many chances for something to go wrong.

Grace didn't say thank you—she didn't even glance his way. She climbed into the backseat with her phone already pressed to her ear, her voice sharp as she rattled off directives to her team. Caleb climbed into the driver's seat and adjusted the rearview mirror, catching her reflection for a split second.

"You ready?" he asked, betraying none of the irritation simmering beneath his surface.

Grace ended her call, her eyes locking on his in the mirror. "Just drive."

He clenched his teeth but didn't argue. The engine growled to life, and he eased the SUV onto the main road, the silence between them heavy and charged.

The drive wasn't long—ten minutes, maybe twenty with the protest—but it felt like hours. Grace tapped away on her phone, ignoring him, while Caleb kept his focus on the road, his senses heightened. Every intersection, every passing car, every shadow warranted a second glance.

When they reached the House, Caleb pulled into the private garage, shutting off the engine. He opened his door, launching out to assess their surroundings before opening Grace's door.

"We're here," he said.

She stepped out, the sound of her heels echoed sharply against the concrete., her attention still glued to her phone. Caleb's eyes swept the area once more before falling back to her.

"You're going straight to your meeting," he said, stepping into her path. "No stops, no detours."

Grace's eyes flicked up from her phone, her expression incredulous. "Excuse me?"

"You heard me."

Her lips pressed into a tight line as she tilted her head, studying him like he was some kind of puzzle. "Agent Knight," she said, her tone dripping with sarcasm, "I wasn't aware I needed your permission to move about freely."

"You don't," Caleb replied. "But I've got my orders, and if you think I'm letting you cruise around in this climate, you're mistaken."

For a moment, she didn't respond. Then, to his utter surprise, she let out a sharp laugh—cold, humorless, and biting.

"You really take this whole protector thing seriously, don't you?" she said. "Newsflash, buddy—I don't need saving. I don't need you."

Her words hit harder than he wanted to admit, but he didn't let it show. Instead, he fell into step behind her, his eyes scanning the path ahead. "You might not need me," he said, his voice low enough that only she could hear, "but someone out there wants this president to drop dead before he gets re-elected. And that's extending to anyone helping him. So until I know for sure you're safe, you're stuck with me."

Grace froze mid-step, her shoulders stiffening. She turned, her eyes narrowing as they locked onto his. For the first time, Caleb saw something there—something beneath the layers of confidence and defiance. Fear, maybe. Or doubt.

"Fine," she said, her voice quieter now. "But don't get comfortable. This isn't permanent."

Caleb nodded. "Wasn't planning on it."

As they walked toward the elevator, the tension between them settled into something heavier.

But as the elevator doors slid shut, trapping them in a small, silent space together, he couldn't ignore the way Grace's presence filled the air around him. Strong. Unrelenting. And for the first time, just a little bit vulnerable.

He didn't say anything. He didn't need to.

Chapter Two

It was a cool October morning. The DC campaign war room was a hive of activity. Less than four weeks left before the election — and the clock was ticking.

Grace Williams sat at the head of the table, elbows propped up on the edge, her laptop open and glowing with data. The room was cluttered with strategy maps, polling reports, and team members pacing back and forth as they fine-tuned the approach for the next round of battleground states. Grace was in her element, sharp and unyielding. There was no room for hesitation, no time for fluff. Every minute mattered, and she wasn't about to waste any of them.

"Ohio's slipping," Jordan Simmons muttered, his eyes glued to his tablet screen. "But Pennsylvania's holding steady. If we—"

"Push a last-minute ad buy in Cleveland and double down on canvassing in Pittsburgh," Grace interrupted without looking up, already calculating the moves in her mind. "We saturate both markets. We get boots on the ground and start dialing in those voters. I don't care if it's a holiday. We're pushing forward, no more second-guessing."

Jordan nodded, firing off a series of emails to his team. Grace could already tell that he was one of the few people who understood the stakes as well as she did—no nonsense, no time for games. They were on the same wavelength, and it made everything easier.

Before she could push forward with more ideas, the door to the war room slammed open, jolting her attention from the data. Wyatt Steele, her boss, stood in the doorway, his posture rigid. He was followed by Caleb Knight, a hulking figure whose presence filled the room like a storm cloud.

Grace didn't bother with the pleasantries. She had enough on her plate. "Whatever this is, make it fast," she said, her fingers still flying across the keyboard.

Wyatt stepped forward. "We've got a security problem. One you can't afford to ignore."

Grace didn't flinch. "We're restructuring Pennsylvania's ground game right now. Can this wait?"

"It can't." Caleb stepped into her line of sight, his eyes unwavering. "You need to watch your tactics. Things are getting too heated out there."

Grace's mind immediately raced to calculate what this meant for the campaign. "And what's new?" She didn't have time for paranoia, and Caleb's imposing presence wasn't helping her focus.

Wyatt nodded, his face grim. "People are getting crazy. We've seen more social justice warriors with weapons. We're escalating protection immediately."

"That's your job," Grace said, barely looking up from her laptop. "Our job is getting Armstrong re-elected. I don't have time for this." She didn't mean to sound bitchy, but she couldn't afford to be distracted. The election was her focus—nothing else.

Jordan sighed, clearly frustrated but not surprised. He leaned back in his chair, rubbing his temples. "Wait, what? Are we seriously considering axing events for this?"

"This isn't negotiable," Wyatt cut in, raising his hand to silence the room. "We're not here to debate this, Grace. We've got a serious situation emerging, and you're going to have a full-time detail starting today. Caleb's going to be with you everywhere. Your safety is now a top priority."

Grace shot Wyatt a look that could've frozen him on the spot. "I'm not canceling events," she snapped. "I'm not rearranging my schedule for this, and I sure as hell don't need someone following me around."

She could feel Caleb staring at her — like a weight on her back. The silent judgment, the disapproval. It irritated her more than she wanted to admit.

Wyatt sighed. "Grace —"

"No," she interrupted, holding up a hand. "We're not making this bigger than it is." Her gaze flicked to Caleb, the man who'd somehow found his way into this mess. "Can I fire you?"

Caleb's gaze remained locked on hers, steady and unblinking. His presence was suffocating, the quiet intensity practically radiating off him. "It's not a matter of if something happens," Caleb said, calm but blunt, "it's a matter of when. And if you want to be around long enough to win this election, you're going to have to adjust."

Grace's jaw clenched, her temper flaring. "Let me be clear," she bit out. "Stay to the side. Shut your mouth. Stick to your job, and let me do mine."

Caleb didn't flinch. "I am doing my job. You might hate it, but you're stuck with me."

"We'll see about that."

The silence between them was thick with tension. Grace could feel the frustration building, her chest tightening with every word. There was something about Caleb's bluntness that rubbed her the wrong way. Maybe it was the fact that he wasn't intimidated by her, or that he seemed so sure of himself — like he knew something she didn't. But he didn't get it. She wasn't some delicate flower who needed protection.

Grace tried to look away, but she couldn't. It was like he had this gravitational pull, drawing her eyes back to him every time. His presence was infuriating — so damn commanding, like a force of nature, and she hated how effortlessly he had this effect on her.

His dark blond hair, a little too boyish, fell perfectly across his forehead in that messy yet deliberate way. She hated how it caught the light, how the warm, golden strands seemed to highlight everything about him — especially his eyes. Those eyes. A piercing green, intense and unreadable, as though he could see through her. And it was maddening. He was too good-looking, the kind of handsome that made her pulse stutter and her thoughts scatter.

His gaze was fixed on her, unflinching, like he knew exactly what he was doing to her. And it drove her insane. The connection between them was undeniable, but she hated that it was so raw — so real.

Her eyes drifted down to the broadness of his shoulders, the muscles of his chest straining against the fabric of his suit. She should have looked away, but she couldn't. The sight of him, so strong and powerful, made her feel like a coil wound too tightly. This was not helping.

Caleb was everything she should avoid — and everything she couldn't seem to resist.

"Fine," she snapped, pushing back from the table with a flourish. "But don't slow me down. I don't stop for anyone."

"Noted," Caleb replied, as if nothing she'd said had made a dent.

Wyatt clapped his hands together, clearly relieved that they hadn't turned this into a shouting match. "Good. Now that we're on the same page, we'll let you get back to it. Caleb, stay close."

As Wyatt and Caleb made their way to the door, Grace turned to Jordan, her frustration bubbling over. "Can you believe this? As if we don't have enough to do."

Jordan smirked, shaking his head. "At least he's easy on the eyes. Could be worse."

Grace shot him a look that could've burned through glass.

Jordan shrugged, unbothered by her lack of reply. "Maybe you'll both get what you want. Just try not to kill him before then."

Grace turned back to her laptop, her fingers tapping quickly over the keys, but despite herself, she couldn't shake the feeling of Caleb's presence lingering in the room. It was as if an invisible weight hung in the air, always just out of sight—his watchful gaze lingering even when he wasn't physically there. She hated the way it made her feel—like she was suddenly being scrutinized. She couldn't let him get under her skin, no matter how much he irritated her. This was business, nothing more.

But that didn't stop her mind from drifting to him as she worked. Caleb Knight was a mystery wrapped in a storm of contradictions. Dangerous. Unyielding. And maddeningly effective at his job. He might be focused on the security of a hundred staffers, but right now, she was more concerned about the political fight that would determine the future of this country—and she didn't need anyone getting in her way.

Still, a part of her wondered if this was the beginning of something else. Something she wasn't sure she was ready for.

November couldn't come soon enough.

* * * *

The ride back to her condo felt endless. The rhythmic hum of the engine and the occasional tap of Caleb's knuckles against the steering wheel did little to drown out the thoughts swirling in Grace's mind. The day had been a marathon—back-to-back meetings at the White House, campaign strategy sessions, speeches, endless logistics. And now, her exhausted body finally wanted to collapse, to shut off for a few hours before the madness started again.

But as they navigated the streets of DC toward her place, something else gnawed at her. She hadn't expected Caleb to drop her off. She hadn't expected him to show up at all, really—not after everything that had gone down that evening. She hadn't anticipated the closeness—the intimacy of him driving her home, the silent tension that seemed to hang in the air every time he glanced her way. She wasn't sure if it was exhaustion or something else, but she could feel it, deep in her gut, the crackling energy between them. Something unsaid. Something dangerous.

She glanced out of the window, the lights of the city flashing by in a blur. She could feel Caleb's gaze on her, even though he wasn't looking directly at her. His focus was always outward, always scanning, always aware of everything around him. Always in control.

She wasn't in control now.

"Here we are," Caleb said, his deep voice breaking through the silence as he pulled up in front of her building.

Grace's stomach tightened, the familiar tension creeping up again. She didn't want him to see her place—not like this, not after a day that had drained her of any pretense of put-togetherness. Her condo had always been a reflection of her work—cold, functional, a place to sleep and reset before diving back into the chaos of the campaign. Nothing more. Nothing personal.

She hated it.

"I can manage from here," she said, opening the door before Caleb could even shift the car into park. "Thanks for the ride."

Caleb didn't move. His jaw tightened as he watched her, and for a moment, it felt like the world had stopped. His eyes—those piercing blue eyes—met hers, and something unspoken passed between them. Something that made her heart race and her mind retreat into itself.

"You're not going to just disappear into your building after a day like today," Caleb said. "I'm coming up with you."

Grace froze. The command in his voice made her blood run cold.

"No," she said, her tone sharper than she'd intended. "I'm fine. Really. I just need to rest. I don't need you to—"

"I insist," Caleb interrupted, his voice firm, unyielding. "I've been responsible for your safety all day, Grace. You don't get to send me off now like this. You're not leaving me with no intel. I'm going to check out your place."

She could hear the logic in his words, the professionalism that underpinned everything he said and did. But she hated it. Hated the way he imposed himself on her life, the way his presence was always there — silent, watching, inescapable. He was everywhere.

She let out a frustrated breath and slammed the door shut behind her.

"Fine," she said through clenched teeth, the words leaving her mouth before she could stop them. "If it'll shut you up, then fine. Come on in. See for yourself."

They walked together up the steps to her building in a silence that felt too thick, too weighted. The glow of the streetlights outside did nothing to soften the tension between them. She kept her head down, focused on her steps, her pulse thumping in her ears.

When they reached her condo door, she turned the key and stepped inside, forcing herself to ignore the shiver of discomfort crawling up her spine as Caleb followed her in. She could feel his presence in the small entryway, and for the first time, she couldn't ignore how empty it all felt. The apartment was stark — sparse, with cold metal furniture and dark wood floors that only seemed to amplify the silence. There were no personal touches — no pictures, no knick-knacks, no signs of a life outside of work. It was functional, but it wasn't home.

"This is..." Caleb's voice trailed off as he stepped inside, taking in the bare walls, the lack of decoration. It wasn't disorganization, it was just emptiness.

"Yeah," she said, shrugging off her jacket and tossing it onto a chair. "This is it. Not much to see."

He didn't say anything, but she could feel his eyes on her — on the place, on her. He walked around, checking the rooms, windows, vents and doors. The only thing that seemed to stand out to him was her red dress—something fancy—hanging on the bathroom door.

"It's for the Presidential charity ball in New York." She sighed.

Caleb grinned. He reached out and felt the dress. She knew what he felt. It was soft and silky. Very unlike her.

He turned to her.

"Is this really all you need?" he asked quietly, his gaze settling on her in a way that made her skin prickle. "No pictures? No...personal life? I mean, you're twenty-eight."

"Twenty-eight?"

"I read your whole file."

"Well, how convenient. Any other questions, then? Let's get it out of the way. What's my favorite position?"

He stifled a snort. "What do you do when you're not playing political strategist?" he asked. "Or should I expect to only be following you to work."

His words hit harder than she expected, knocking into the wall she'd carefully built around herself. She didn't want to answer. Yes, she was a workaholic. Why did he need to know?

She didn't want to tell him about the emptiness that sat between the political battles she fought, the strategy sessions that consumed her days, and the moments she didn't know how to fill.

The silence had stretched. She fumbled to fill it.

"I don't have time for a life outside the campaign," she said flatly, crossing her arms over her chest in a defensive gesture. "I've got the president's re-election to manage. That's it."

Caleb raised an eyebrow. "No boyfriend? No family to go home to?"

"Why do you care?" The question hit Grace like a sharp pang in her chest, but she quickly masked it. "I'm saving that for after the election," she replied. The words felt empty, but she didn't want to admit to the loneliness that crept in at night when the campaign office was closed and the streets outside were silent. The loneliness she fought to ignore every day.

"No one in your life who can pull you out of the chaos for a second?"

She didn't answer. She couldn't. She didn't want him to see the truth, the vulnerability beneath her armor. She spoke again, her voice quieter, teasing even. "And, what about you—are you married? Or are you one of those guys who's married to the job?"

He blinked, caught off guard by the question. "That's...none of your business," he replied, as if trying to maintain his usual detached tone.

She shot him a sideways glance. "Ah. I see. You're good-looking, competent, and always serious. Someone must've snatched you up by now. If there wasn't something wrong underneath the hood."

He chuckled dryly, the sound surprising her. "I'm not... I don't think I've got the time for anyone." He didn't expand. "I don't really *do* relationships. And there is nothing wrong underneath the hood. I can assure you."

Grace raised an eyebrow, interested. "So you're single, then?"

Caleb shot her a look. "Stop."

She smirked, her gaze shifting to the window. "I don't know. I'd think someone like you might be hard to keep up with. All that...danger and focus. Must be exhausting."

"You'd be surprised," he said, the hint of a smile returning to his lips. She wasn't sure why he was talking to her like this, but it didn't feel wrong. It felt easy, in a way. He added, "Maybe you're the one who would be exhausting."

She was trying not to laugh. She shifted her weight, looking around the apartment like it might offer her some escape. "Can we just get this over with? I really should sleep."

Caleb stepped closer, a silent force of nature, but he didn't press. Not this time. He just looked at her, his gaze lingering for a moment longer than necessary.

Finally, he nodded. "I'll leave you to it. Just…stay safe. And if you need me, don't hesitate to reach out."

"Please, go home. I have to pack."

"Just remember — anywhere you go, I go."

"Then bring something nice. We've got a big event in New York on Friday. Before then, we have Georgia. A little small town. Rustic. Rough. You'll fit in there."

She nodded at the door and made a show of annoyance.

"Stay," he said, with the slightest semblance of a killer grin.

Grace nodded, her heart pounding in her chest as she watched him turn and leave. As the door clicked shut behind him, she allowed herself a breath. The silence was suffocating.

Chapter Three

Cobb County, Georgia. Swing state.

The rally was everything Grace had planned for. The crowd roared in approval, every cheer a testament to her calculated precision. The president was in his element—charismatic, commanding the stage with ease. He even wore the Georgia Kings basketball jersey in honor of the venue hosting them. The energy inside the court was palpable, building like a thunderstorm on the horizon. But Grace knew this wasn't enough. Not anymore.

The stakes were too high. Georgia was more than just a swing state—it was *the* state. Winning it would be a statement, the momentum the campaign so desperately needed. She could feel it in the air, the tension thick with potential.

She pushed through the crowd of staffers and security, her eyes scanning for any opportunity, any opening to make the next bold move.

Then she saw him.

Caleb stood across the court, his figure imposing, a silent sentinel in the crowd. Every inch of him radiated control, from the rigid posture to the unflinching focus in his eyes as he scanned the room with military precision. Grace knew that look. He was already calculating, assessing, always a step ahead. He was too composed, too stoic, like a wall she couldn't break through.

Her mind raced, trying to reason with herself.

He's a risk. He's too dangerous. It's not the right time.

But none of that mattered. Caleb didn't understand. He played everything safe, tucked behind his walls, keeping everything in check like he always did. And that was the problem. Grace wasn't here to play it safe. She wasn't going to let him control everything, to let his caution choke the campaign. She needed him to see her, to let down those defenses, to stop treating her like a liability.

The ache in her chest grew tighter as she forced herself to move, marching with purpose, though every step felt heavier than the last.

Why does he have to be so damn attractive?

Her body betrayed her as she closed the distance between them. The way his broad shoulders filled out his suit, the tension in his jaw, the strength in his posture — all of it made her pulse quicken. And yet, as much as she hated it, the thought of him, of his presence, kept pulling her in. She couldn't ignore it. Couldn't ignore him.

The closer she got, the more she struggled to keep her composure. She had to stay focused. She couldn't let him distract her like this, not when there was so much at stake. But still, she couldn't help herself. Caleb, with his quiet intensity, was impossible to ignore.

"Caleb," she said, her voice cutting through the noise. She didn't bother with pleasantries. "Make sure the perimeter is secure. You know how the enemy is. They're already gunning for him. We need more eyes on the crowd. More cameras on the president." She glanced at the stage where the president was wrapping up his speech. "I want him to come down into the crowd. Let them touch him. Let them feel like he's real. Let the media eat it up."

Caleb's gaze hardened instantly, a flicker of anger flashing in his eyes. His voice was low, controlled, but his words were sharp. "It's too dangerous, Grace. We're in a high-risk zone. We don't know who these people are. You want him to walk straight into a potential situation?"

"That's exactly what I'm asking," Grace shot, her patience already wearing thin. "You think locking him on stage behind a wall of Secret Service is going to make him more popular? He needs to connect with the people, Caleb. Not just stand there looking like he's in an ivory tower."

His jaw clenched. "What the hell do you think I'm here for? The people will get what they need, but they don't need to touch him to feel it."

Grace stood her ground, meeting his hard gaze with equal force. "You're not getting it. This isn't about security. It's about sending a message. Showing the president as human. Accessible. One of them. We can't win from behind a barricade. He needs to be out there with them. With them, Caleb."

His eyes narrowed, his body bristling with frustration. He took a step closer. "We don't do stunts. We don't make the president a target for the sake of some damn photo op. His life is not your campaign tool, Grace."

The words hit like a slap, but Grace didn't flinch. She was used to this—his constant pushback, his protectionist instincts. But she couldn't back down. Not now. The election was on the line.

"I'm not talking about stunts," she snapped. "I'm talking about winning. The people don't care about your overblown sense of security. They care about how the president makes them feel. And if he's not out there with them, shaking hands, kissing babies, showing up in their lives? They'll forget about him. And we lose."

Caleb's lips pressed into a thin line, his entire body radiating tension. She could see the internal battle playing out behind his eyes—protecting the president at all costs and holding on to control. But she was used to fighting a different battle. She fought for power. She fought for votes.

And no one—especially not Caleb Knight—was going to stand in her way.

"Grace," he said. "You're pushing him too hard. You're pushing all of us too hard."

"I'm not pushing him," she shot back. "I'm pushing you. And you can't keep holding him back just because you're scared. We need to take the risk. He needs to be with the people."

Her words were cold, sharp, cutting through his defenses. She knew he hated them, hated how much they were getting under his skin. But she couldn't afford to soften. She couldn't afford to back down.

Caleb opened his mouth to respond, but the sound of applause broke the tension between them. The president was on the move, stepping down from the stage, walking into the crowd.

Caleb's posture immediately straightened, his eyes locking on the president. Grace knew the drill. He'd be shadowing the president, eyes scanning every face in the crowd, his instincts hyper-vigilant, ready to protect.

"Look at him," Grace muttered, her lips curling into a smile as she watched the president connect with the people, his charisma undeniable. "Perfect timing. This is exactly what we need."

Caleb glanced at her, his eyes hard. "He'll be fine. I've got him."

Grace didn't respond. She knew he'd be following the president, obsessing over every little detail, scanning for threats that probably didn't exist. He wasn't wrong to be worried, but he was wrong about the bigger picture.

The president needed to be seen. Needed to show he was one of them.

Without another word, Grace stepped into the aisle, moving swiftly toward the front. Her heels clicked sharply against the floor, making her way to a strategically placed position just in front of the president. She wasn't waiting for permission. She didn't need Caleb's approval. She knew exactly what she was doing.

Caleb's hand shot out, grabbing her elbow with a grip that was firm, almost painful. "Grace —" His voice was a low command.

"Don't touch me." She jerked her arm out of his grip. His touch felt like a restriction she couldn't afford.

She pushed forward, the crowd parting like the Red Sea, the security detail flanking the president. When he reached her, she positioned herself just before him, allowing him to stand tall and confident, yet within arm's reach of the people. He reached out, shaking hands, kissing babies. The cameras flashed, the media eating it up.

Grace's lips curled into a smile. This was her moment. She was right.

But when she glanced over at Caleb, she saw the fury in his eyes, the hard set of his jaw. He was already moving toward her, cutting through the crowd, and she knew he was coming to stop her.

She didn't care.

This wasn't about Caleb. This was about winning.

The president posed for a few more pictures, the media frenzy reaching a fever pitch. Grace didn't let her eyes wander from the scene for a second. The campaign needed this.

It was time to take control.

And as the crowd surged around them, Grace couldn't help but feel the heat of the fire they were all playing with. But she wasn't the only one.

Caleb was, too.

The rally was loud — too loud. The kind of noise that scraped at his nerves, every cheer and shout driving his thoughts further into the dark corners of his mind. Caleb stood at the edge of the crowd, keeping a careful eye on the president, watching his every move like it was the only thing that mattered. It was his job to protect him. His job to make sure no one could get to him.

But the truth was, it wasn't just the president he had to worry about. It was her, too.

Grace.

He watched her now, moving with that unflappable confidence of hers, weaving through the crowd like she owned the place. She was already making her way toward the stage, toward the heart of the action, where the risk was highest. She didn't care about the danger.

Didn't care about the precautions. Didn't care about anything except pushing forward, no matter the cost.

And damn it, it was starting to get under his skin.

She was too reckless. Too driven. Too ambitious for her own good. He had seen people like her before—that same hunger in the eyes of soldiers who didn't understand that there was a time to push forward and a time to hold back. And right now, she wasn't holding back. She was leading them straight into a potential disaster.

His job was to keep the president safe, to make sure no one got close enough to do harm. But with Grace charging ahead, like the rules didn't apply to her, it felt like he was standing in the middle of a goddamn hurricane.

He watched her give orders, moving behind the scenes, strategizing. Every step she took felt like a challenge. Every word that left her mouth was a dart aimed at him. She was testing him—testing his limits. And he hated it.

"You need to make sure the perimeter is tighter before proceeding," he had told her earlier, but she had brushed him off. Naturally, she had. It was the same thing every time. Her eyes would flash that sharp, dangerous light when she disagreed, that look of determination that made him feel like he was the one holding them all back. Like he didn't understand the bigger picture. Like he was just some soldier who only knew how to follow orders.

But he wasn't just a soldier. He was the one who kept people alive. He was the one who saw threats before they happened.

"Caleb, you're just being paranoid," she had snapped at him a few days ago, after he'd raised concerns about one of her bold moves. She hadn't even looked at the full security report. Hadn't taken a second to consider the risks. And now, here they were, in the middle of a high-profile rally in a swing state, surrounded by a crush of people, and she was pushing for more.

More exposure. More interaction. More risk.

Caleb's grip tightened on the radio at his side, his eyes fixed on Grace as she worked the crowd, positioning herself right in the heart of it all. The knot in his stomach twisted tighter, the warning bells in his head growing louder.

The president was nearing the front, waving to the crowd, working the media like he always did. But Caleb's focus never wavered from Grace. He had to keep her safe, too. He couldn't just look out for the president and let her wander off like that.

But then he lost her.

Shit.

"Where's Grace?" he said, his gaze scanning for her.

He found her just as she reached the front row, pushing forward, ignoring the security line meant to keep everyone at a safe distance. Her focus was sharp, intent on the next press opportunity, on making the next big move to keep the campaign momentum alive.

She wasn't thinking about security. She wasn't thinking about the risk. "Goddamn it," Caleb muttered under his breath.

He was already moving, his hand going to his earpiece, signaling his team to lock down the perimeter. He needed to get to her before things went too far.

But of course, she was too fast. Already too deep into the mix.

"Grace," he called, pushing his way through. He could feel the heat of her presence even before he saw her clearly. The tightness in his chest deepened. "You're too close."

She didn't turn around at first, not until she'd reached the president's side, where a horde of people were already reaching out, trying to touch him, to get close to the man they'd come to see.

"Caleb, I've got it under control," Grace said, her voice cool, dismissive, as though he was just another annoyance in her path. She did not bother to glance at him as she moved further into the fray.

He stopped dead in his tracks.

"You don't have it under control. I'm telling you, it's too dangerous."

Her head whipped around, her eyes flashing with that familiar fire. She wasn't used to being told no. Not by anyone. Least of all him.

"Caleb, I don't have time for this," she snapped. "We need this. We need the people to see him. They need to feel like they're part of this. You're just…overthinking it."

He had to bite back a laugh. "You think I'm overthinking it? You're throwing him right into a potential target zone. You're asking for trouble."

She didn't blink, just pushed past him, her back straight, her focus unwavering.

Her words were clipped, but they stung. "I'm not here to play it safe, Caleb. This is the only way we win. And if you're not with me on this, then get out of my way."

Caleb stood there for a moment, the heat of her defiance burning him. He wanted to argue with her, wanted to tell her she was being reckless, that he wasn't going to stand by and let her put the president in danger. But a voice inside him told him to hold back. To wait.

She was a force, Grace. A whirlwind. And as much as he hated to admit it, there was something about her — something magnetic. Something that made him want to pull her back from the edge and shake sense into her, but at the same time, something that made him want to keep her close.

That thought didn't sit well with him.

He couldn't afford distractions. Not with the stakes this high. And Grace was a damn distraction.

As the president continued to shake hands and press the flesh, Grace stood beside him, positioned exactly where she needed to be. The cameras were flashing. The crowd was roaring. The media was eating it up.

But there was no way in hell Caleb was going to let her play with fire like this. Not while he had a job to do.

And as he watched her standing there, right at the center of it all, pushing the boundaries as usual, Caleb couldn't help but feel that familiar tightness in his chest. He was supposed to protect her, too. But damn it, she didn't want his protection. Not now. Not when she was chasing her own goals.

He wasn't sure which one of them was more stubborn, but he was damn sure they were on a collision course.

Chapter Four

The Georgia rally was finally over. It was time to get onto the next thing. The president had already been flown back to the White House.

Of course, Grace had demanded to stay behind and measure sentiment from the rally-goers. Caleb had been forced to stand for hours as she'd talked to supporters, asking questions and gaining insights.

Now, they were finally back on the road. Caleb's knuckles tightened on the steering wheel of the SUV, his eyes sweeping the Georgia landscape. The route back to the airport was remote — just cornfields and the occasional farmhouse. It was the kind of place that made a man feel exposed. Vulnerable. The stillness hung heavy, the kind that made his instincts prick with unease.

And they were alone.

Wyatt was two miles ahead in another vehicle.

The hum of Caleb's SUV was almost too soothing, a low, steady rhythm that seemed to match his thoughts. The wheels glided over the cracked asphalt, the only sound cutting through the still October air. The road stretched out in front of him, flanked on both sides by rows of corn, tall and brittle, their golden-brown stalks swaying gently in the breeze. It was the calm before the storm, and Caleb had learned long ago to never trust the calm.

In the back seat, Grace's voice sliced through the silence. She was on the phone with Jordan Simmons, her campaign co-lead. But it wasn't the words she was saying that held Caleb's attention. It was the way she said them — sharp and authoritative. She was all business, her voice unwavering, rattling off strategy points as though nothing else in the world existed. As if the vast fields outside, the quiet hum of the SUV, or the danger they were constantly under, couldn't touch her.

It was something Caleb had never seen before. Her focus was unshakable, and it made her so damn attractive. She was the embodiment of fierce determination, of loyalty. Every ounce of her energy was dedicated to the president, to the mission, and nothing could distract her. Not even him.

As she spoke, Caleb stole a glance at her in the rearview mirror. His gaze lingered on her, his chest tightening, as he took in the way she carried herself. There was an intensity about her, a fire in her that made him admire her in a way he couldn't explain. Her jaw was set, her eyes narrowed with purpose, and every inch of her screamed strength. She was hot. Unapologetically powerful. She wasn't just a woman with a mission — she was a force.

Caleb exhaled quietly, his focus flickering back to the road ahead, but a part of him stayed rooted to her. Grace. She was everything he respected, but there was something else there, too. Something he couldn't fully grasp yet. All he knew was that she wasn't like anyone he'd ever known before.

And as much as he tried to remind himself of the lines they both had to draw, he couldn't deny the magnetic pull she had on him. She was fierce, loyal, and capable — everything he respected — and that, more than anything, made her irresistible.

The radio on his dashboard crackled to life.

"Knight, this is OPS. Potential threat. Two unidentified individuals moving through the corn to the north, closing in on your route."

Caleb's pulse quickened, but his voice stayed steady. "Armed?"

"Unconfirmed," came the reply. "One appears to be carrying something long — potential rifle. We're tracking, but you need to move. They're about half a mile out, heading south toward your location."

Caleb glanced in the rearview mirror. Grace was still talking, oblivious. His jaw tightened as he reached for his earpiece, adjusting the volume.

"Stop. You might need to turn around," Wyatt said into his earpiece. "I'll double back to you."

Caleb immediately eased the SUV to a halt. The silence pressed in, thick and unnerving. He scanned the wall of corn on either side, the stalks swaying in the wind, too tall to see through. His hand drifted instinctively to the weapon at his side.

"What's going on?" Grace's voice cut through, sharper now. She was watching him, her campaign notes forgotten.

Caleb didn't respond. He swung the door open and stepped outside, the dry autumn air hitting him like a sharp reminder. This was what they were trained for —

to protect the VIP, neutralize the threat. Ideally, they'd capture the threat alive, extract information, and follow the trail to the source. "Stay in the car," he barked, his tone leaving no room for argument. "Let us deal with this."

"Caleb—"

"Stay. Here."

But the sound of her door opening made him whirl around. Grace was already stepping out, her heels crunching against the loose gravel at the road's edge.

"What the hell is going on?" she demanded, crossing her arms as if daring him to send her back.

Caleb took two long strides toward her, his expression dark. "Get back in the car. Now."

She didn't move. "Not until you tell me what's happening."

The rustling in the corn grew louder. Caleb's head snapped toward the field, his hand flying to the radio on his shoulder. "OPS, sitrep."

"Movement's confirmed closer, roughly two hundred yards. Shooter's still unconfirmed. We're repositioning your backup."

Caleb swore under his breath and turned back to Grace, his voice low and tight. "This isn't a negotiation. Get back in the car, or I'll put you there myself."

Her eyes widened slightly, but to her credit, she didn't argue. She hesitated for just a beat, then climbed back into the SUV, slamming the door behind her. Caleb exhaled sharply, his focus snapping back to the cornfield.

The next moment, the crack of a gunshot split the air.

"Down!" Caleb shouted, lunging toward the SUV as the bullet ricocheted off the road a few feet away. He reached for the driver's door and yanked it open, crouching behind it for cover. Another shot hit the windshield, cracking it.

Grace's face was pale now, her defiance replaced with shock.

"Fuck," Caleb said curtly, scanning the corn. The stalks waved gently, the perfect cover for someone lying in wait. Another crack — a third shot — and Caleb's heart thundered in his chest. The SUV was taking damage. He couldn't see the shooter, but they were close, too close.

"OPS," he barked into his radio. "Confirm shooter's position."

"Northwest edge of the field," came the reply. "Closing in. We're moving backup, but you need to get her out of there."

Caleb didn't wait. He yanked open the rear door and grabbed Grace's arm, his grip firm but careful. "Out. Now. Stay low."

"What —"

"Do as I say," he snapped, dragging her from the car. The tension in his voice left no room for argument. He couldn't let them ambush them in the SUV. They needed to hide.

Grace stumbled slightly as her heels sank into the dirt beside the road, but Caleb didn't let her fall.

He pulled her toward the edge of the field, running south, ducking low as the rustling in the corn grew louder. Caleb didn't stop moving. He guided her toward a dense patch of stalks, the tall corn offering some cover.

"Stay here," he ordered, crouching beside her. His eyes swept the horizon, his hand steady on his weapon. "Hide."

The world around Grace was chaos wrapped in silence, the kind that settled in after the sharp ring of gunfire. He stood between her and a world of danger, but what terrified her most was how much she needed him there.

She stood frozen behind Caleb as he scanned the horizon and spoke with Wyatt through his mic.

Her heart slammed against her ribs, each beat loud enough to drown out the distant rustling of the corn. She had always prided herself on being unshakable, unyielding. But this—this wasn't something you outmaneuvered with clever words or a strategic pivot. This was raw, terrifying reality. Someone out there wanted her dead.

Her legs felt like they didn't belong to her as she stood in the dirt, barely breathing, her back pressed against the brittle stalks of corn. She clenched her hands into fists to stop their trembling, but it didn't work. The chill of October air felt like a blade slicing through the silk of her blouse, but the cold wasn't what made her shiver.

It was Caleb.

Not just his presence, though that alone was a force. It was his precision, his calm in the storm, the way he had reacted without hesitation. She hadn't fully registered the first shot before he was yanking her from the SUV, his hand firm around her wrist, dragging her to safety.

If safety was even a word that applied here.

She risked a glance at him now. He was holding ground in front of her, his frame tense and unmoving, like a statue carved from steel. Every muscle in his body seemed primed for action, his weapon steady in his hands, his eyes scanning the horizon with a predator's focus. There was no trace of doubt in him, no hesitation, only certainty.

It should have made her feel better. Instead, it made her feel exposed.

He'd told her to stay with him. His voice had been a low growl, firm but laced with a kind of care she wasn't used to hearing. She hated that care. She hated how much she noticed it.

Her breath hitched, and she forced herself to focus on anything but him. On the corn swaying in the breeze. On the dirt beneath her fingers. On the undeniable fact that Caleb had thrown himself into the line of fire without a second thought—for her.

It wasn't the first time he'd protected her, but it was the first time she'd realized what it cost him. This wasn't about duty anymore.

"Caleb," she whispered, unsure why she was even speaking. She wasn't the kind of woman who whispered anything.

He didn't turn. He didn't acknowledge her at all, his focus locked on the distant stalks, his body still blocking hers like a shield. She could see the tension in his shoulders, ready for whatever came next.

Her fingers itched to grab him, to pull him back and make him explain why he was so willing to put himself between her and a bullet. But she didn't. She stayed frozen, too aware of the weight of the moment, the fragility of it.

"Stay down," he muttered, his voice sharp but quiet. "Behind me."

Her chest tightened at the command, anger bubbling beneath the fear. She didn't take orders. Not from anyone, not even him. And yet, for once, she didn't fight back. Not because she agreed, but because she didn't trust her voice not to shake.

Another shot cracked through the air, closer this time. She flinched, her fingers digging into the earth as if it could anchor her. Caleb shifted immediately, his body moving to shield her, and something inside her twisted painfully at the instinctive gesture.

She wanted to hate it. She wanted to hate him for making her feel like this—small, vulnerable, out of control. She wanted to snap at him, to demand answers, to remind him that she didn't need saving.

But she did.

She hated how true that was, how much it hurt to admit.

When she looked at him again, his jaw was set, his profile like stone. There was something raw in the way he carried himself now, something that made her stomach flip. It wasn't just professionalism. It wasn't just the job. It was him—Caleb. And the way he made her feel things she didn't want to feel.

"Why are you doing this?" The words slipped out before she could stop them, soft and jagged, almost lost in the chaos.

He glanced at her then, just for a second, his eyes dark and steady. "Because it's my job."

But there was more to it, she could see it in the way his gaze lingered a moment too long, in the tight line of his mouth, in the way he positioned himself so completely between her and the danger.

Her throat tightened, the words she wanted to say tangling together, refusing to come out. She hated him for being this person, for making her feel like she needed him.

Because she did.

And that terrified her more than the bullets.

Wyatt's voice crackled into Caleb's earpiece. "I'm coming down on the north side. You stay there. Hold onto her. I'll get them."

The plan was clear—Wyatt would neutralize the threat while Caleb was tasked with keeping Grace safe. Simple enough, but Caleb had learned never to trust a simple plan in a situation like this.

Grace's grip tightened on his arm as they moved through the darkness of the cornfield. Her earlier bravado was gone, replaced by a palpable tension. She glanced up at him, her breath shallow. "Caleb—" Her voice was unsteady, unsure, like she was struggling to hold it together.

"We've got this," Caleb replied. "Stay close. You're safe. Don't think about anything else."

For once, she didn't argue, and Caleb was surprised at how much that unsettled him. He didn't want her scared. He didn't want to feel responsible for her fear.

"Wyatt, what's your position?" Caleb scanned the dark expanse of the field. The wind howled around them, but the static coming through his earpiece was too loud. He hated the silence, the lack of confirmation.

No response. Just static.

"Wyatt." Caleb's voice lowered, urgent now. "What's going on?"

Still nothing. The silence in the earpiece made Caleb's skin prickle with unease. Something wasn't right.

Grace stumbled beside him, barely keeping up with his quick pace on the uneven ground. He caught her arm to steady her. Her heart was pounding, he could feel it through the fabric of her jacket, and her breathing was coming in short bursts.

"Caleb—what's happening?"

Caleb's gaze shifted quickly, scanning the field, eyes sharp, body taut. There was something off. His jaw clenched as he gripped his sidearm tighter.

Then—*crack*—a sudden snap of a twig.

Caleb went rigid. He moved before she could react, shifting to shield her.

"Down!" he barked.

But, before she could, a figure emerged from the shadows of the corn, a rifle leveled at them.

"Don't move," the man rasped, voice raw with adrenaline. "Both of you, stay where you are."

The gunman's finger twitched against the trigger, but Caleb was already in motion. A blur of muscle and speed, he dove to the side, rolling hard into the dirt, angling himself between the rifle and Grace.

The shot rang out, the crack of gunfire deafening. Caleb didn't hesitate. He surged forward, a vicious collision of body and force. The man was knocked back, his rifle flying from his hands, spinning into the dark, and Caleb was on him in a heartbeat.

The two men hit the ground in a chaotic mess of limbs, Caleb's pounded into the attacker's face with cold, brutal efficiency. The sound of flesh meeting flesh echoed through the night, harsh and raw.

The gunman fought back, scrambling for a knife at his side. But Caleb was faster. His boot slammed into the man's wrist, a sickening crack sounding through the air, and the knife fell to the dirt.

Without hesitation, Caleb pressed his forearm against the man's throat, cutting off his breath. Seconds passed, the fight leaving the man's body. His eyes glazed over, and soon, he was unconscious, limp beneath Caleb's hold.

Caleb pulled out zip ties, his movements quick, calculated. He bound the man's hands without breaking his focus.

"Stay down." Caleb's voice was low, commanding, almost cold.

Grace nodded, her limbs heavy, her body shaking, but instinctively, she dropped to the ground, pulling herself into the cover of the cornfield. Her heart was still racing, her mind struggling to catch up.

Caleb didn't look back at her as he checked the man's pulse. He'd survive. Whatever. Caleb didn't care. He was already moving, eyes scanning the surrounding field, every muscle coiled tight.

"Police are on their way," he muttered into his mic, his voice steady but laced with urgency.

His gaze flicked to Grace, her chest rising and falling rapidly as she slowly stood, shaky but determined.

"You okay?" He felt the cortisol high in his face.

She nodded, swallowing the lump in her throat. "Yeah... I think so. Is he?"

Caleb didn't wait for more. His hand pressed to her back, urging her forward. His eyes didn't leave the man on the ground.

"Let's go. Now."

No time for hesitation. No time for questions. Caleb was already moving, scanning the dark field, his senses on high alert. They weren't safe — not yet. But for now, he had her.

And that was all that mattered.

Chapter Five

New York City

It had been a week since Georgia — since the ambush in the cornfields. Grace could still feel the tightness in her chest every time she thought about it. The sound of the gunshot, the way Caleb had moved, his body between her and danger. It was still fresh, too fresh, despite her attempts to bury it.

She stared at her reflection in the mirror, fingers lightly tracing the soft, silky fabric of her red dress. The deep hue contrasted with her pale skin, the minimalist cut of the dress both daring and elegant. Her hair — dark chestnut curls that cascaded in soft waves — had been styled professionally. She rarely allowed herself the luxury of someone else's hands in her hair, but tonight was different. Tonight, she had to be more than just the strategist. Tonight, she had to be the vision of confidence.

But underneath the polished exterior, everything felt off. The armed men in Georgia — desperate, unpredictable. The news coverage had been relentless, speculating about who was behind the attack and why they had targeted her. No one had the full story, and they sure as hell didn't know *her*. It wasn't about her. She repeated that in her head like a mantra, over and over, until it almost felt true. They weren't after *her*.

Still, the whispers were there. The panic. The uncertainty. Grace had buried it all, determined to move on, to focus on the campaign. The president's numbers were rising. The polls were favorable. Tonight, they needed to show strength.

She gazed at herself again, adjusting the neckline of the dress. There was no time to focus on lingering doubts. Not tonight. The hotel ballroom awaited, a major stop on the president's campaign. They didn't often win this crowd. But tonight, they had to. Tonight, they had to look like winners.

Just as she turned away from the mirror, there was a knock at the door. It was seven p.m. on the dot — Caleb was never late. She inhaled deeply before opening the door, instinctively straightening her posture.

And there he was.

Caleb. In a black suit, sharp as ever, a dangerous kind of precision to every step he took. His eyes locked on her, and for a second, she saw the flicker of something in his gaze. He blinked, and his mouth parted, only slightly. She knew the reaction was mutual.

He offered her his arm and, without thinking, she took it. They walked together in silence, heading down to the ballroom, the weight of what happened in the cornfield hanging between them.

The elevator doors opened, and the sounds of the ballroom hit her like a wave — clinking glasses, the murmur of political chatter, the heavy thrum of power in the air. It felt electric. A world apart from the quiet tension that had settled between her and Caleb since the incident in Georgia.

But Grace didn't have time to dwell on that. She stepped into the room, heels clicking sharply against the polished marble floor, every step calculated. *Confidence*, she told herself. *Show them strength. Show them a woman who has it all together, despite the chaos.*

The ballroom was alive, full of the kind of people who never took a step without it being deliberate. The kind of people who could make or break careers with a single word. Grace could almost taste the power in the air — rich, heady, intoxicating. It was the kind of room that made you believe anything was possible. Even the impossible.

But as she walked, she couldn't shake the feeling that she was balancing on a razor-thin edge. One wrong step, and everything could fall apart.

She swallowed hard, pushing the thought away. Tonight wasn't about fear. It was about getting the job done. It was about three weeks left — and the campaign was going well, despite the stories from Georgia. She'd make sure of it. Even if the threats lingered in the background. Even if Caleb was still a shadow behind her, his presence both a comfort and a reminder of the danger lurking out of sight.

Grace's gaze flickered to Caleb as they moved through the crowd. His face was unreadable, his posture rigid, every inch the protector. He stayed a step behind her, always alert, always watching.

But tonight, they both had a role to play. And Grace was determined to play hers perfectly.

Caleb stood in the corner, scanning the room with practiced precision. The crowd was thick with New York's elite — donors, influencers, campaign backers — each one of them a key to the president's re-election, each one with their own agenda. He could feel the electricity in the air, the weight of expectations pressing down on them all. This was the kind of event where a single wrong move could change the entire trajectory of the campaign.

And yet, there she was — Grace, as always, at the center of it. Her presence in that red dress, so polished, so assured, perfectly complimented her dark hair and blue eyes. She had the ability to make even the most hardened political players sit up and take notice of her. She was good at this. Damn good.

He had seen Grace in countless settings — dressed for meetings, for work, even in casual attire — but nothing compared to this. The gown was elegant yet bold, its neckline a perfect balance between sophistication and allure. It swept the floor behind her like something out of a dream, and the way the soft light from the chandeliers seemed to dance on the fabric made it appear as though she were walking in a world of her own creation.

Her hair, dark and shimmering, cascaded down her back in soft waves, the strands catching the light as if they had been kissed by fire. Her makeup, subtle but striking, brought out the natural beauty of her face, highlighting the sharpness of her cheekbones and the softness of her lips. And those eyes — those eyes that could pierce through any barrier, any guard he tried to put up. She was a vision, and Caleb's chest tightened with the overwhelming need to protect her, to keep her safe.

But more than that, he wanted her—wanted all of her, in a way he hadn't fully allowed himself to acknowledge until this very moment.

As she glided through the crowd, her presence commanding attention without even trying, Caleb's breath caught in his throat. He had seen her look confident, strong, and capable in countless high-stress situations, but tonight—tonight she looked like something else entirely. She was the embodiment of grace and strength, elegance and power, all wrapped up in one beautiful woman.

For a brief moment, he stood there, just watching her, his hands tightening around the glass in his hand without him realizing it. He knew the risks of this life. He had always known them. But seeing her like this— so radiant, so full of life—made everything else seem insignificant.

His job was to protect the president and his inner circle, and right now, that meant keeping them away from the spotlight.

But Grace… Grace was already working her magic, weaving her narrative, trying to shift the story in her favor. Caleb could see it in her eyes, the fire, the determination. She wanted the people's attention, up on a pedestal, wanted them to see the president as untouchable. But she was pushing too far, and he wasn't going to let her put them all at risk.

"Hey," Caleb said quietly, stepping toward her as she moved through the crowd, already heading toward the front where President Armstrong was chatting with donors. His voice was low but firm—he wasn't going to let her walk this dangerous line without a fight. "We need to keep things calm tonight."

She barely looked at him, continuing to smile at a donor as she passed, but he saw the flicker of irritation in her eyes.

"Of course. We'll be careful," she said, brushing past him with a dismissive flick of her hand. "But tonight, we are brave in the face of media exaggerations."

His jaw tightened. She wasn't getting it. This wasn't about bravery. It wasn't about bold moves or dramatic gestures. This was about safety.

"This isn't about boldness, Grace." His tone was sharper now. He stepped closer, his eyes never leaving her. "We don't have time for stunts."

Grace stopped, her back straightening, a flash of anger crossing her face. "If we don't show strength, if we don't take control of the narrative, the polls can turn. And tonight, he's showing he's untouchable."

Her words were like daggers, sharp and pointed. Caleb's pulse quickened, but he forced himself to stay calm, to stay on task. She turned away, moving toward the stage where the president was preparing to speak. The woman never fucking listened.

Caleb stood at the edge of the grand hotel ballroom, arms folded across his chest, doing his best to fade into the background. The place was all polished floors and glittering chandeliers, buzzing with excitement for Armstrong's re-election. Caleb had seen plenty of rooms like this — too-bright smiles, cheap pleasantries — and he'd never cared for any of it. But he wasn't here for the party — he was here to watch over Grace. She stood across the room, chatting with the president's staff, her smile warm and genuine, her eyes darting to him every now and then. He knew what that look meant—she was checking in on him just as much as he was guarding her.

His gaze shifted, skimming the crowd until he found Wyatt seated near the back, a bandage peeking out from under his jacket, his crutches leaning against the wall. The fallout from that fiasco in the Georgia cornfield still weighed heavily on both of them. They'd unearthed a tangle of threats that night—enough to keep Wyatt's head buried in intel for weeks. Wyatt had taken a hit, literally and figuratively, and was still recovering, both in body and spirit.

Caleb moved closer to Wyatt, slipping through the throng without drawing attention. Wyatt glanced up as he approached, offering a small, tired grin that didn't quite reach his eyes. "How's it going?" Caleb asked quietly, scanning the room to ensure no one was eavesdropping.

Wyatt let out a slow breath. "Slow. We got a few names from those burners we pulled after the cornfield raid, but nothing rock-solid yet. Some middlemen, maybe a compromised staffer here or there. Whoever set that up knew how to cover their tracks." He ran a hand gingerly over his ribs—still sore. "I'm working through chain-of-command leads, financial records, coded comms, but it's a slog."

Caleb nodded, jaw tightening. The ambush in that Georgia field had nearly cost Wyatt more than a few bruised ribs, and the frustration of hitting dead ends clearly gnawed at him. "You need more time?"

"Time, more intel, a miracle. We'll see. Grace okay?" Wyatt asked, his tone softer.

"Yeah," Caleb said. "She's good. Safe."

Wyatt cleared his throat, dropping his voice. "We'll get them," he said. "Whoever was behind that Georgia mess — we'll nail them down. I promise."

Caleb nodded once, grateful for Wyatt's grit. "I know," he said. "Just keep me posted."

Somewhere in the deep recesses of offices and dark corners, Wyatt would keep digging, keep pushing until the truth came to light. And Caleb would be there in the background, watching over Grace, the president, and everyone else who mattered — just as he always had.

And then, out of nowhere, a viper from his past appeared.

Caleb's stomach sank. Adrienne Amoroso.

He sensed her before he saw her, cutting through the crowd like a blade — fluid, confident, and dangerous. Just what you'd expect from your CIA ex-girlfriend. Adrienne had a knack for getting what she wanted, whether she earned it or not.

He stiffened the moment she stepped into view, wearing that dress that clung to every curve. Her eyes found his instantly, and the faint, knowing smile on her lips made his pulse spike with anger.

"Caleb," Adrienne said, voice low and disturbingly familiar, layered with a gentler note he knew better than to trust. "I thought I would see you here."

He didn't respond right away. He shouldn't even be engaging, not with her, not here. He wasn't going to let her pull him back into whatever manipulation she had in mind. But the rage was still there — the rage of betrayal that hadn't gone away, no matter how much time had passed.

"I've been trying to get a hold of you," Adrienne said, stepping a little closer, but not too close. Just enough to draw his attention, to test him. "But are you really going to ignore all my calls? Is that where we are at?"

He held the gaze of his ex, his jaw tightening. He didn't want to talk to her, not really. Not after everything. Not after how she'd cheated on him, how she'd left him in the mess that followed. The wounds were still raw, too fresh for him to pretend they were just going to talk like everything was fine.

"Hear me out, okay?"

"You made your choice," Caleb muttered, his voice colder now, more controlled. "I'm not interested."

She tilted her head, taking in the words like a slow burn. Adrienne knew how to play this game better than anyone, but this time, Caleb wasn't biting. She'd lost that privilege a long time ago.

"I see things are still the same."

"Go," Caleb shot back, his voice icy. He wasn't interested in talking about the past—he didn't want to reopen old wounds. Not when he had other, more pressing matters on his mind.

Adrienne's expression shifted, just a little. A hint of frustration flashed in her eyes, quickly masked by a glance around the room. She was still looking for a way in, a crack in his armor.

"Babe," Adrienne began again, quieter this time, leaning in just a fraction. "Hm, what if I have something for you—perhaps, information?"

"No," he cut her off, firm. "Don't care for your strings." His words were direct, no room for misinterpretation. He had no intention of letting this conversation go any further.

Adrienne's gaze flicked across the room again, her lips parting as if to say something more, but she stopped herself. Her eyes lingered on him, unfortunately familiar — full of regret.

She gave him one last look, eyes lingering, studying his face as if searching for any sign that he might crack, but Caleb stood firm. No cracks. No doubts. He wasn't interested in going back to the past.

He quickly scanned the room again, finally landing back on Grace, still talking to the president's staff. She didn't look over, not yet. But Caleb knew — he could feel it — that she knew something was off. She always did.

He pushed away from the column, straightening his posture. He gave one last nod to Wyatt. There would be no more distractions. He had a job to do. Grace was safe, and she was his priority now. Nothing else mattered. Not even the ghosts of the past.

With a final glance toward the door where Adrienne had just vanished, Caleb turned and walked back to Grace, his heart heavy, but resolute.

He focused on Grace. She was in her element, effortlessly commanding attention without even trying. Grace moved through the crowd with the kind of grace that made people gravitate toward her. Her laughter rose above the low hum of conversation, and her smile — perfectly curated — never wavered. She navigated the web of donors, influencers, and campaign backers with ease.

He'd done this job a thousand times before — watched over politicians, secured high-profile events, kept threats at bay. But with Grace, it was different. He wasn't just watching the room, he was watching her. And the more he did, the more he realized how much control she had, how easily she wielded it. It made his job harder than it had any right to be.

His role tonight? Simple. Keep her safe. Keep the president safe. Nothing more, nothing less.

But the longer Caleb observed Grace, the more the line between duty and something else blurred. There was a sharpness in her — something he hadn't noticed before. Her ability to charm, to read a room, to make connections, to lead — she was more than a campaign strategist. She was a force.

And it bothered him.

Not because Grace was a threat — no, she was a risk to his focus. His resolve. His ability to do his job right. And that, more than anything, set his nerves on edge.

His gut tightened as he saw a woman approaching grace. Caleb clocked the woman instantly — the crisp white suit, the sharp angles of her short silver hair, the way her smile cut as much as it charmed. Predatory. Calculated. Dangerous.

Marisol Rhodes Stewart.

She was leaning in close to Grace now, whispering something just loud enough to draw a flicker of unease across Grace's face. Most people wouldn't notice it, but Caleb had trained himself to see the moments others missed — the way her posture stiffened like she wanted to pull away but wouldn't give Marisol the satisfaction of retreat.

Marisol was pressing her, demanding something with that too-smooth smile. Caleb didn't need to hear the words to know what was happening. He could read it in the way Marisol tilted her head, like a lion sizing up a weaker animal, testing for weakness.

He didn't like seeing Grace boxed in like that, didn't like the way Marisol's presence seemed to cast a shadow over the room. He stayed rooted where he was, though, his muscles taut with restraint. He never moved until he was sure — sure of what was being said, sure of what he'd have to do.

For now, he watched, his eyes sharp and calculating. Because if Marisol was as dangerous as she looked, then she wasn't just Grace's problem — she was his, too.

Moving toward her, Caleb watched a rich-looking man lead Grace onto the dance floor. The man was older — too old — and the man's fucking hand lingered too long on her waist. Grace's smile never faltered, but Caleb could see the subtle shift in her posture, the way her body stiffened, just slightly.

Grace was fine. She had to be fine.

The music swirled around them, the beat slow, intimate. Grace's dance partner pulled her in, his hand moving up her back in a way that Caleb didn't like. The sharp pang in his chest grew. He was getting caught up in this — letting his emotions cloud his judgment.

Get it together, Caleb. She's fine. She's doing her job.

But the irritation in his chest wouldn't release.

He watched as the man leaned in to whisper something in her ear, and Grace responded with that same practiced, pleasant smile. It was the smile she wore when she was playing a part, keeping things on her terms. But Caleb could see it now — just a flicker of discomfort in the slight way her shoulders tensed.

The realization hit him hard. He wasn't just frustrated. He was worried.

"No," Caleb muttered, almost angrily, to himself. This wasn't his job. He wasn't supposed to care about this. He was here to keep her safe, to protect her from external threats. Not to get tangled up in whatever this was.

But something gnawed at him, deep in his gut. *Something isn't right.*

Caleb felt the weight of it settle in his chest, making every step toward Grace feel heavier than the last.

"Grace," he called out as she brushed past him.

She paused, turning. "What?"

"What's going on?" Caleb pressed, his gaze flicking to Marisol, who was now holding court with a small cluster of prominent figures.

Grace hesitated. "You know who she is. Everyone does," she said, her voice flat. "She controls influence like it's her personal chessboard. Tech, lobbying, PACs — you name it, she has a piece of it."

Caleb's jaw tightened as his eyes locked on Marisol again. The way she moved through the crowd, the effortless authority in her every gesture — it didn't sit right. He'd seen power like that before, and it rarely ended well for anyone caught in its orbit.

Then Jordan Simmons appeared, sliding into the conversation like he'd been waiting for his moment. "Did you get her support?" he asked Grace, his tone impatient, his words biting.

Grace's expression hardened. "No," she said, curt and final.

Jordan wasn't having it. "No? Grace, do you know what she could do for us? Her name, her connections — "

"I know exactly what she could do," Grace interrupted. "And it's not worth the cost."

Jordan frowned, clearly not ready to drop it. "You're being idealistic," he argued. "We need her, Grace. The stakes are too high to play this your way."

"We don't need her." Grace's tone was steel now. "We've built this campaign on authenticity. On trust. If we bring her in, everything we've worked for — everything the president stands for — is gone."

The tension between them was suffocating. Caleb stood off to the side, silent but watchful, reading every flicker of their expressions. Jordan was desperate, pushing harder than he should, while Grace stood her ground, unyielding.

Caleb stepped forward, his presence deliberate, his voice cutting through the charged air. "Is there a problem here?"

Both of them turned to him, but Grace didn't answer. Instead, she shot him a look that said *not now* and turned on her heel, walking away without another word.

Caleb watched her retreat, the tension still buzzing in the space she left behind. Jordan muttered something under his breath before stalking off in the opposite direction, leaving Caleb standing there alone.

Caleb's jaw tightened, and he matched Grace's pace, his footsteps deliberate. She wasn't taking him seriously, and that wasn't something he could allow.

"Are you running from me?"

"Not everything is about you." She spun to face him, her fiery gaze piercing. "Just fuck off for one minute, please."

The words hit him harder than they should have. His fists clenched, but he kept his face calm, the anger simmering beneath the surface. This was his job. It wasn't about her defiance — it was about his control, his responsibility to protect her.

"Fuck off?" he repeated, voice colder now.

"You heard me," she snapped, taking a glass of champagne from a tray as if she could shake him off with that simple gesture. He didn't miss how her voice slurred.

She walked to the edge of the ballroom, downing the glass in one drink.

"You are a real piece of work," she said as he caught up to her side. "Coming in hot with that suit."

Caleb couldn't hold it back anymore. "How much have you had to drink?" he asked, his voice a low growl.

She didn't respond immediately, but Caleb could see the defiance in her gaze. She was poised to retort, yet before she could, his instincts kicked in. His eyes scanned the room, landing on something unusual — something amiss, a subtle movement near the back exit.

Without a word, he moved swiftly, his hand grabbing her elbow and pulling her back. Grace stumbled, but Caleb didn't release his hold. Speaking rapidly into his mic, he issued orders to his team to secure the president.

As their eyes met, the tension between them was thick, an unspoken charge filling the space. But Caleb pushed it aside. He couldn't afford to dwell on that.

His mission was still within his grasp.

Grace's body flushed with heat as Caleb guided her on the edge of the crowd, his fingers tightening around her arm. His touch was a constant pull, a silent demand for her attention, and it burned into her skin with every step. The moment his hand grazed her skin, the crowded room vanished, leaving only him — too close, too commanding. She was spinning.

He moved her farther from the ball, the weight of his presence surrounding her, pressing her against the cool walls of a deserted, closed stairwell. The air between them thickened, heavy with something neither of them could deny. She hated it. She hated how her body responded to him, how every inch of her skin screamed for more of him.

He was pretty fucking hot. She couldn't deny it. All that army muscle and brawn — it was just *mmm*.

As they reached the bottom steps, Caleb's grip on her arm shifted, pulling her in so close she could feel the heat radiating from him.

She stumbled off the last step and he caught her.

His breath sent a shiver down her spine. "The night's over," he murmured, voice low, thick with something dangerous, something that made her pulse race.

"Says who?"

"You've had too much to drink."

She barely shook her head, her heart pounding as his hand slipped down to her waist, his fingers grazing her skin with agonizing slowness. She wanted to pull away, to regain control, but her body betrayed her. She leaned into his touch, the warmth of him drawing her in like a magnet.

She moaned into him as he pressed her against the wall.

"What are you doing?" she whispered, her lips trembling just inches from his.

His eyes darkened, his jaw clenched. "Watching out for you." His voice was a husky growl, rough and intimate, making the air between them crackle with tension. "You're about to fall over."

Her breath caught in her throat, the space between them charged with a heat she could barely comprehend. She closed her eyes, leaning into him. The hard length of his body, solid and unwavering, left no room for escape.

Her skin tingled where he touched her, and she couldn't stop herself from leaning in closer, her lips brushing against his jaw. "You're too close," she breathed, the words more of a plea than a protest.

"Not close enough," he rasped, his voice low, laced with something darker, more urgent.

Her hands were shaking, her body burning with a need she couldn't ignore. She could feel every movement of him, the tension in his muscles, the heat that pulsed between them. "Caleb," she moaned softly, the word slipping from her lips before she could stop them. "Don't do this."

His eyes locked onto hers, intense and searing. He was so close, his breath mingling with hers, the space between them nonexistent. "I didn't like that man touching you," he growled, his hand sliding down her back, pulling her even closer. Her pelvis met his and she would swear there was something hardening to greet her.

She felt his body against hers — strong, commanding, unrelenting — and she couldn't breathe. She didn't want to.

"You are too possessive," she said. "It's making my head spin."

"I'm not letting you go."

Her lips parted, inches from his, her chest rising and falling in quick, shallow breaths. "Don't," she whispered, her voice low, shaky with need.

"Bad girl."

"Come closer."

That was when everything shifted — again. Caleb surged forward and claimed her lips. Their first kiss wasn't gentle, it was a slow ignition of unspoken want, a molten collision that made her moan into his mouth, desperate to taste every inch of him. It was fierce and sudden and stole Grace's breath, leaving her caught between resistance and surrender. The hard line of his body, the scent of him, the warmth of his mouth—she felt it all in a dizzying rush.

For a few stolen seconds, she let herself sink into the moment. His hand cupped the back of her head, his fingers curling into her hair, pressing her against the wall. She responded without thinking, rising onto her toes, her hands fisting in his shirt as if to keep him from slipping away. The frantic beat of her heart, the tension that had hovered for weeks finally ignited into something they both desperately needed.

But then, just as abruptly, Caleb pulled back. He broke the kiss, leaving her breathless and off-balance. His chest heaved, and regret flickered in his eyes. "I'm sorry," he managed, voice strained. The intensity of what had just happened lingered in the air, heavy and hot.

Grace stood still, shock and hunger colliding inside her. She wanted to protest, to drag him back, to demand why he would give her that taste of something she so desperately wanted only to snatch it away. But he had already stepped back, forcing himself to return to that careful, detached role.

"Grace," he said, his voice cold, businesslike again. The sultry tension between them shattered in an instant. "I'm going to get you home."

Grace stood frozen, her heart still racing, the heat between them lingering like an open flame. She didn't move. She couldn't. She wanted to say something, anything, but the words were gone—swallowed by the ache that burned in her chest, the unanswered desire still hanging in the air.

Chapter Six

Cheeseman Farm Pumpkin Festival, Lawrence County, Pennsylvania
15 days to the election

Caleb stepped out of the SUV and the scent of frying onions and hot oil hit him with the force of a freight train. It was the unmistakable scene of a small-town fair — greasy, pungent, but oddly comforting.

This was the last stop on a series, visiting Allentown, Scranton, and Reading — and rallying supporters in Pittsburgh and Philadelphia.

He squinted into the late afternoon sunlight as he stepped onto the cracked pavement. This wasn't New York City. Hell, it wasn't even a town where big political speeches were made. This was a backwater Pennsylvania town, the kind that clung to its faded industrial roots like a long-lost relic. The streets were lined with old storefronts, their windows filled with dust and memories, and every porch seemed to sport an American flag, fluttering lazily in the warm breeze.

New York came and went. He got out alive despite her drunken ass tempting him more than he could ever admit. They'd learned to keep a good distance from each other since then.

As Grace stepped out of the SUV, Caleb couldn't help but watch. She had that kind of walk — the kind that demanded attention. Her body was lean, toned, the way a fighter's might be, and she carried herself with a strength that couldn't be ignored. The town felt like it shrank around her as she moved through it, effortlessly owning the space. Grace wasn't just walking — she was commanding the crowd, her every step pulling people in.

Her hips swayed just enough to catch the eye, her shoulders straight, and that confident, knowing smile? It wasn't just for show. She knew exactly what she was doing, how she could make everything feel important, even in a town like this. The older men tipped their hats, the younger women whispered as she passed — Grace had an effect on people. And it wasn't her looks. It was her power.

She wasn't just strong, she was magnetic. There was a fire in her, a focused intensity that made it hard for Caleb to look away. The way she moved, the way she carried herself, told him everything — Grace wasn't here to play. She was here to dominate. And damn, it never failed to captivate him.

Caleb, on the other hand, hung back. His eyes darted from one corner of the street to another, scanning for anything out of place. Easy.

But Grace wasn't concerned with any of that. She was already on the move, effortlessly engaging with the crowd. Caleb let out a soft sigh and stepped in line behind her, trying not to let his discomfort show. There was no danger here, not yet—but the nagging feeling in his gut told him that it wouldn't be the first time something had slipped through the cracks.

As Grace approached a booth selling local jams, the elderly woman behind the counter beamed at her. "Miss Williams, it's so good to have you here! I make all these myself, you know. Special recipe passed down from my grandmother."

Grace smiled back, a little too brightly, Caleb noticed. "I can tell! These look delicious." She reached forward, grabbing a jar of strawberry jam and inspecting the label with exaggerated interest.

Caleb stayed a few paces behind her, his eyes sweeping across the crowd. It was strange, this kind of campaign stop. The only thing remotely political here were the few lawn signs, leaning awkwardly against tree trunks and fence posts, as if they'd been set up in a rush and hadn't been properly installed. The air was thick with the smell of caramel apples, pumpkin pies, and the distant rumble of a tractor pulling a parade float. It didn't feel like a political event. It felt like...well, a pumpkin fair.

"So, what do you think of the town?" Grace asked, catching his eye. She'd turned away from the booth and was now studying him, her expression slightly too amused. Caleb forced a smile, not letting the suspicion in his gut show.

"It's...charming," he said, betraying nothing. "It's got that small-town vibe." He didn't add that he hated it. He hated the way it made him feel like he was watching a ticking clock in slow motion. The town seemed unaware of the massive campaign machine moving through it, unaware of the kind of people Grace and her team had to constantly be on the lookout for.

"Charming," she repeated. "That's the word everyone uses. Like a page from a picture book."

Caleb nodded, scanning the crowd again. A family walked past, kids tugging at their parents' shirts, each one more excited about the fair games than the fact that a presidential candidate was in town.

The sound of cameras snapping photos pulled him back to the present. A couple of photographers had appeared from nowhere, their lenses trained on Grace, capturing the scene like she was a model at a photo shoot rather than a political figure. He could already feel the buzz of social media taking off in the background, people tagging pictures and posting live updates. It was all part of the show, and Grace was the star.

"Do you miss it?" Grace asked suddenly, her tone quieter now as she picked up a jar of homemade apple butter. She wasn't looking at him, but Caleb could feel her gaze shifting in his direction, like she was weighing him. "DC, I mean. The fast pace. The big crowds."

He raised an eyebrow. "Why?"

She shrugged, still scanning the label on the jar. "I don't know. You just seem..." She trailed off, then looked at him, half-smiling. "You don't seem like you're from around here."

"Not exactly," Caleb replied, his voice dry. "And you do?"

She laughed softly. It was the kind of laugh that sounded genuine but had an edge to it. "I've lived all over. But this? This is as far removed from what I'm used to as possible. I can't imagine what it must be like for someone like you, though."

"Someone like me?" Caleb glanced at her, confused.

"A guy who spends his days looking for danger. The dark corners. The threats," she said, a little more reflective. She paused, her eyes narrowing. "I get it. I've seen the way you watch people. Like you're always waiting for something bad to happen."

Caleb blinked, taken aback by the sudden clarity in her words. "It's my job," he said, his voice hardening slightly. "It's what I do."

"I get that." She gave him a look then, one that felt like she was actually seeing him for the first time. "But it's not just a job, is it? There's more to it than that. People who live that way...it's like they don't know how to turn it off."

"People who live what way?" Caleb asked, his brow furrowed.

"The way you live." She tilted her head, as though considering how much to reveal. "The way you're always watching, always anticipating, always on edge. It's not just about keeping others safe. You're trying to protect yourself too, right?"

Caleb shifted, feeling suddenly exposed. He wasn't used to talking about himself — not with anyone. Not with Grace. "It's not a lifestyle choice. This is my day-to-day — my job," he repeated, a little more sharply than intended.

She didn't press. Instead, she handed him a jar of the apple butter, a playful glint in her eye. "You know," she said, almost teasing, "you could try something different for once. Take a break. Let someone else do the looking."

"I'll pass." Caleb took the jar from her, his fingers brushing hers briefly. There it was again — but he quickly pushed the feeling down. He wasn't supposed to be thinking like that.

Grace smiled at him, her eyes lighting up as the next round of cameras flashed. "You know, if you ever want to take a day off from the danger and just, I don't know, enjoy the pumpkin pie...you could join me. But then again," she added with a wink, "maybe you're too much of a hard-ass for that."

Caleb didn't know how to respond. He wasn't sure if she was joking, but he wasn't sure if he wanted to find out either. Instead, he said nothing, handing the jar back to the booth owner, who was still grinning like he'd won the lottery.

The crowd thickened, the energy of the fair buzzing around them, but Caleb couldn't quite shake the feeling that this—this whole thing—was just a performance.

The sun hung low, casting long, golden shadows across the small town square. Caleb walked a step behind Grace, his eyes scanning the quiet surroundings, but his attention was on her. She was different now. There was an ease to her stride, a subtle shift in her posture that made her seem less like a politician and more like...well, a person.

He wasn't sure when it happened, but something about Grace was starting to grow on him. She'd always been sharp, too polished, too calculated for him to get a real read. But today? Today, she seemed almost...human. More herself, maybe. And Caleb couldn't quite put his finger on it, but he found he liked it.

"Did you like the giant pumpkin?" Her voice pulled him from his thoughts, light and teasing, a sharp contrast to the seriousness she wore like armor. She wasn't giving him the usual political spiel, wasn't sizing him up. She was just...talking.

He raised an eyebrow, surprised by the question. "I don't know if 'like' is the word I'd use," he answered dryly, then smirked. "But it's not the worst thing I've ever seen."

She laughed, the sound unexpected and genuine. There was no rehearsed charm in it. "Not a fan of small-town stuff?"

"Not when the locals act like I'm the tourist," he said with a grin, the edge of irritation melting away.

"Well, you are a spectacle," she shot back, her gaze running over him for a second, but it wasn't the kind of look that made him want to squirm.

"Come on," he said, feigning offense, though the playful banter felt oddly comfortable.

She didn't let up. "Yeah, most guys don't look like you."

He gave her a mock-serious look. "Eyes up here." He motioned to his face, his lips curling into a half-smile.

Her laugh came again, full and easy. Caleb couldn't help but feel it—something about her was getting under his skin, but in a good way. She wasn't playing the game with him anymore. There was no edge, no power struggle. Just two people walking through a quiet town.

They walked for a while in companionable silence, Caleb noticing the subtle changes in her body language, the way she seemed to drop her guard just a little more with each step.

"Tell me more," Grace said after a beat, her voice softer now, curious. "I know you're with the Secret Service now, but you were in the Army before, right?"

The question caught him off guard, and instinctively, Caleb tensed. He didn't like talking about the past. It wasn't something he shared. But Grace didn't pry, didn't push—she just asked, her voice casual, like she was genuinely interested, not trying to get the next piece of useful information.

"Yeah," he said, his voice shorter than he meant. "Army Rangers."

Her eyes flicked over to him, but the look wasn't judgmental.

"That's impressive," she said, nodding slightly, her tone sincere. "What was that like?"

He shifted, taking a deep breath. It wasn't something he was eager to relive, but she was different. She wasn't just probing for dirt. She was…asking. Like she wanted to understand. And that made it easier to talk.

"It was intense," he said. "I was with the 75th Ranger Regiment. Deployed a lot. Did a lot of things that don't exactly make the papers." He hesitated, then added, "You learn quick that you either trust your team, or you're dead. That's the kind of pressure I'm used to."

Grace's eyes softened, a brief moment of understanding passing between them. "Must have been hard," she said, quieter. "I mean, seeing things like that, the kind of stuff you never really get over."

Caleb swallowed, feeling the weight of her words in a way he wasn't expecting. "You don't get over it," he said, like he was offering a truth she wasn't prepared for. "You learn to live with it. It's…part of the job."

There was a silence between them then, the quiet of the park stretching on, a couple of ducks waddling by the pond as they walked. For the first time since they'd met, he felt like she was seeing him—not as a Secret Service agent, not as some guy who was just there to keep her safe, but as someone who had lived, had seen, and carried things with him.

It wasn't comfortable, but it was real.

And for the first time, he found himself appreciating it.

They continued walking, side by side, the tension between them gone, replaced by something more tangible. Human. Grace wasn't hiding behind her strategy, her polished exterior. She was just being Grace. And Caleb liked it.

They approached the municipal hall, and as they slowed, Grace glanced at him, her expression softer than it had been before. "Thanks for walking me over," she said, without the usual formality.

Caleb nodded, a small, unexpected smile tugging at his lips. "Of course."

She turned toward the door, her eyes meeting his one last time before she stepped inside, and Caleb lingered for a second. The conversation had been easy—nothing earth-shattering, but it had felt different. It had felt real. Something he hadn't expected, and certainly hadn't anticipated enjoying.

But now, as she disappeared into the building, Caleb found himself wondering just how much of this—her— he could keep ignoring. Something told him, maybe, he didn't want to.

But that was a thought for another time.

Chapter Seven

Caleb stepped out of the town hall, the cold October air hitting him like a slap to the face. His shoulders squared, he was still locked on the meeting that had just wrapped up. It was supposed to be a good day. Everything was going according to plan. Until it wasn't.

He glanced down the street, and his stomach sank. The protestors were everywhere. What had been a quiet town square just a few hours ago was now a boiling cauldron of chaos. They'd appeared out of nowhere — hundreds of them, packed tight, their chants slicing through the air like knives. The noise was deafening, a chorus of rage that reverberated in his chest.

The smell hit him next — the burning plastic, the stench of a trash can fire somewhere down the block. His jaw clenched. This wasn't supposed to happen. Not today. Not when everything had been so damn perfect up until this point.

He adjusted his earpiece, trying to keep his voice steady even though his patience was already wearing thin. "Status."

"South flank secure." Wyatt's voice crackled in his ear. "President safe in the motorcade."

"Eyes on the west alley. It's a blind spot," Caleb snapped. His tone was clipped, controlled, but inside, a knot was forming in his gut. Something was off. This wasn't just a protest. It was the kind of situation where the wrong move could set everything on fire. And for the first time today, Caleb wasn't so sure he was in control.

The chants thundered against the old brick walls, each cry echoing down the narrow street. "Systemic corruption ends today! No justice, no peace!" At the head of the crowd, TVC operatives masked in black were already testing the barricades, shoulders braced, intent clear. *Shit.* Protesters waved signs, shouting about everything — abortion rights, safe injection sites, poverty. You name it, they were furious about it. The riot police held their line, shields raised, batons ready. But the tension crackled in the air, and everyone knew it — this was about to explode.

Caleb's grip tightened on the gun at his hip. The air around him felt like it was on the edge of snapping, the tension so thick it put him into war mode. TVC wasn't known for playing nice. They liked big surprises and bigger headlines — better if fire was involved.

And of course, it had to happen now. Just when he thought he might catch a damn break.

"Well, fuck," he muttered under his breath. The anger that had been simmering all day was bubbling up, and for the first time, he wasn't bothering to hide it.

He turned, barking orders into his comms. "Get eyes on every corner. We're not letting this shit spill over."

As the chants grew louder and the crowd pushed forward, Caleb's eyes narrowed. It was going to be a long night.

"Caleb."

The sound of Grace's voice cut through the chaos like a steady current in a storm, a calm amidst the madness. Caleb turned instinctively, catching sight of her emerging from the town hall, moving with purpose toward the armored SUV. Her dark coat sliced through the gray backdrop of the scene, her eyes scanning the scene with that sharp, calculating focus that had become all too familiar. There was something about her — something fierce. And it made everyone else look small in comparison.

"You shouldn't be out here," Caleb said, stepping toward her without thinking. His words were sharp, his concern obvious. "Get in the truck."

Grace didn't miss a beat, her tone unshaken as she met his gaze. "The president needs to make a statement. Put these people in their place."

Caleb's jaw tightened, irritation flaring. "Not here. Not now. For fuck's sake, Grace. He stays in the motorcade."

"It worked in New York," she shot back, her voice unwavering, the hint of defiance already rising in her.

"Those were his supporters. These are not," Caleb countered, his eyes narrowing, his posture bracing against the tension that crackled in the air.

Grace didn't stop. She didn't even slow down. She flicked a glance toward the motorcade, where President Armstrong was waiting behind reinforced glass, the Chief of Staff at his side, gesturing animatedly, but the president's eyes were locked on the riot unfolding before him.

"They need to see his face," Grace insisted, stepping closer to Caleb, her voice firm with conviction. "He's stronger than you think."

Caleb's patience thinned, his words coming out clipped, sharp. "It's not about how strong he is or isn't."

Her gaze locked onto his with a flash of irritation. "You don't know how politics works."

Caleb's voice hardened, a command cutting through the air. "The president is staying in the motorcade. That's final."

Grace was unyielding, her stance a perfect mirror of loyalty, of fierce protection. She wasn't backing down, and Caleb knew, without a doubt, that she never would. That was when it hit him like a punch to the gut. Grace wasn't just here for the president. She wasn't just doing her job. She was ride or die. And for the first time in his life, Caleb realized he had someone like that beside him. Someone who would follow through. Someone who believed in him as much as she did in the president.

Before he could respond, a firecracker exploded near the front of the crowd. The sound jolted him, adrenaline spiking in his veins. The protesters surged forward, pushing against the barricades, and the tension in the air snapped, shifting violently. Caleb's body moved before his mind could catch up, instinct driving him to step in front of Grace, his form shielding hers from the chaos.

Her breath hitched slightly, her eyes flicking to his as she looked up at him. He could see it now — the way she didn't flinch, the way she stood her ground with that same intensity that had been there from the beginning. She wasn't afraid. Not of the crowd. Not of the threat. And certainly not of him.

"Grace," Caleb said, his voice low but firm, "get back in the truck."

She didn't budge, her jaw tightening as she looked at him, her gaze never wavering. "I need to be out here," she said, her voice steady, but Caleb could see the tension in her fingers. She was beyond this moment now—beyond the orders, beyond the politics. She was in it for real. With him.

"Why is it always you lingering past everyone else?" Caleb asked, softening his tone just enough to try and understand. "Let me handle this. Not every protester deserves your time."

For the first time, he saw a crack in her armor. Just for a second, a vulnerability flashed in her eyes. It was gone as quickly as it appeared, replaced by the same unshakeable confidence. But it hit Caleb harder than he expected—this woman, this force of nature, wasn't just playing her part. She was in it, heart and soul. The president, the politics, the campaign—it was everything to her.

"Go. Now," he urged, his voice quiet but commanding.

She hesitated. But when their eyes met again, the moment was charged. Something shifted. Caleb didn't know what. It wasn't just duty. It wasn't just loyalty to the job anymore.

Grace exhaled sharply, and her gaze softened, just a touch. "You better not let anything happen to you," she said, her voice low. "These types hate veterans."

Caleb's chest tightened at her words. "I won't," he said. "Just go."

The comms crackled urgently, pulling him back to reality. "North perimeter breached! TVC militants with weapons — requesting backup!"

"Wyatt, pull your team to the north line," Caleb barked, his attention snapping back to the chaos.

The crowd surged again, pushing forward. He moved swiftly, guiding Grace toward the vehicle. His hand brushed her arm as he did, and the contact — brief as it was — sent a spark through him. He didn't have time for distractions, but she was right there, close, impossible to ignore. As she climbed into the truck, he caught a glimpse of her face. Their eyes met for a brief, electrifying moment. Her expression — grateful? Wary? He couldn't be sure.

But it was undeniable.

Then the door slammed shut, and she was gone.

Caleb turned back to the chaos in front of him, the sound of the crowd, the sharp tension in the air, all pulling him into the present. But Grace's face lingered in his mind. The way she had stood there — unfaltering, loyal, a ride or die in every sense of the phrase.

It was something he had never known before. And for a fleeting second, it unsettled him in ways he couldn't explain.

But there was no time to dwell on it now. He had a job to do.

He focused, his mind narrowing to the task ahead. But in the back of his mind, Grace was there, steady and unshakable. And for the first time, Caleb thought maybe he didn't mind it one bit.

* * * *

Whiskey and steak. That's how Caleb did the debrief. No bullshit. Wyatt knew the drill.

The hotel room was dim, the heating unit rumbling softly in the background, the only noise other than the occasional clink of glass. Finding his way beside his teammate Duke, Caleb dropped into a chair near the table, yanked off his tie with a quick tug and tossed it on the tabletop like a useless rag. He dug his fingers into his temples, trying to erase the tension of the day.

Across the room, Wyatt was already at work. The guy was a machine — smooth and efficient, even when it came to pouring whiskey. He set two fingers of bourbon in a glass and extended it toward Caleb with the casual confidence of a guy who knew he'd earned it.

"Well," Wyatt drawled, "that was a damn circus." He refilled Duke's glass.

"Those people need to get some fucking jobs," Duke said.

Caleb grunted and picked up his glass, but didn't immediately sip. His eyes were still glued to the table, his mind replaying the scene outside the town hall. The protesters pushing forward. The breach on the north perimeter. The adrenaline that had been pulsing through his veins.

And Grace. Damn it. Grace.

She had been all about getting Armstrong to make a statement. He could still hear her voice in his head, firm and insistent. But he knew better than anyone that things weren't always so black and white.

Wyatt lowered himself onto the couch with a groan, stretching out like a man who'd been through hell and back — and had a few stories to prove it. "You think they're getting bolder?" he asked, his tone matter-of-fact. "TVC, I mean. They came damn close to making their move today."

"They're escalating," Caleb muttered, his voice as cold as steel. "That wasn't just a protest—it was a dry run. Testing our defenses, seeing how far they could push before we pushed back."

Duke leaned forward in his chair, the creak of his boots making a quiet, ominous sound as he scowled. "Hell, I've been in some sticky situations. But today? That wasn't just a bunch of pissed-off civilians. They were organized, Caleb. Too organized."

Caleb glanced over at Duke. The guy had been in the game longer than most people, and he wasn't one to overstate things. When he said something was off, it was worth paying attention.

"Yeah. Someone's pulling the strings," Caleb agreed, his eyes narrowing as he ran a hand over his jaw. "It's not just some random cells causing trouble anymore. They've got leadership. They've got a plan."

Wyatt swirled his whiskey, the ice clinking in the cup like a reminder of the calm before the storm. "You think it's personal, or just a political statement?"

"Could be both," Caleb said with a slight shrug, finally taking a drink. He didn't flinch at the burn—it was the only thing keeping him grounded at the moment. "But it's more than just the usual political rhetoric. There's too much coordination, too many moving pieces. They're playing a longer game."

Duke grunted and took a long pull from his own glass. "Longer game, huh? I can respect that. But let's be real here for a sec. It's about making noise, making Armstrong look weak, right? This isn't just some protest—they're testing how far they can push. And they know that's going to rattle the cage."

Caleb nodded slowly, thinking about the look on Grace's face when she'd stepped out of the hall, when she'd insisted that Armstrong needed to face the crowd. She wasn't wrong. The optics were everything. But it had felt like something more. And he couldn't quite shake it.

"That's the thing," Caleb muttered, his voice quieter now. "They don't care about optics. They're willing to make a move when the stakes are highest — get people to doubt everything."

Wyatt chuckled darkly. "What's that say about you, then, if you're sitting there thinking about them instead of your dinner?"

Duke snorted. "Yeah, Caleb. You've got a steak, but I'm betting you're chewing on something else."

Caleb shot them both a look that could freeze a man in his tracks. "Well, what the hell do you want me to say? If we're gonna keep doing this job, we need to keep our heads in the game. And right now? This job doesn't give a damn about your whiskey and steak."

But he couldn't help the small, knowing grin that tugged at the corner of his mouth. Wyatt and Duke were right. That was the way of the game. Big men doing big things, fighting for the bigger picture, and damn it, the only thing that kept them sane was cutting loose every once in a while.

And maybe...just maybe, a little humor went a long way in staying sane.

"Besides," Caleb said, slapping the table and leaning back in his chair, "you two jackasses can't even make a proper steak. I don't trust you with my dinner anymore."

Wyatt smirked and raised his glass in a mock toast. "To poor culinary decisions."

Duke laughed, his deep chuckle echoing off the walls. "Hell yeah. And to keeping us all alive long enough to make more bad decisions."

Caleb shook his head, a real grin breaking through. "You two are impossible."

But he didn't mind it. These guys were family now. His crew. And no matter how bad it got out there, they'd have his back. Just like he'd have theirs. Even if it meant laughing in the face of a warzone and ordering up another round.

This was what being part of something was all about. That kind of loyalty.

Before Wyatt could say anything, a sharp knock at the door cut through the silence. Caleb stiffened, his eyes flicking to Wyatt. Neither of them was expecting anyone.

Wyatt, ever the cautious one, reached for his weapon instinctively, but Caleb was already up and moving, striding toward the door with his jaw set. He peered through the peephole, and his stomach dropped.

Adrienne.

His ex-girlfriend was standing there like a goddamn vision of trouble—dark hair perfectly tousled, leather jacket hugging her like it was made for her, eyes sharp as razors. And that smile—he'd never quite trusted it.

Caleb didn't even flinch as he opened the door. "Are you fucking stalking me?"

"I'm with the agency. All I do is stalk." She pushed her way inside without waiting for an invitation, her gaze flicking over him with the precision of a sniper's aim. When she saw Duke and Wyatt, she paused, giving them the briefest of nods, but not enough to make it civil. "Good. You're here too," she said, her tone clipped. "That will keep this clean."

Wyatt grunted. "Always a pleasure."

"No, it's not," Duke said.

Adrienne ignored him, focusing all her attention on Caleb. "I've got intel from today's operation. First-hand surveillance. Am I still unwelcome?"

"Yes." Caleb crossed his arms, barely hiding the irritation bubbling up. "I'm sure your boss at the CIA could just email that over?"

She flashed him a humorless smile, not missing a beat. "Not the kind of intel you email. I needed to deliver it personally." She tossed her bag onto the table and fished out a tablet, setting it down with precision, like she was about to make some grand announcement.

"Personally," Duke repeated. "Got it."

Caleb leaned against the doorframe, too tired for games. "So, what's the real reason you're here, Adrienne?"

"Before we get into that," she said, "you should know something. I saw you today, Caleb. With her."

He felt the blood drain from his face, his muscles going taut. "With who?"

She wasn't letting up. "The campaign chick. You two were practically joined at the hip. And don't act like I didn't notice the way you were looking at her."

Wyatt let out a whistle from the couch, a grin spreading across his face. "Well now, this just got interesting."

Caleb shot him a glare that could've cut glass before turning back to Adrienne. "I was doing my job. Protecting her is most of it." His voice was low, controlled, but the words didn't land the way he wanted them to.

Adrienne tilted her head, a cruel smile dancing at the corners of her mouth. "Protecting her," she repeated, dripping with sarcasm. "Sure. That's what we're calling it now?"

"What the hell is that supposed to mean?"

She stepped closer, her eyes flashing with something — anger, maybe, or something worse. "It means I know you, Caleb. I know how you get when you get too close to someone. You let your guard down, and people get hurt."

Caleb took a step back, his fists clenching involuntarily. "That's enough. Get the fuck out of here."

"Make me," she said.

"You know how to make things personal."

"For once, don't be so self-involved. This isn't just about you and your chiseled abs. It's about the president. If your head's not in the game because you're too busy trying to fuck the campaign assistant, you're a liability."

The words hit harder than he wanted to admit. The tension in the room was palpable. Caleb could feel the old weight of distrust between them — every moment they'd shared in the past seemed to come crashing back like a freight train.

But he didn't let it show.

He clenched his jaw. "You have intel or not?"

Adrienne didn't miss a beat, her fingers flying over the tablet's screen. "Fine. Let's talk about the TVC." Her eyes were locked on the device, but her voice was as steady as ever. "Their operatives weren't just testing your defenses today. They were scouting for a high-profile hit. And I've got evidence that their next target isn't Armstrong."

Caleb's frown deepened. "Who, then?"

Her eyes flicked to a name on the screen, and Caleb's gut twisted. "Her. Your campaign chick. Grace Williams. They want her dead."

The room went silent. Caleb's heart stuttered, but he forced himself to hold it together. *Not now. Not here.* He didn't let it show, but inside, he was seething.

Wyatt broke the silence with a low whistle. "Who the fuck cares about some campaign assistant?"

"They do," Adrienne replied, her voice hardening. "The TVC thinks she's too close to getting Armstrong re-elected. If they take her out, it sends a message. To everyone watching." She leaned in slightly, eyes narrowing. "They're going after what hurts."

Wyatt snorted. "Nice. Killed for being too good at your job. Classic."

Adrienne shot him a look of contempt before turning back to Caleb. "They were after her in the cornfield. It's been the TVC this whole time."

Caleb didn't respond. His mind was already working, moving faster than he wanted it to. Grace was a target. Grace, the one person who could be the key to Armstrong's re-election.

Wyatt's voice broke through Caleb's thoughts. "What do you want us to do with this info, Adrienne? Spell it out for us."

Caleb didn't even look at him. His focus was all on Adrienne. But his fists were clenched, and his eyes narrowed.

"We handle it," Caleb said, his voice as tight as a wire. He was ready to move, to act, but something gnawed at him. "But this doesn't end with intel, Adrienne. You can't just walk back into my life and expect me to trust you again."

Adrienne didn't flinch. "I'm not asking for your *trust*, Caleb. I'm asking you to be professional — and listen."

"Listen, to you?"

"I'm trying to help you."

"I'm sure you are.

"Stop ignoring my calls," she said.

Caleb stared at her. "Fuck you."

Duke sighed from the couch, clearly enjoying the show. "Well, this just turned into a hell of a reunion. How about we all agree not to kill each other before we finish dinner?"

Caleb shot him a look, but couldn't help the corner of his mouth pulling upward. If anyone could keep the peace, it was Duke. At least, for now.

Chapter Eight

Grace sat at the hotel bar, the dull light overhead casting deep shadows across her tired face. The amber liquid in her glass swirled in lazy circles as she stared into it, the hum of voices around her nothing more than a distant murmur. The weight of the day — the protest, the threats, the constant tension — gripped her chest like a vise, and no amount of whiskey could ease the pressure.

Her mind buzzed with fragments of the chaos — the violent surge of protesters, the near breach of security, and, of course, the way Caleb had been there — close, protective, but distant. She sighed, tipping the glass to her lips for another sip, hoping it would drown out the rest.

Jordan Simmons slid into the seat beside her, the smooth rustle of his tailored jacket louder than any of the background noise. His eyes were focused, calculating as always, but there was something else there—an unspoken awareness of just how close they'd come to losing control today.

"You're late," Grace muttered, not bothering to turn her head. She stared ahead, tracing the rim of her glass with her finger, feeling the chill of it against her skin. The burn of whiskey didn't seem to cut through the fog of exhaustion and frustration that clouded her mind.

"Had to make sure the motorcade was secure," Jordan said, his voice low, steady. It wasn't an explanation—it didn't need to be. They both knew what had happened outside the town hall, and neither of them was in the mood to relive it.

Grace let out a breath, the tension in her shoulders settling a little. "That was a mess out there."

Jordan shifted in his seat, his gaze lingering on her for a moment before he replied, his voice softer than usual, "You okay?"

It was too damn soft, and it made her flinch. Jordan wasn't the type to ask if you were okay. He was the type to make sure you stayed on task, to push you when you hesitated. But today...today was different.

"I'll be fine," Grace muttered, her tone flat, dismissive. She didn't want to admit she was rattled. Didn't want to admit how much of her focus had slipped today—not just on the situation, but on the feeling that something had changed in the way she'd been looking at Caleb. Something she couldn't shake. Something that felt...dangerous.

Jordan didn't push her. Instead, he slid a file across the bar to her, a silent gesture that didn't need words. She didn't hesitate. Her fingers flipped open the file, scanning the contents without really reading them. She'd seen it all before—threats, surveillance, another escalation. They were always a step behind the TVC. Always reacting.

"You know they're escalating," Grace murmured, tracing her finger over the lines of the report, though her mind was miles away. The protest, the crowd, the violence — it was still fresh in her mind. But Caleb was there too, his presence unsettling in a way she hadn't expected.

Jordan's voice was tight, a touch of frustration leaking through. "Yeah. It's not just a protest anymore. They're testing the waters. Pushing until they figure out what's going to make us break. This is just the start."

"I know," she whispered, her voice thick with the weight of the truth. "Two weeks. Just two weeks left, and we need to keep these protests off the damn radar. They can't be part of the narrative."

Jordan's eyes narrowed, his frustration showing through. "This is bigger than politics now, Grace. These people are relentless. They won't stop until they've made their point, and we're just one damn spark away from it all going up in flames."

Grace reached for her drink again, the burn of whiskey doing little to ease the gnawing ache in her chest. She didn't answer immediately. Instead, she crumpled the napkin beside her in her fingers, squeezing it tight until it was a little ball of frustration. "I'm sick of these goddamn warriors showing up to everything. Every single protest, every rally, like they're the only ones who matter."

Jordan exhaled a low breath, clearly ready to vent himself. "God, I'm so ready to be back in DC tomorrow. Debate time. Let's get back to taking on a real opponent. These protesters are just a fucking distraction."

Grace shook her head, the weight of the day pressing down even harder. "I'm not ready for that. I'm too distracted. Too tired." Her voice trailed off, and for a second, she allowed herself a moment of vulnerability. The exhaustion from today, the weight of the fight ahead — it was all starting to feel like too much.

Jordan didn't respond immediately. Instead, he took a sip of his own drink, the silence between them comfortable in its own way. He knew when to push and when to give space.

"I get it," he said, his voice quieter now. "It's a hell of a lot. But we're in it now. And we'll keep pushing forward, Grace. We have to."

She nodded but didn't reply. She wasn't sure if she was just too tired to argue or if, for the first time in a long while, she actually needed someone to tell her it was going to be okay. The quiet stretched out, broken only by the sound of ice clinking in glasses and the hum of the world continuing around them.

For now, it was enough to sit in, let the weight of the day settle, and brace for whatever came next.

"Everything all right?" Caleb was a presence before he even stepped into view, and Grace's heart skipped a beat. His eyes flicked between them, unreadable. He'd just come from the chaos outside, his military precision still written all over him.

Grace wasn't prepared for him to step into the room like that. She couldn't stop the flutter in her chest, couldn't stop the way her body responded to him, even though she tried to push it down.

He was standing there, just beyond the door, his eyes flicking between her and Jordan. There was that unreadable intensity in them again, that look he always had, as if he was calculating everything around him. But Grace couldn't look away. He was too damn present—too strong. She couldn't stop noticing how every inch of him seemed designed for power. His jaw was set, his broad shoulders filling the doorway like a wall, like he could take on anything, anyone.

"Ready for tomorrow?" Caleb asked, his voice steady, yet it seemed to carry weight. It felt like it wrapped around her, making her feel small, and she hated how much she responded to it.

His eyes lingered on her, steady and unyielding, and her pulse tripped again, racing now. She wasn't prepared for this—not for the way he could affect her with a simple glance. The man was a force, and it made her flustered in a way she hated to admit.

"Mostly," she managed, her voice coming out steadier than she felt, but she couldn't deny the way her body responded to his proximity. The heat of his presence felt too close, too demanding. The unspoken words between them, the space that seemed to narrow the more he stood there, making her want to scream.

Caleb didn't break the stare, his gaze flicking over Jordan, then back to her. His eyes hardened, and the air seemed to thicken. "Good. Because the next round's gonna be worse. And I need everyone sharp."

Jordan nodded, but Grace could feel the underlying tension, the silent understanding that had nothing to do with words. Caleb was here to protect, to keep everyone safe. But it wasn't just that. The way his presence dominated the room made her second guess everything she thought she knew about herself. She felt him—strong, demanding. It made her head spin.

And then he stepped closer. It wasn't far, but it was enough that she could feel the heat coming off him. His stance was wide, solid, like he could hold the world on his shoulders if need be. His scent hit her — clean, sharp, uncompromising. It felt like she was suffocating, and yet, she wanted more.

His lips parted like he was about to say something, but the moment was broken by the shrill beep of his comms. Frustration flashed and for just a second, Grace saw the weight of his job press down on him, the responsibility etched in the hard lines of his face.

"Stay here. Have a good night," Caleb said, his voice low, but that look he gave her — just a beat too long — had her frozen in place. It was like a promise, or a warning. Maybe both. He didn't need to say more.

He turned, his broad back retreating from her line of sight, and it took everything in her to not call after him, to not let herself linger on the way his body moved, how effortlessly powerful he was. But she did. She turned to Jordan instead, trying to focus on anything but the man who had just walked out. She wasn't prepared for how much Caleb had thrown her off balance tonight. But that was the thing with him. He was always there, always pushing her boundaries in ways she wasn't ready for, making her question everything she thought she knew about herself.

Jordan, however, was watching her now, the curiosity clear in his eyes. "You good?" he asked, half teasing, half concerned.

Grace nodded, forcing herself to clear her throat. "Yeah. Just fine." But the flush creeping up her neck betrayed her. She had never been good at lying to herself, especially not when it came to Caleb.

"What's going on between you two?" Jordan asked, his tone light but with an edge of something deeper.

Grace didn't answer right away. Her lips parted, but the words didn't come. Instead, she leaned back, feeling the tension ebbing from her shoulders in the stillness that followed.

"Nothing," she said quietly, the weight of her own uncertainty hanging in the air. "He's the bodyguard."

Jordan threw some money on the table. "For the drinks. I'm heading to bed. Get an early night, Grace."

* * * *

Hours later, Caleb walked back into the bar, pausing at the edge for a moment as he watched Grace sitting alone in a booth. She traced the edge of her laptop, her eyes distant, her fingers absentmindedly.

The dim lighting of the bar softened the sharp edges of the world, but it couldn't stop the pull he felt toward her. He'd had a few drinks already, the warmth spreading through him, a devil at the back of his mind urging him to go to bed. But something about Grace kept him from walking away.

Grace hadn't noticed him yet, so he let her stay lost in her own world for a moment. She had a way of doing that, of retreating when things got heavy. He could see it in the tightness of her shoulders, the way her gaze flickered across the room without truly seeing anything. But even in this moment of distance, she was still magnetic. He couldn't stop himself from wanting to know what was happening inside her, especially when she wouldn't tell him.

He walked forward and slipped into the booth beside her, perhaps a little too close. Her eyes snapped up when he slid into the booth next to her, the faintest flash of surprise flickering across her face before she quickly masked it with something unreadable. Annoyance, maybe. He couldn't tell.

"Haven't moved?" he said, voice low, as if the words themselves might be too much for the space between them. His own breath felt a little too heavy, his chest a little too tight. He'd meant to go to bed, meant to take the night off. But now that he was here, so close, he couldn't walk away.

"Not yet—but it's getting late. I should go." Grace's lips curved into a thin, nonchalant smile, but the tension in her eyes told him everything. She wasn't as unaffected as she was trying to seem.

"Have a drink with me."

"Funny," she replied, her voice smooth but edged with something Caleb couldn't quite place. "I didn't think you were allowed."

"I'm not working right now."

"Aren't you always working?" Her gaze flickered to his, then quickly back to her wine glass. There was something in the way she held herself that was impossible to ignore. She wasn't quite pushing him away, but she wasn't welcoming him either. Still, it didn't stop him from leaning in slightly, drawn by her presence, the familiar tension between them settling in.

"Grace."

She sipped her wine slowly, as if trying to find time.

Her message was clear, and he could have easily turned away, could've left before it got messy, but that wasn't what he wanted. Not tonight. Maybe it was the drink, maybe it was her, but Caleb found himself unable to pull away from her. Every instinct told him to go, to cut the tension and walk out—but it felt like something inside him was caught. Trapped, but in a way he didn't want to escape.

"You want me to leave?" His tone was a challenge, but it came out softer than he intended.

Grace didn't answer right away. Instead, she just studied him, as if weighing her next move. The silence stretched out, thick and suffocating, before she finally spoke. "Well, when you put it like that, it sounds rather rude."

"One drink," he said.

"Fine."

He motioned to the bartender and turned back to her. "Tell me why you're still sitting here?" His voice was barely above a whisper now, the pull between them becoming impossible to ignore. He was beyond trying to fight it.

After a beat, she met his eyes again. The deflection was gone, and all that remained was the raw honesty between them. "Because I didn't want to be alone."

The bartender arrived, serving them two red wines and taking her empty glass away.

As Grace sampled her new wine, Caleb felt the last of his resistance fall away. Whatever the hell this was, whatever was between them, it was always going to draw him to her. And maybe that was a mistake, but in this moment, he didn't care. He didn't want to be alone either.

"Excellent pinot."

"Delicious," he said, his voice a little rougher than he intended after he took a long swig. "So, let's not change the subject."

"I've just been thinking tonight," she replied, but he could hear the edge to her voice. "It's been a lot lately and I'm reflecting."

"On what?"

She met his eyes for a moment, a flicker of something there—something he couldn't quite place. Then, like always, she masked it with a quick glance downward. "About how much has been...out of my control," she said, her words crisp, like she was trying to force them into something more manageable. "The protest, the TVC, the president—and you."

Caleb's pulse quickened, though his face stayed unreadable. "Me?"

"Yeah. You," she repeated, eyes sharp. "It's...complicated."

Caleb didn't lean back, didn't give her any space. "Complicated is one way of putting it." He let the words linger, just enough to keep the tension tight.

"What does that mean?" she asked, her voice suddenly quiet, like she was trying to draw him out.

"Means I don't believe you," he replied with a small smile. "You're holding something back. What do I have to do to get you to talk?"

"You aren't really an interrogator, are you?"

"Never was my thing."

"It's hard to let it all out," Grace met his gaze again, her breath catching slightly before she said, "I don't want to be a damsel. I don't need saving."

A low chuckle escaped him, but there was no humor behind it. "Never said you did. But said it yourself— you are tired of being alone." He leaned forward just enough for her to feel the weight of his presence, the edge of something that wasn't quite professional anymore. "Ever thought maybe you could use someone to watch your back for once?"

Her eyes darkened, and he saw something— defiance, desire, maybe both—crossing her face. "You think you're the one to have my back?" she asked, her words sharp, but her body betraying her.

Caleb's lips curved upward, just barely, like he was enjoying this more than he should. "I think I'm the best option."

The corner of her mouth twitched, and for a second, he thought she might say something—argue, snap, make it clear she wasn't about to let him get away with that kind of arrogance. But instead, she just leaned back, her eyes holding his for a beat longer than was strictly necessary.

"Why are you here, Caleb? Why did you really show up here, at the end of the night, demanding I have a drink with you?"

He knew what she was really asking. Why him? Why now?

He leaned back in his seat, his gaze flicking over her once more—assessing, weighing, but never fully revealing. "Because I'm trying to figure you out."

"For work or personal reasons?"

"Can it be both? You are a mystery that I want to solve."

Her breath hitched slightly, just enough for him to notice. But she recovered quickly, her walls slamming back into place. "What do you think you're gonna find?"

He leaned in again, this time his hand dropped on her thigh, and just for a second. "Maybe I'll find that you like someone else being the boss."

Grace's breath caught, her fingers curling tighter around her glass, but she didn't pull away. For a moment, neither of them moved—too close, too charged, the line between them finally too thin to ignore.

"I should get to bed." She stood up abruptly and waltzed away, leaving him hungry as fuck.

Grace's hand shook ever so slightly as she swiped the key card at her hotel room door, her mind still racing from the conversation at the bar. Her heart wasn't exactly settled either—more like a knot of tension, tight and pulling at her insides. She wasn't used to feeling this...unsettled.

She didn't expect him to follow her, but the sound of heavy footsteps behind her made her pause before the door even fully opened. She didn't have to look to know who it was. Caleb's presence was unmistakable. It always had been.

She turned the handle with a quick twist, the door swinging open, and without a second's hesitation, she grabbed his arm—strong and warm—and yanked him inside. The hallway light flickered for a moment before the door clicked shut behind them, cutting off the outside world in a quick sweep of silence.

Caleb didn't flinch, didn't hesitate. He stepped inside, his eyes scanning the room, but the moment they locked onto hers, something shifted. His expression was unreadable, his jaw tight in that familiar, calculating way. But Grace could see the way his gaze narrowed, how the air between them thickened.

She hadn't wanted to make a scene in the hallway, didn't want to have to explain anything to anyone who might wander by, so she'd acted on instinct. Pulling the door shut behind them was supposed to create some distance—some kind of barrier between her and whatever was happening with Caleb.

But the space between them only seemed to shrink, his heat filling the small room, his presence almost too much to ignore. Grace's back hit the door as Caleb stepped closer, a quiet tension in his movements that mirrored her own.

"Grace..." His voice was low, rough—an undertone of something more dangerous beneath it. Whiskey and wine left them more careless than before.

She swallowed, her breath catching in her throat as she looked up at him, the dim light casting shadows across his face. It was the way he looked at her, like he was trying to peel her open, see inside, and she hated how much she wanted him to.

He was already too close, his chest just brushing hers as his hand moved up to touch the side of her face. His fingers lingered there, teasing, before sliding down the curve of her jaw to her neck.

"You followed me," she said. She ran her hand up his chest. "Why?"

"I don't know."

"Tell me."

"You sure you want to do this?" he asked, his voice a mere whisper, his breath warm against her skin. There was no need for an answer.

Grace's pulse quickened—just a soft push, but it was barely a suggestion as he leaned in even closer, until she could feel a wall of muscle against her. She pressed her lips together, trying to steady herself, but her body betrayed her—responding to him in ways she couldn't control.

"I... I'm not sure what I'm doing anymore," she muttered, her voice strained. She could feel him so close, the heat of him like a fire threatening to consume her, and she hated how much she wanted to burn.

Caleb didn't answer at first. Instead, his lips brushed against her ear, sending a shiver down her spine. "You need to let go," he murmured, his voice low and husky with something far deeper than just desire. "Let someone else be in control."

"Of me?"

"Hell yes."

Her breath hitched as his lips trailed down her neck, a slow, deliberate kiss that made her stomach flip. His hands were everywhere—firm against her waist, pulling her closer, guiding her, as if trying to erase all the space that had ever existed between them.

He growled as he explored, telling her wanted to taste more than just her tongue.

"Caleb…" Her voice cracked, the sound of his name like a warning on her lips, but it came out more like a plea than a protest. She wasn't sure what she wanted, but in that moment, her body knew exactly what it was craving. He pulled at her shirt, her pants—tearing everything off until she was up against the wall in her bra and panties. His touch made her feel like she was spinning—like she was losing control and couldn't quite find the ground beneath her.

His eyes locked onto hers again, something feral in his gaze now. "Tell me to stop," he said, his voice barely a whisper, but the challenge in it was unmistakable. "You don't want me to."

She opened her mouth to speak, but the words caught. She didn't want him to stop. God, she didn't want him to stop. But she wasn't ready to admit that— not yet, not in this moment when everything was on the verge of breaking.

Instead, she reached up, threading her fingers into his hair, tugging him down to meet her lips in a kiss that was messy and desperate, as if she were trying to savor the heat before it consumed them both. Caleb groaned, the sound low and primal, as his hands slid down her sides, pulling her flush against him.

This time, there was no hesitation, no space between them. It was nothing but heat, nothing but the raw, unspoken tension that had been building for days now, finally igniting into something that felt too dangerous to ignore.

She kissed him harder, her body pressing into his as she felt his hands moving lower — sliding over her hips, pulling her closer. The way he touched her felt like it was meant to set her on fire. Her head spun with it, the overwhelming warmth of him flooding her senses, making it impossible to focus on anything other than him, other than the way his mouth moved against hers, the way his body seemed to envelop hers completely.

But just when she thought she couldn't take it anymore, when she thought her heart might explode with how badly she needed him — he pulled back, just enough to look at her, his face inches from hers.

"I can't be trusted with y—" She started as he yanked his shirt over his head in one smooth motion, tossing it onto the bed without a second thought. Grace froze mid-sentence. Whatever words were coming out died on her tongue as her eyes landed on Caleb's bare chest.

She was not prepared for the sight of him like this — broad shoulders, defined pecs, and abs that looked carved from stone. His tan skin gleamed faintly with a sheen of sweat, and a faint scar trailed along his side, adding a roughness that only enhanced the image.

"You've been hiding that under a suit this whole time?" she said, half-joking but entirely unable to look away. Her tone was light, but her voice betrayed her surprise — and appreciation.

Caleb turned, his brow furrowed in confusion until he caught the way her gaze lingered. A slow, amused smile tugged at the corner of his mouth. "Didn't know you were keeping tabs on my wardrobe."

She rolled her eyes, trying to recover her composure, though her cheeks flushed pink. "I'm not. But seriously, do you live in a gym or something?"

Caleb chuckled, taking her mouth in another long kiss before replying. "I've got more important things to do than impress anyone."

Her lips quirked into a smirk. "Too bad. It's working anyway."

That earned her a glance, his expression unreadable but his eyes sharp. Grace wasn't sure if she'd managed to fluster him — or if he was just amused by her boldness — but she didn't care. She just felt him — and every hard muscle. He groaned, reacting in response. She was turning him on.

"You sure about this?" he asked, his voice a little raspier, a little more strained than before.

The room seemed to shrink around them, the air thick with desire and the weight of everything they hadn't said. Grace's breath was shallow, her chest rising and falling quickly as she met his gaze.

"This isn't right," she whispered, her voice trembling, her body aching for more. "But I'm done pretending I don't want it."

The corner of Caleb's mouth quirked up into a half-smile, a flicker of something — amusement, or maybe satisfaction — in his eyes. "Good," he murmured. "Me too."

And before she could say anything else, he kissed her again — this time, there was nothing gentle about it. It was heated, relentless, a storm that neither of them was trying to stop.

Caleb's mind was a blur. One moment, he was standing there, barely able to breathe with the heat between them — his hands on her, his lips on hers — and the next, it was like the world had tilted. Everything else faded. The weight of her body against his, the way she kissed him back with such fierce need, was all that mattered.

His hands were on her now — every inch of her soft skin, the curve of her waist, the sharpness of her collarbone under his fingertips. She was better than he'd expected. Warmer. Softer. The way she reacted to him. The tension in his chest had exploded into something much hotter, much more demanding. He couldn't slow down.

Grace's breath hitched as his hands skimmed up her sides, over her full breasts bursting out of her bra. Fuck, they were perfect. And then she was pulling away from his mouth, gasping, eyes wide with something like surprise, like shock, but there was no fear in her expression. Only want. The kind of raw hunger he couldn't deny, the kind he knew all too well.

"Caleb…" Her voice was a low plea, but she didn't stop him. Didn't push him away. His lips were on her again, tasting her skin, her neck, his breath heavy as he worked to get closer, to strip away anything between them.

His heart hammered in his chest, adrenaline coursing through his veins like fire. The thought of stopping, of holding back, vanished as quickly as it had appeared. There was no turning back now. He needed this. He needed her, and he wasn't going to apologize for it.

"Grace..." he muttered her name like a prayer, a command, his hands now at her waist, yanking her closer, his body pressing against hers. The feel of her softness, the way she trembled under him, sent a rush of heat through him. It was dizzying, suffocating, in the best way. He kissed her again, deeper this time, his mouth demanding as he peeled away more layers — more of the walls she'd built around herself. He felt her tongue against his and immediately hardened to the point of pain.

Her bra followed quickly. His hands roamed freely now, desperate and greedy as he traced the lines of her back, her breasts, her nipples — feeling the heat radiating off her skin. She didn't move away, instead, she pressed against him harder, her breath matching the frantic rhythm of his.

Caleb pulled back just long enough to look at her. She was wild — eyes dark, lips swollen, chest rising and falling with shallow breaths. His stomach tightened, the need to possess her, to feel her closer than ever, surging through him.

Without warning, he scooped her up, lifting her in his arms with ease, and she gasped, her arms locking around his neck. She was smaller than he expected — lighter, fragile in the way a storm could be, swirling with power under the surface. He was quick, the urgency in every movement as he laid her down on the bed.

Her eyes followed as he stood over her, chest heaving, desire like a physical thing crawling beneath his skin. Her hands were still on him, touching him, pulling him toward her. The heat between them was unbearable, and he knew they wouldn't last much longer like this — teasing, taunting.

"Caleb..."

He didn't wait for permission. She wasn't shy, wasn't holding back. Her body pressed into his, desperate for more.

Grace's legs wrapped around him as he moved on top of her, his body heavy, but her touch made him feel weightless, like he was floating and falling all at once. Her lips were on his again, wild and searching, and Caleb's pulse raced as he let the sensation swallow him whole.

He didn't want to stop. Didn't care about anything else. There was only this — only her. The way she felt under him, the way she responded to every touch. Every kiss.

"Girl," he said, his voice a gravelly whisper as his hands slid beneath her, fingers tracing the curve of her spine, pulling her tighter to him. "You drive me insane."

But her answer was only a soft gasp, her lips finding his again in a kiss that was all fire, all need. She was everything he'd ever wanted — wild, untamed, full of passion and fire.

Grace was trembling — not from fear, but from the overwhelming energy radiating from Caleb. His mouth was claiming hers in a kiss so fierce, so consuming, it stole the breath from her lungs. Her hands instinctively clutched his shoulders, her fingers digging into the solid muscle. He tasted like wildness and heat, his lips demanding, his teeth grazing hers as though he couldn't get close enough.

"You drive me insane," he rasped against her lips, his voice thick with hunger and frustration. "Do you even know what you do to me?"

Grace couldn't answer, couldn't think. All she could do was feel—his hands sliding up her thighs, opening her legs to his exploration. His piercing blue eyes burned into her, unrelenting, his jaw clenched as though he were battling a war within himself. She knew what this was. She could feel it too, a magnetic pull that refused to let either of them stop.

"I'm done pretending," Caleb growled as he kissed down her jaw and throat. "That I can hold back. That I can let you look at me like this, and not lose my goddamn mind." She shivered at the raw possessiveness in his tone, but she didn't flinch.

"Maybe I like driving you crazy," she shot back, her own voice breathless but defiant.

He moved lower on her, sucking on her nipples and massaging her breasts. "You like pushing me until I can't hold back? Time for my revenge." He bit at her nipple.

Her breath hitched as his nip sent a thrill racing through her. She could only moan in response. The way her body arched into his, the way her lips parted in anticipation, said everything about their connection.

Caleb settled down further, his mouth finding the mound of her pussy, softer this time but no less consuming. He parted her sensitive folds and licked her clit like she was his air, like he couldn't breathe without her. And when he finally pulled back, his gaze up and locking with hers, his voice was raw and unguarded.

"Like that?" Caleb asked, his voice low, the words thick with meaning.

Grace didn't answer immediately. She couldn't. She was moaning and twisting. He was pinning her down. The way he was savoring her—like he was tasting something far more than just pussy—had her transfixed. She was watching his lips, his tongue darting in and out. Moving up and down.

There was something hypnotic about the way he pleasured her, the way he didn't rush, letting her juice drip down his fingers and over his lips, his eyes never wavering from hers. His hands were rough, calloused from years of hard work, but the way he held her ass, angling her pussy to his mouth was deliberate, sensual, like it was a small, fleeting indulgence.

Grace's lips parted, her breath barely audible, and she could feel pleasure building inside her. He was bringing her to the edge with every lick and pulse. And the show was damn fine. She could see the muscles in his arm flexing as he raised her closer to his mouth, determined, his movements purposeful, drawn out, every little motion meant to make her explode.

"Take your time," she said, her voice lower now, teasing. "You seem to enjoy it."

Caleb's eyes darkened, his smile turning into something more dangerous. "I enjoy a lot of things," he replied, his tone rich with intent. "But, this. This is beyond enjoyment."

And then he launched his final attack. Moving faster and faster, he pulled her pussy harder to his mouth. His tongue and fingers worked in a professional rhythm. Like he knew exactly how to make her sing.

And God, he fucking did.

Then, he hit a sweet spot. She was spinning. Tumbling. Calling out his name.

Caleb's lips curled into a knowing smile, a flash of amusement flickering in his eyes. "That's the idea," he said, before taking another slow lick, letting her rock back against his fingers. His gaze never wavered from hers.

She actually screamed when the orgasm hit her. Her whole body rocked. She spun out, unable to catch her breath. He licked every last moment out of her until she fought back tears.

She hadn't come like that…ever.

As she was trembling post-orgasm, Caleb pulled away and wiped it all from his mouth, clearly savoring her flavor. She curled up on her side, humming with a mixture of complete calm and serenity.

And still wanting him close.

Caleb had a way of doing that to her — making her want him with every touch, every glance, every quiet, teasing word.

As if reading her mind, he laid down behind her, spooning her. He held her close to his chest, breathing into her hair. She was in a different dimension.

She was losing whatever game it was. And she didn't care.

* * * *

The room had grown quiet, save for the soft hum of the air conditioning and the occasional rustle of the sheets as Caleb shifted behind her. Grace lay on her side, her back pressed against the warmth of his chest. She hadn't realized how much she needed the quiet, how much she needed to unwind until this moment.

Caleb's presence was a grounding force, steady and reassuring. He was close, so close that she could feel his breath against her skin. His body was relaxed, a comforting weight against hers, and as his arms snaked around her waist, pulling her even closer, Grace felt her tension melt away. The heat from his body seeped into hers, filling every inch of space between them, and for the first time in what felt like forever, she felt completely at peace.

She could hear his breathing deepen, slow and steady, a rhythm that soothed her, lulling her into a trance-like state. His arms were firm but gentle around her, one hand resting on her stomach, the other tucked beneath her chin, holding her close. His chest rose and fell with each breath, and the sound of it was as constant and comforting as the ticking of a clock.

Grace shifted slightly and she felt his lips brush against the back of her neck. It was a soft kiss, almost absentminded, as if he didn't want to disturb the calm they'd found in each other's presence. She didn't respond to it with words, but her body relaxed further into his embrace, her muscles unwinding.

His touch was like a balm, a quiet reassurance that the chaos of the day, of the world outside, was far away now. There were no protests, no threats, no demands on them — just the silence of the room, the warmth of his body, and the steady rhythm of his breathing.

Grace felt her eyelids grow heavy, the pull of sleep becoming irresistible. Her body was so relaxed, her mind so quiet, that she couldn't remember the last time she'd felt so completely at ease. She let out a soft sigh, her fingers curling loosely around his hand as it rested on her stomach. The pressure of his touch was grounding, a reminder that she was safe, that she didn't have to be the strong, controlled version of herself right now.

His lips grazed her ear, and she felt the faintest smile tug at her lips.

"Sleep, girl," he murmured, his voice low and thick with exhaustion. "I've got you."

The words were simple, but they carried a weight that sent a shiver down her spine. It wasn't just the promise of protection. It was the quiet, unwavering certainty in his voice, the knowledge that he meant it.

She let herself go then, her body sinking into the warmth of the bed, the softness of the sheets, and the strength of his embrace. She could feel the tension that had held her captive for so long finally loosen its grip. With each slow, steady breath, she sank deeper into relaxation.

The world outside felt so distant now—like a memory, a place she no longer needed to worry about. Caleb's presence was the only thing that mattered, and in that moment, with his arms wrapped around her, she knew she was safe. The soft murmur of his breathing behind her was the lullaby she'd been craving, and as sleep finally overtook her, Grace let herself drift away, her heart lighter than it had been in weeks.

* * * *

Caleb woke slowly, his body still heavy with sleep, his mind sluggish as he became aware of the soft sheets around him. The smell of her—citrus and something warmer, sweeter—lingered in the air. For a moment, he let himself savor the stillness, the quiet intimacy of the space, before his eyes fluttered open.

The dim glow from the streetlights outside filtered through the blinds, casting faint shadows across the room. He blinked, adjusting to the soft light, and then, as the fog of sleep cleared, he realized what had pulled him from his slumber—the sharp, insistent pull of reality.

The clock on the nightstand read 4:03 a.m.

Shit.

He had to get back to his own room. His mind jolted into focus, heart rate picking up as he carefully untangled himself from the sheets. Grace lay in front of him, her back still turned, the slow rise and fall of her chest signaling that she was deep in sleep. Her hair splayed across the pillow, her skin soft under the moonlight.

He stared at her for a long moment. A part of him didn't want to leave—couldn't imagine stepping out of this bubble they'd created, this fragile moment that was theirs alone. But the other part of him, the part that was always aware of duty, of the mission, knew he couldn't stay.

With quiet care, Caleb slid out of bed, careful not to disturb her. He dressed quickly in the dark, his movements practiced and efficient. Every movement was precise, but as he stood, taking one last look at Grace, a knot tightened in his chest. He hadn't planned this. He hadn't planned any of it.

Stepping out into the hall, he let the door click shut behind him, swallowing the uneasy tension in his chest. The hallway was silent—empty. He walked down the narrow corridor to his own room, his mind racing.

What the hell had just happened?

He'd crossed a line. A line he hadn't even known existed between them until it was too late. And now, in the cool, detached quiet of the hallway, it felt real. Felt like a mistake, like something he couldn't easily undo.

But then again, he hadn't exactly been trying to stop it, had he?

His stomach tightened as he slid his key card into the door of his room. The familiar sterile feel of the suite greeted him—nothing like the warmth he'd just left behind. He took a deep breath, exhaling slowly as he tossed his jacket onto the chair and stripped out of his clothes.

The cold water of the shower hit him like a jolt of clarity. As it warmed, steam fogged up the mirrors, the heat stinging against his skin, but it didn't clear the haze in his mind. He stood there for a long moment, the water running down his body, trying to scrub away the tension, the warmth of Grace's touch that had still lingered on him like an aftertaste.

But nothing could erase what had happened between them. The way she'd looked at him, the way he'd felt her body against his, the way everything in the room had faded into a blur of heat and desire. He hadn't been in control. Not entirely.

And then there was the conversation—barely spoken, but so much more than just their words. The quiet urgency in her eyes, the way her breath had hitched when he'd kissed her. That had been real, undeniable.

But he'd crossed the line. And now, he had to figure out what to do next.

He turned off the water, stepping out of the shower then toweling off quickly. His reflection in the mirror looked like a man who had spent the night doing everything he'd promised himself he wouldn't.

He swiped a hand through his damp hair, staring at his reflection like it could give him some answers. But it didn't. The only thing he saw was a man who had let his guard down for the first time in years. And for what? A moment of clarity, or just a fleeting rush of something he hadn't expected?

No, he reminded himself, this was a complication. It was nothing more than a complication.

His thoughts were tangled, knots of conflicting emotions that didn't seem to have a place to go. He didn't know what to do next. He didn't know if it was even possible to pretend that nothing had happened. He didn't even know if he *wanted* to.

But what he did know was that he couldn't be the kind of man who let this pull him in deeper. He had a job to do. And as much as he wanted to keep drifting back into the warmth of the bed, the comfort of her, he had to stay focused.

The mission had to come first.

With a last glance at his undisturbed bed, Caleb left the room, the door clicking shut behind him. The hallway was quiet again. His thoughts were anything but.

And as he headed down the corridor to the elevator, he realized there was only one thing he knew for sure. He wasn't ready to let her go.

Chapter Nine

The TV studio was alive with energy — chaotic, controlled chaos. Bright lights flashed overhead, cameras moved in and out like hungry beasts, and reporters clustered together, their voices rising in a blend of excitement and curiosity. The atmosphere was thick with the tension of a live debate — expectation hanging in the air like a storm waiting to break.

Grace sat at the edge of the president's prep room, a laptop open in front of her as she reviewed the final talking points. She felt the weight of the world pressing down on her shoulders. The protest from the town hall still hung in the air like a lingering aftertaste. It was a spectacle. And now, the press was turning its eyes on her. The political strategies she'd built for President Armstrong's campaign were being questioned, her every move dissected and analyzed in real-time. She had to be flawless tonight—no room for mistakes.

She was used to the pressure, but today, it felt different. Everything had felt different for days.

The kiss. The moment in her hotel room. The softness of Caleb's touch, the heat in his eyes, the way he made her feel alive in a way no one else had. She could still feel the ghost of his presence against her skin, and it was distracting. The vulnerability it had sparked—something she didn't like to acknowledge, something she wasn't sure she knew how to handle.

She shook her head, trying to push the thoughts aside. *Focus, Grace. You've got a job to do.*

The door creaked open, and Caleb's presence filled the room like it always did—heavy, suffocating. Grace didn't need to look up to know it was him. The familiar scent of his cologne and the sheer force of him had her tensing before he even spoke. She hated how much she could sense him now.

"Everything ready?" she asked, voice clipped, sharper than she'd intended.

"Just about," Caleb replied, his tone as cool and detached as ever. He moved toward the corner of the room, checking the monitor like she wasn't standing there, like she wasn't trying to hold it together. His eyes flicked to her, but he didn't meet her gaze. She could feel the weight of them anyway.

Grace pressed her lips together, forcing herself to stay composed. She refused to let him see any weakness. Not now. Not after everything that had happened between them. She couldn't let him back in, not when she was still so damn pissed at him.

"So, after the election, you'll be reassigned?" she asked, barely more than a murmur, but she knew he heard it. It wasn't even a question for him. It was just her acknowledging the cold distance between them.

He didn't answer right away, of course. Caleb never did. He was a master at retreating into silence when it suited him. It drove her insane.

Instead of replying, he stepped closer to her desk, blocking her view of the screen. The heat from his body radiated toward her, but she stiffened, refusing to let it affect her. She couldn't—she wouldn't let him do this again.

"The president's going to be under a lot of pressure tonight," Caleb said, his voice low, controlled, like he was speaking to a subordinate. "Let's stay focused."

Grace's hands tightened on the edge of the desk, the words a slap in her face. *Focus*. She didn't need a lecture from him. This was her job. This was what she did. She didn't need him questioning her ability to do it.

"I've got it under control," she said, forcing the calm into her voice, forcing herself not to snap. "We've prepped him for the tough questions. He just needs to stay calm and stick to the message."

"You think he's going to be able to do that with everything that's going on?" Caleb asked, finally locking eyes with her, his expression unreadable. "The protest, the noise… It's a lot. Too much."

Grace felt the knot tighten in her chest. He was right, of course. The noise was deafening. The headlines. The questions. The uncertainty creeping in like a shadow. But she couldn't let him see that. Not now.

"Then we make the noise work for us," she said, her voice firm, her words cutting through the tension between them. "We use it. We show the public we won't back down."

The anger between them flickered in his eyes. She saw it, but she didn't react. She couldn't. His gaze lingered on her longer than necessary, and her pulse skipped, but she refused to let it show. She wouldn't let him back in. He didn't get to leave in the middle of the night without a word—especially after making a show about having her back. Lofty words just to get her undressed.

"You've got a plan for everything, don't you?" he said, voice tinged with something—sarcasm? Frustration? She couldn't tell. But there was an edge to it, a reminder of what happened between them. The heat. The words unsaid.

Grace bit her lip, tearing her eyes away from his. She couldn't do this. She couldn't let him distract her again.

"I know what I'm doing," she snapped, the sharpness in her voice betraying her. Damn it, why couldn't she just keep it together?

Caleb's reply was calm, too calm. "And I know what I'm doing," he said. But the way he said it—there was a hesitation in his voice, like he wasn't so sure anymore.

For a beat, everything hung in the air, raw and unresolved. Neither of them moved. Neither of them backed down. The tension between them crackled, thick and suffocating. The words they hadn't said, the distance they'd both put between them, had only made it worse. And yet, neither of them seemed ready to walk away.

The door to the prep room opened with a soft creak, and President Armstrong walked in with a calm, almost nonchalant air, his presence filling the room like a familiar weight. Grace didn't flinch, didn't miss a beat. Instantly, she was all business, the shift in her demeanor seamless. She smiled, the expression practiced, warm but just a shade too tight at the corners. The façade of confidence and professionalism slid into place.

"Mr. President," she greeted, her voice smooth, as she moved to stand in front of him. "We're all set for the debate. The strategy we've discussed is ready to go. Just need you to stay calm, stick to the key points, and let the momentum work in our favor."

President Armstrong, the man who held the office, gave a short nod. His hands were stuffed casually in his pockets as he leaned back against the chair, already looking more relaxed than anyone in the room. He wasn't worried, not in the way Grace was. Not in the way he should be.

"Got it, Grace," he said. "Let's just get this over with. I'm ready. We've prepped enough."

Grace nodded, pushing back echoes of concern that threatened to break through. His dismissive tone wasn't unexpected, but it still rattled her. This wasn't just any debate, this was a turning point. The public perception was on a knife's edge, and Armstrong seemed to brush it off like he was heading to another casual meeting. But she couldn't show any of that. She couldn't show the doubt that nagged at her as she thought about how badly this could go if he didn't stay focused.

"You're more than ready, sir," she said, her tone polished, upbeat, hiding the worry beneath layers of practiced control. "You've got this. Just keep your cool, stay on message, and don't let the distractions pull you off track."

"Distractions?" The president raised an eyebrow, a smile playing at the corner of his lips as he glanced over at the staff moving behind him, adjusting lights and cameras. "I've had worse distractions than this. It's a cakewalk." He gave a soft chuckle, completely at ease with the weight of what was about to happen.

"Of course," she said, nodding, pushing all emotion from her voice. "But it's important to remember that tonight could shift everything. Your answers need to hit hard, and we need to show the public that you're in control, no matter the noise outside."

She kept her eyes focused on him, but her mind was elsewhere, lingering on the fact that the president was, as always, unshakable. And as always, that made Grace's job harder.

"You worry too much, Grace," he said, offering her an easy smile, clearly oblivious to the undercurrent of stress in her. "You've trained me well. I know my lines, I know my points. Let's get this done."

Grace swallowed her frustration, forcing her voice to stay even. "I'm not worried about your lines, Mr. President. I'm worried about the next few hours. This is about perception as much as policy."

A flicker of recognition passed through his eyes, but it was gone as quickly as it came. "I've been in worse spots," he said nonchalantly, his hand brushing at his jacket as if everything were already handled.

The ease with which he dismissed everything struck a chord in Grace. He'd never been someone who felt the pressure in the same way she did, never cared enough to show it. But tonight was different. She knew it, and deep down, she needed him to know it too.

But Grace had learned long ago how to push her emotions aside when it mattered. She didn't have the luxury of reacting. Not now.

"All right," she said briskly, keeping her voice steady, forcing the warmth back into her expression. "I'll be here, monitoring everything. We'll be ready."

The president stood, giving her one last easy smile, before he straightened his tie and headed toward the exit, not sparing a glance at the staff still working behind him. As he moved toward the stage, Grace's gaze followed him. Her thoughts were a jumbled mess — concern for him, concern for the campaign, for the country. But she didn't have time to let it show. There was too much riding on tonight.

"Good luck, Mr. President," she said softly, even though she wasn't sure he could hear her.

She just hoped it would be enough.

* * * *

The harsh flicker of the fluorescent lights overhead did little to ease the tension that was building inside Caleb. He and Wyatt were pressed against the concrete wall of the TV studio lobby, their eyes scanning the chaos unfolding just behind the thin glass door. Caleb's mind raced, still caught in the aftermath of the protest and the mounting pressure of tonight's debate. The job had always been tough, but tonight felt different.

It wasn't the work. It wasn't even the threat of violence hanging over President Armstrong's head.

He couldn't shake the memory of her — of the kiss, of the way her body had responded to him. Every minute spent with her, no matter how brief, felt like it was pushing him off course. But now? Now was no time for distraction. The president's life was on the line, and his own feelings had no place here.

"Everything's quiet," Wyatt muttered, scanning the crew and technicians moving frantically behind them. "It's a circus back there, but perimeter's solid."

Caleb didn't respond. His mind was elsewhere—on the threat that was lurking just beneath the surface. *What the hell is going on with the TVC?*

Before he could think through it, the click of heels rang out, sharp against the stillness. Caleb turned instinctively. There she was—Adrienne Amoroso, all confidence and sharp edges. Her eyes cut through the room, taking in every detail, every movement. It was what he'd once loved about her.

Until she'd fucked him over.

"You again," Caleb greeted, his voice flat. "What do you have?"

Adrienne's lips quirked, a small, knowing smile tugging at her mouth. "TVC's been busy. More than just protests. They've got plans."

Caleb's stomach dropped, and he exchanged a tense glance with Wyatt. "What kind of plans?"

"Assassination," Adrienne said, her voice dropping low, as though the words themselves could be dangerous. "A credible plot against Armstrong."

Caleb's heart skipped a beat. *Shit.* His blood ran cold. "Are you sure?"

"Multiple sources confirmed," she said, her eyes locking onto his with that familiar intensity. "They've made Armstrong a target—he's their symbol, the embodiment of everything they're fighting against. And they're not going to stop until they get him."

The weight of her words hit Caleb like a punch to the gut. This was real. Too real.

Wyatt didn't wait a second. "We need to pull him. Now."

Adrienne shook her head. "We don't know when they'll strike. It could be now, could be later, or not at all. TVC isn't known to have great tactical plans."

Caleb's gaze hardened. He stepped in front of Wyatt, blocking him. "Pull him now and you hand the TVC exactly what they want—a headline saying the president was too weak to finish the debate. They'll use that as fuel."

"I don't care about their damn narrative," Wyatt snapped, his voice sharp. "I care about keeping the president alive."

"And I care about keeping Armstrong in the White House," Caleb shot back, his jaw clenched. "We can't just yank him off that stage without causing chaos. We need to control this. Not let it spiral."

Wyatt's nostrils flared. "Sounds like you're taking *her* side."

Caleb knew who he meant. "Who?" His voice was tight.

Adrienne stepped forward, eyes glinting with a mix of suspicion and knowing. "Grace."

"Don't start," Caleb warned, his patience thinning.

"She's clouding your judgment," Wyatt growled.

Adrienne snickered to the side. "Ahh, young love."

Caleb shot her a serious look. She could fuck all the way off.

"Then it's your call," Caleb said to Wyatt, his voice a low rasp. "But make sure it's because you can handle the heat, not because you're running scared."

Adrienne leaned in, her hand resting on Caleb's arm. "This is your job, Caleb. Your mission. You're here to protect Armstrong, not play favorites with your new plaything."

Caleb didn't answer, too focused on the shift in the room. And then, out of nowhere, she appeared. Grace.

Her presence was a jolt, cutting through the tension like a blade. Caleb couldn't mask the rawness that hit him seeing her — his chest tightened, emotions tangled, and for a second, he forgot everything else.

"What's going on?" She locked eyes with him.

"Intel that there's a real assassination plot. Get him out of there."

Grace stared into him. He knew what she was asking. "Caleb, *please*," she said.

"We need to move," Wyatt said, his voice quieter now, more urgent. "Now."

Caleb nodded, but before he could take a step, Grace's hand landed on his arm, stopping him dead in his tracks.

Her touch was subtle, but it was electric, sending a shock straight to his core. "Help me," she murmured, her voice low, softer than he expected. "We can't pull him off that stage. Not over a vague threat. If we do, we're giving the TVC exactly what they want. We need to stand strong, not let them see us flinch."

His heart stuttered. *Damn it.* She was right. He knew she was right. The risk was too high, but if they pulled Armstrong now, the damage to his reputation — and to their efforts — would be catastrophic.

But Wyatt was already moving. Caleb couldn't let him go. He couldn't let her down, either. He was stuck, torn between duty and something else — something he wasn't ready to confront.

"Grace…" His voice cracked, barely a whisper.

She stood firm, her gaze locked on his. "Do something. You said you'd have my back."

But the wall between them went up, fast and hard. Her eyes turned cold, like a door slamming shut. Caleb's chest tightened as he realized she was already pulling away, both physically and emotionally.

He'd just lost her again.

"Damn it," he muttered under his breath.

The moment hung between them, suffocating. Caleb had to turn away, his mind a tangled mess of duty and something darker — something deeper — that he didn't know how to deal with.

Wyatt was already on stage. It was too late to change course.

Adrienne sidled up to him, a small, satisfied smile on her lips. "That was the right choice, babe," she said, her tone too sweet, too certain.

Grace's gaze cut through Caleb like a blade. Hurt. Betrayal. It was all there, written clear across her face.

* * * *

7 days to the election

It felt like the clock was counting down to something inevitable, but Grace wasn't sure if that something was victory or total collapse.

The DC campaign war room had become a second home for her. She spent more time here than anywhere else, surrounded by the hum of machinery, the soft glow of screens filled with numbers and polls, and the constant shuffle of staffers in and out. Maps lined the walls, pins marking battleground states and red zones, the areas that could make or break everything. The air was thick with the weight of responsibility, the stakes higher than they'd ever been. Each step forward felt like it came with a cost, each gain came with another price to pay. The pressure had started to suffocate her, and she could feel it closing in.

The president pulling out of the debate had been a bad move, one Grace had fought fiercely. But now, seven days from election day, it felt like more than a mistake.

It was a catastrophe.

The phones rang nonstop, advisors buzzed around her like bees in a hive, all with one goal—save the campaign. Jordan was across the room, pacing as he slammed his fingers on his phone, barking into the receiver as he coordinated with the communications team. He was normally the picture of control, but even he had started to crack under the pressure.

Grace rubbed her temples, trying to focus through the fog of exhaustion that had settled in her brain. She needed a solution, but the answers weren't coming. And then, Caleb walked in.

His presence hit her like a punch to the gut. He was still the calm in the storm, the one person she could count on to keep his cool when everything else seemed to be unraveling. But now, she could see the tension in his stance, in the way his jaw tightened, the furrow between his brows. He didn't need to say anything— she could read it in his posture. He was just as worn down as she was.

Jordan snapped her out of her thoughts. "Grace," he said, his voice sharper than usual, his eyes flashing with frustration as he hung up his phone. "We need to pivot. We can't let the narrative from TVC gain more traction. All anyone is talking about is how Armstrong fled the debate. They're calling it a 'weak' move, a 'scared' move. And it's working. It's hitting the polls hard. Sentiment is tanking, Grace. This is bad. Really bad."

"I know," Grace muttered, barely sparing him a glance. Her focus was still on the campaign notes spread out before her, as if the scattered pages might somehow contain the solution to their growing crisis. "I'm not blind, Jordan. I see the polls. I see the numbers. But there's no time to—"

"You don't get it," Jordan cut in, voice rising with every word. "This isn't just some little dip in the numbers. The press is having a field day. They're painting Armstrong as a coward, someone who can't take the heat. It's bleeding into the public perception. Every day we don't respond, every day this narrative gets more traction, we lose ground. We're not just playing catch-up here, Grace. We're on the edge of losing everything. Everything."

Grace bristled at his words, her temper flaring. "And what the hell do you want me to do about it, Jordan? Snap my fingers and fix it? I don't have that kind of magic."

Jordan didn't answer. Instead, he clenched his jaw, frustration seeping into his features as he glared at the papers in front of her. But before either of them could say another word, Caleb stepped forward, his voice low and firm.

"All right, that's enough," he said, his voice cutting through the tension like a blade. He looked between them, his gaze sharp, focused. "Jordan, take a breather. Grace, breathe. We're all under pressure, but shouting isn't going to help."

Jordan shot him a look, frustration still simmering in his eyes, but he didn't argue. With a stiff nod, he turned on his heel and stormed out of the room.

Grace let out a long, exhausted breath and ran a hand through her hair, her mind racing.

They still had not talked about what had happened. They hadn't talked about anything either than what time she needed to be somewhere.

Caleb stayed where he was, watching her closely. "You all right?" he asked, his voice quieter now, gentler. His question wasn't about the campaign — it was about her.

Grace didn't answer immediately. She didn't know how to. Everything felt like it was slipping through her fingers, and no matter how many solutions she tried to put together, it felt like the pieces just wouldn't fit.

Instead of answering, she stared at the papers in front of her, her gaze unfocused. "I was right," she murmured, her voice soft but resolute. "Pulling him out of the debate was the wrong call. And now the whole thing's falling apart. I can't keep up with this. I don't know what else to do."

Caleb leaned against one of the maps, folding his arms across his chest. "This is too much," he muttered, his voice quieter now that they were alone. "Everyone's losing their damn minds."

Grace didn't answer right away. Her fingers tapped impatiently on the table, a thousand thoughts swirling in her head. There were too many questions, too many things left unsaid between them. And her frustration had nowhere else to go.

Finally, she snapped. "I can't keep doing this — pretending that everything's fine, pretending like you didn't fuck me over."

Caleb's eyes narrowed, and he stepped closer to her, the space between them electric. "Grace, this isn't the time —"

"I don't care if it's the time," she shot back, her voice rising. "You made a promise to me — to *this*."

"What the hell are you talking about? There's no time for whatever *this* is. You've got your campaign to run, I've got my job to do. We don't have room for anything else."

Grace had a thousand things she could say, but there was one question she needed the answer to, one that had been gnawing at her for longer than she wanted to admit. "So tell me, Caleb…who exactly *is* Adrienne?"

The question landed like a punch. Caleb froze, looking away before he could meet her eyes again. He didn't answer right away, but Grace could see it in the way his posture shifted — the way he was retreating.

"Why the hell would you bring her up now?"

"Because I need to know," Grace pressed, the words slipping out before she could stop them. "Who is she? Why does she get to stand next to you in the middle of this shitstorm, while I'm left out here to do the dirty work?"

Caleb's eyes darkened, unamused. "She's my ex-fiancée. She wasn't interested in waiting around for me when I was overseas. That's who she is."

Grace's heart clenched at the rawness in his tone, but she pushed forward. "So you were with her? When?"

Caleb's eyes flashed, his face a mask of frustration. "Six months ago. It blew up. There. Happy?"

The words hung in the air between them like smoke, thick and suffocating. Grace's breath caught, her mind reeling.

"You still love her?" she asked, disbelief twisting her words. She couldn't help the way her voice shook, the edge of vulnerability creeping in.

"No."

"I doubt that."

"We were together for a long time. You want everything to be neat and perfect, but it's not. It's messy. It's complicated."

Grace swallowed hard, the weight of his words pressing down on her. She knew he was right. "I don't *want* perfection, Caleb. I just want...*something real.* Something I can count on."

"Count on this — it's over between me and her."

She chewed her lip, trying to halt the tears. The silence between them was deafening. Caleb ran a hand through his hair, his shoulders sagging as if the weight of everything had just hit him full force.

"This —" he started, but she cut him off.

"I can't count on you. You didn't have my back. You said you would and you didn't. That's all I know."

Grace's eyes stung with unshed tears, refusing to let him see her like that. She was so close to the edge, and she hated it. She hated feeling like she was losing control — of her campaign, of the people she cared about, and of the one person who had started to mean more to her than she was ready to admit.

With a long, exhausted sigh, she turned away from him. "I am not doing this, Caleb. Not like this."

She knew the moment she said it, it would change everything.

Caleb stood still for a long moment, watching her, but saying nothing. Then, he turned and left, his footsteps heavy against the cold tile floor.

The sharp sound of the door clicking shut echoed through the empty campaign room, the air heavy with the weight of Grace's decision. She didn't turn to watch Caleb leave — didn't want to see the look on his face when he left her alone to pick up the pieces. Her heart felt like it was splintering, but she swallowed it down. She didn't have time for weakness, not now. The campaign needed her to be strong, and the stakes had never been higher.

She sat down at the desk, fingers pressing into the cool surface as she stared at the campaign data on the screen in front of her. Polls had been slipping for weeks, and every time she thought she had a plan to turn it around, something else came crashing down—distractions, threats, the press. There was no breathing room. She didn't even know what victory looked like anymore.

The door opened again, and she looked up, expecting the inevitable—a staffer with more bad news or an urgent message. But instead, it was Jordan, his tall frame filling the doorway. His usual confident smirk was gone, replaced with an intensity Grace didn't miss. He was no longer the smug strategist, now, he had the weight of the campaign, the president's wishes, and the future of the country pressing down on him.

"We need to talk," Jordan said, his voice low and clipped, the urgency pulling Grace's attention away from her laptop.

"For fuck's sake. What now?" Her tone was sharp, masking the exhaustion that threatened to crack her composure.

Jordan stepped fully into the room and shut the door softly behind him, his face carved into lines of tension. "The president's made a decision. He's going for a Hail Mary. He refuses to lose this election, and he wants us to leverage Marisol Rhodes Stewart's connections to make it happen."

Grace's stomach dropped, the name alone enough to send a chill crawling up her spine.

"You're kidding me." She looked at him, her disbelief cutting through the air. "Again?"

Jordan crossed his arms, his jaw tight. "The polls are tanking, Grace. TVC is hammering us into the dirt, and the attacks are sticking. The president wants us to use Marisol to hit back, hard."

Grace stood abruptly, her chair scraping against the floor as she faced him. "Marisol isn't a weapon, Jordan—she's a loaded gun aimed at everything we've built. You know what she's like. The second we give her an inch, she'll own us."

Jordan took a step closer, his voice dropping to a near growl. "She already owns half the people in this room. You think we're winning any of this clean? Look outside, Grace. We don't have the luxury of principles anymore. Not when we're this far behind."

Grace's mind raced, her frustration and dread tangling into a knot in her chest. Marisol wasn't just an ultra-donor. She had charm, money, and the kind of influence that could turn public opinion on a dime. But she was a puppet master, too, pulling strings that left everyone tangled in her web.

"You want me to go to her," she said flatly, folding her arms across her chest. "You want me to ask for her help."

"The president does," Jordan said, his tone softening slightly, though his eyes remained sharp. "I'm asking you to swallow your pride and do what's necessary. Marisol can get us on prime time, rewrite the narrative, and stabilize the polls. She's not a risk we can afford to avoid anymore."

"She's a liability," Grace countered, her voice rising. "You think she's going to help us out of the goodness of her heart? She'll come for the campaign, the platform—hell, she'll probably aim for the president himself if it benefits her. You're handing her the keys to everything."

Jordan let out a slow breath, his expression unreadable. "And if we don't? We lose. There's no victory speech without her. No second term."

Grace turned away, her jaw tight as she stared out of the window, trying to swallow the bitter truth of his words. She hated this — hated the idea of bending to Marisol's will, of giving her even a shred of power over something Grace had worked so hard to keep clean.

But it wasn't about her. It was about the president, the campaign, and everything they'd fought to stand for.

After a long moment, she turned back to Jordan, her expression cold and resolved. "Fine," she said, her voice like steel. "I'll do it. But on my terms."

Jordan gave her a small, grim smile. "Fair enough. Just make it quick. The clock's ticking."

He left without another word, his footsteps echoing down the hallway. She sank back into her chair, her thoughts swirling with unease.

This wasn't the campaign she'd signed up for. But it was the one she was stuck in. And if Marisol was the only way forward, Grace would play the game.

But she'd play to win.

* * * *

6 days to the election — early morning

Caleb's fingers trembled slightly as he gripped the cup of black coffee, the warmth spreading through his palm. The familiar scent of his usual spot, just around the corner from his place, a mix of rich espresso and baked goods, was a stark contrast to the heavy, suffocating thoughts swirling in his mind. He was used to working early mornings — he had to, for the job. But today, the routine felt off, like everything was out of place.

He was packed and ready for New York. He just needed to get Grace. This was his one moment before the storm of the day.

The café was quieter than usual. The sound of soft conversation, the clinking of spoons on ceramic, and the hiss of the espresso machine were all background noise to his racing thoughts. He didn't expect company, not here. But then, as he found a seat at a table in the corner, he heard the scrape of a chair and looked up to see her.

Adrienne.

She was dressed casually, a light jacket over a blouse, her dark hair falling in soft waves around her shoulders. Her sharp, dark eyes locked onto his as if she'd found exactly what she was looking for. Caleb froze, the cup halfway to his lips, a sinking feeling in his chest.

"Hey," she said, her voice low but steady. She slid into the seat across from him without waiting for an invitation.

He stared at her for a moment, surprised by her appearance.

"Adrienne," he said curtly, setting the cup down in front of him. He didn't smile. He didn't move. "What are you doing here?"

She studied him, her gaze piercing through him like she could read every inch of his mind. There was something different about her today — something more determined, maybe even desperate.

"I want you back," she said bluntly, no preamble, no softening the blow.

Caleb's heart skipped a beat, though he didn't show it. His mind raced, and the words that slipped from his mouth were almost mechanical. "That's not a good idea."

But Adrienne didn't flinch. She leaned in slightly, her fingers drumming on the table between them as she met his eyes. "I need you to listen." Her voice was a little softer now, but her resolve was unmistakable. "I never stopped loving you. And I know you still feel something. You can't tell me you don't."

Caleb's throat tightened as he looked at her, trying to keep his emotions in check. He couldn't think straight. *She can't be serious. Not now.* His pulse quickened as he spoke, his words clipped and cold. "Adrienne, you know this isn't the time. We're both —"

"Don't." Her hand shot out, stopping him mid-sentence. "I know what you're going to say. I hurt you. You've moved on. We're different people now." She made air quotes around the words, her voice sharp with a mix of frustration and determination. "I've thought a lot about it. And you know what? It doesn't matter. You're still the one I want. You've been through hell, and so have I. But we would be better together."

He shook his head, trying to process her words. *What the actual fuck.* "Not even an apology, then?"

The slippery minx grinned. "Apology? For what? You ran from me as much as I ran from you. Now, look what you're doing — same mistakes. You already have someone else to fix, something else to fight," she continued, her voice quieter now, but still firm. "Grace, she's not right for you. Don't do this to yourself."

Caleb felt the weight of her words. For a split second, he couldn't breathe. His thoughts tangled. His relationship with Adrienne had been complicated —

passionate, but destructive. There had been love, yes. But there had also been mistakes, too many to count.

"I'm not the man you want," he muttered, his voice rough with emotion. "You made that clear. I came home and you were gone."

Adrienne's lips quirked into a faint, almost sad smile. "I made a mistake. I shouldn't have left."

"You more than left—you were fucking my best friend the next day." His gaze faltered for a moment, and in that split second, the old feelings he'd buried beneath layers of work, duty, and self-preservation rose to the surface. But just as quickly as they emerged, he shoved them down again.

She remained silent. *Classic. No remorse.*

"Adrienne, the answer is no," he said, his voice hardening. He looked at her with an intensity that made it clear he wasn't going to budge. "We are done here."

Her eyes flickered with something like disappointment, but she didn't back down. "You think you're doing the right thing by pushing me away?" She leaned back in her chair, her arms crossing in a defensive gesture. "Let's see about that."

Caleb closed his eyes for a moment, his jaw tightening as the weight of his past with her pressed down on him. She was right about one thing—he had been running. Running from everything that mattered, including her. But that didn't mean he was going to let her back in now. Not after everything.

"You need to leave."

Adrienne stared at him for a long time, as if trying to gauge whether he was being honest or just pushing her away again. But she knew him too well, and she saw right through the walls he'd built around himself.

"Then I guess that's it," she said, her voice low and steady. She stood up, smoothing down the front of her jacket as she looked at him one last time. "You'll see, though. I'm not wrong."

He watched her walk away, the soft jingle of the café door announcing her departure. He didn't know what to think. Didn't know what to feel.

All he knew was that Adrienne's words lingered in his mind, echoing like a whisper in the café.

How the fuck would that cheating bitch know if Grace was right for him or not? He was learning that Grace was everything Adrienne was not — loyal, for one thing. Grace was fiercely loyal to what mattered to her.

And he admired the hell out of that.

He took a slow sip of his coffee, trying to push everything aside, to drown out the noise of his own heart. The job needed him. Grace needed him.

And they were heading to New York to see the Queen.

Chapter Ten

Fifth Avenue, Midtown Manhattan, New York City
6 days to the election

The elevator's soft hum was the only sound between Caleb and Grace as they ascended to the fiftieth floor. Each passing second felt heavier than the last. The stakes were colossal. And so was the woman waiting for them at the top.

Marisol Rhodes Stewart.

Grace had spent weeks trying to avoid this meeting, but now, there was no choice. The president's life was at stake. The campaign was teetering. And Marisol was the wildcard they needed – if they could handle her.

When the elevator doors slid open, they stepped into an immaculate lobby of polished stone and glass. The view stretched far beyond Central Park, but Grace couldn't appreciate the grandeur. Not when her stomach churned at the thought of what awaited her.

Marisol's assistant ushered them into the office, where Marisol herself was seated at an imposing walnut desk, backlit by floor-to-ceiling windows. She looked up as they entered, a smile playing on her lips that didn't reach her calculating blue eyes.

"Grace," Marisol said, standing with a measured grace that came from years of commanding attention. She extended her hand, her suit a pristine cream, more armor than fashion. "And this must be your shadow."

Her gaze flicked to Caleb, lingering just long enough to dismiss him.

"Marisol," Grace said evenly, shaking her hand. Caleb stayed silent behind her, his presence a wall of tension. "Caleb Knight is Protective Detail. Not my shadow."

Marisol raised her eyebrows and gestured for them to sit, but her focus stayed on Grace. "Things must be dire if you've come to me. What's on fire this time?"

Grace forced a calm she didn't feel. "You've seen the news. TVC's attacks are relentless, and the assassination threats are escalating. The president needs to show strength, and we're running out of time."

Marisol tilted her head, her expression a mix of curiosity and amusement. "Strength? You mean after pulling him offstage in DC? That looked more like fear."

Grace's jaw tightened, but she kept her voice steady. "We made the call to protect his life. The public doesn't need to see strength if the president doesn't live to fight another day."

Marisol let out a soft laugh, low and sharp. "You don't win campaigns by playing defense, Grace. The public wants a hero, not a man cowering behind threats. Put him on every screen. On the ground. In the streets. You want to win? Make him untouchable."

Grace opened her mouth to respond, but Caleb cut in, his voice steady and hard. "Untouchable doesn't mean invincible. Putting him out there now is reckless."

Marisol's gaze snapped to him, her smile sharpening. "And who asked for your opinion, soldier boy? Your job is to keep him breathing, not dictate strategy."

Grace felt the heat rise in her chest. "Caleb has a point. The risks — "

"The risks," Marisol interrupted, her tone slicing through the room, "are exactly why you need me. You don't have the luxury of playing it safe. You're here because you're losing. I can turn this around. But you'll need to trust me — and stop letting him undermine you."

Her eyes flicked back to Caleb, the disdain palpable.

Caleb leaned forward slightly, his presence suddenly towering. "I don't trust you," he said plainly.

Marisol's smile widened, almost predatory. "Good. I don't trust you either. But we don't have to like each other to get results. Grace understands that."

Grace felt her pulse quicken, caught as she was between the two of them. Caleb's disapproval radiated off him in waves, and Marisol's relentless push made Grace feel cornered.

"Enough," Grace snapped, her voice louder than she intended. Both of them fell silent, their gazes locking onto her. "This isn't about trust. It's about saving the president and this campaign. If you have a plan, Marisol, let's hear it. But we do it my way."

Marisol's expression softened just enough to give the illusion of agreement. "Of course. We'll make Armstrong the hero he needs to be. But you have to let me do what I do best. Optics, narrative, control. I don't play small, Grace."

Caleb exhaled sharply, the sound cutting through the tension. "You don't play fair, either."

Marisol leaned back. "Fair is for amateurs. I win. And if you two want to keep your boss alive and your campaign afloat, you'll get on board. Fast."

Grace stared at Marisol, the weight of the decision pressing on her shoulders. Caleb's silent presence at her side only amplified her doubts. She couldn't afford to alienate him — not when he was her rock in all of this.

But Marisol was right about one thing. They were running out of time.

"Six days," Marisol said, her voice like silk over steel. "That's all the time we have to turn this around. Are you going to waste it?"

"No," Grace replied.

"Good. Then, we are on."

"Fine." Grace chewed her lip, hating this new alliance.

As they left the office, Caleb was a storm beside her, his anger barely contained. Grace didn't dare look at him. She didn't want to see the judgment in his eyes — not when she already felt it in her gut.

* * * *

The SUV rumbled down the highway, the cityscape giving way to the monotony of airport signs and industrial sprawl. Caleb gripped the steering wheel, his knuckles pale against the black leather. Grace sat stiffly in the passenger seat, scrolling through her phone with frantic precision, her jaw tight.

"You don't even see it, do you?" Caleb said suddenly, his voice low but laced with irritation.

Grace didn't look up. "See what?"

"That she's manipulating you. Marisol doesn't care about the campaign. She doesn't care about Armstrong. She cares about control."

Grace sighed, her fingers pausing mid-scroll. "You think I don't know that? You think I don't know exactly who and what she is?"

Caleb shot her a sharp glance. "Then why are you letting her steer this whole thing? Every move she makes pulls you further off course."

Grace dropped her phone into the cupholder, finally turning to face him. "Because we're out of options, Caleb! The polls are in free fall, the president's life is being threatened, and I don't have the luxury of sitting back and waiting for a miracle. If Marisol can help, I'm going to use her. That's what leaders do—they make the hard calls."

His jaw clenched, a muscle ticking in his cheek. "Leaders don't sell their souls to fix a problem. There's a line, Grace. And she's way past it."

"And what would you have me do?" she shot back, her voice rising. "Walk away? Let the campaign implode? Sacrifice everything we've worked for because you don't like the way I'm handling it?"

"Yes!" Caleb snapped, his voice cutting through the enclosed space like a whip. "If it means doing the right thing, yes! You're so focused on winning that you're blind to the cost. You're playing her game, Grace, and it's going to destroy you."

Grace stared at him, her breath shallow as his words hit a nerve she didn't want to acknowledge. "You don't understand," she said finally, her voice quieter but no less tense. "You've never been in a position where everything depends on you. Where every decision you make ripples out and affects millions of lives. You think this is just about me? About my pride? It's about something bigger than both of us."

Caleb's laugh was bitter, devoid of humor. "You think I don't understand responsibility? Every day, I put my life on the line to protect people like you. I know what it means to bear the weight of someone else's survival. The difference is, I don't compromise my integrity to do it."

Grace flinched at the word integrity. "And what does your integrity get you, Caleb? A job where you're always in someone's shadow? Where you're never the one making the call, just cleaning up the mess afterward?"

His hands tightened on the wheel, and for a moment, she thought he might pull over. Instead, he exhaled through his nose, a sound of barely contained frustration. "You think I don't want more? You think I'm content with this? I'm not. But at least I know who I am. At least I don't lose myself trying to be everything for everyone else."

Her throat tightened, the words she wanted to say stuck somewhere between anger and guilt. She looked out of the window, unable to face him. "Maybe you're right," she said after a long pause. "Maybe I am losing myself. But if I don't hold this together, no one else will. And if that means I have to work with people like Marisol, then so be it."

The silence that followed was suffocating. Caleb's jaw was set, his eyes locked on the road. Grace could feel the weight of his disapproval, but she refused to back down. She couldn't.

When they pulled up to the terminal, Caleb didn't even put the car in park. The SUV idled as Grace unbuckled her seatbelt and grabbed her bag.

She hesitated before getting out, her hand on the door handle. "You don't have to agree with me, Caleb. But I need you to trust me."

He looked at her then, his eyes dark and unreadable. "Trust isn't the problem, Grace. The problem is, you don't trust yourself."

The words hit harder than she wanted to admit. She opened the door, stepping out into the cold air. "I'll see you in Alabama," she said stiffly, before slamming the door shut.

As she walked into the terminal, Caleb watched her go, a knot tightening in his chest. He should've gotten out of the car. Should've said something — anything — to fix the rift between them. But he didn't.

Instead, he pulled into the parking lot, his mind racing with everything he'd left unsaid.

Chapter Eleven

Alabama-Georgia football game in Tuscaloosa, Alabama
4 days to the election

Caleb and Wyatt stood in the dimly lit corner of the VIP section of Bryant-Denny Stadium, the excitement of the Alabama-Georgia game raging beneath them while their own world felt like it was slowly imploding. The stadium was packed to the brim, fans in crimson and white shouting, clapping, stomping — living and breathing for the win. On the field, Alabama's offense was taking control, a steady rhythm of passing and power running that was unmistakably dominating. But Caleb couldn't even hear the roaring crowd, despite the electrifying atmosphere that would've had him on his feet if it were any other time.

He was too focused on the things that couldn't be fixed with a touchdown. The president was working the crowd, shaking hands, putting on his best face for the local bigwigs and donors. But Caleb could barely summon the energy to care about the pleasantries. His gaze was fixed across the room, on Grace. She was at the center of a small group of influential donors, laughing politely, her eyes glancing around — alert, but strained. The perfect picture of control. Except it was all a mask. Caleb saw through it. He always did.

Outside the stadium, the noise wasn't all from the game. The protests had escalated. Shouts and chants of angry demonstrators carried over the security barriers, pounding on the gates. The TVC wasn't backing down, and neither was Grace. She was pushing, every hour of the day, doing everything she could to steer the ship. But Caleb wasn't sure anymore if the ship was meant to be steered or if they were all just desperately trying to stay afloat.

Wyatt's voice broke through his thoughts, low and rough, like a sharp jab to the ribs. "Can you believe it? Less than a week left, and it's all falling apart."

Caleb didn't answer immediately. His eyes flicked back to Grace, watching as she played the part, shaking hands, smiling. He could feel it — her fatigue, her struggle, the same fight he was carrying inside himself. It was all getting too heavy, and there was no way out.

"Everything's coming apart at the seams," Caleb muttered, the words barely making it over the noise. "I don't know how she thinks she can pull this off."

Wyatt wasn't fazed. He took a sip from his whiskey glass, savoring it like it was the only thing keeping him from cracking. He set it down with a soft clink and leaned back against the wall, arms crossed, watching the game on the giant screen above the field. "You think she's losing it?" he asked, his voice a mixture of disbelief and cynicism.

Caleb's jaw tightened. He kept watching Grace, noting the stiff way she held herself, the brittle edge to her laughter. She wasn't fooling anyone. "No. But she's trying too hard. Trying to control everything, and it's making everything worse."

Wyatt let out a laugh, but it wasn't light. It was dark, edged with the bitterness of someone who had seen too many things fall apart. "You're too close to her, man. You can't see it straight."

Caleb bristled, his gaze snapping to Wyatt. "I know what I'm doing."

Wyatt gave him a pointed look, his eyebrow arched in that infuriatingly knowing way. "Do you? Because it sure looks like you're losing your shit right along with her."

The words landed harder than Caleb expected. It wasn't just the words — it was the implication. He wasn't just letting things fall apart — he was part of it. He clenched his fists, his nails digging into his palms. "I'm not losing my shit. I'm just trying to keep everything from falling apart completely."

Wyatt snorted, clearly unimpressed. "Yeah, well, good luck with that," he muttered. "You've got four days to keep the president safe, make sure he survives this campaign, and handle the TVC. Meanwhile, Grace is throwing gasoline on the fire every chance she gets."

Caleb's hands gripped the edge of the railing harder, knuckles white. "She doesn't see it that way."

Wyatt's lips curled, but there was no humor in the expression. "She's playing with fire, Caleb. And so are you."

Caleb's frustration bubbled over, the tightness in his chest growing unbearable. "What the hell do you want me to do?"

Wyatt stared at him for a long beat, his dark eyes sharp, calculating. Finally, he let out a heavy sigh and shook his head. "I don't know what the answer is. But you can't keep pretending you're not in over your head."

Caleb's chest tightened as though someone had just slammed a fist against his ribs. But he refused to show weakness. "I'm not."

Wyatt's voice softened, but there was no pity in it — just the raw honesty of a man who had been in the trenches long enough to know the hard truth. "Brother, come on. I know you. You're in too deep now. So is she. And neither of you can see how far you've already fallen."

Caleb wanted to deny it, wanted to scream that they were wrong, that he was still in control. But the tightness in his throat told him everything he needed to know. They were right. Maybe he was losing control.

The game raged on, Alabama up by two touchdowns. Caleb's eyes flicked to the field as the Alabama defense crushed Georgia's hopes with a brutal sack. He should've felt something — pride, maybe — but all he could feel was the crushing pressure building inside him.

"I got this," Caleb muttered, more to himself than to Wyatt, his voice barely audible.

Wyatt studied him with an intensity that made Caleb uncomfortable. His eyes were narrowed, like he was searching for a crack in Caleb's armor. "We'll see," he said quietly.

Without another word, Wyatt turned and walked away, disappearing into the shadows of the VIP section. Caleb stood there, alone for a moment, the noise of the crowd around him still nothing more than a distant echo.

Duke, who had been standing nearby keeping an eye on the room, sidled up next to Caleb, his expression unreadable. He didn't speak for a moment, just watching the game and the crowd. Then, in a tone that felt like it was cutting through the noise of the stadium, he said, "It's not just the job, is it?"

Caleb's eyes snapped to Duke. There was something in the way he said it — something personal.

"What do you mean?" Caleb asked, his voice flat.

Duke didn't look at him, still watching the game unfold. "I mean, it's not just the threats, the protests, the campaign. It's her." He nodded toward Grace, still talking to donors, her posture tense. "You've been around her long enough to know that no matter what you do, she's not going to listen to you. Not now."

Caleb's throat went dry, but he didn't respond. He couldn't.

"Look," Duke added quietly, "I'm just saying, you can't save someone who doesn't want to be saved."

Caleb's stomach tightened. He didn't know if he believed that or not, but he didn't want to hear it. Not now. Not with everything at stake.

He took a deep breath, watching Grace as she spun toward him, her eyes meeting his for a split second before she quickly turned away. Caleb's heart sank.

"We'll see," he muttered again, though this time, it wasn't a promise. It was a question.

The noise from the protesters outside filtered in through the walls, a constant reminder of the tension in the air. The clock was ticking, and there was nothing Caleb could do to stop it.

He looked over at Grace. She was laughing again, this time with more ease, but Caleb saw the strain behind her smile, the exhaustion in her eyes. He wanted to reach out, to tell her they could fix this, that they could make it through. But even he wasn't sure if that was possible anymore.

Because no matter what happened in the next week, no matter what they tried to do to salvage this campaign, one thing was certain – Grace was the one thing Caleb wanted most and that was the one thing that would never happen.

The tension in the air had been building all night, but it hit Caleb like a jolt of electricity when he saw Grace standing there, as if she'd materialized out of the haze of his frustration.

She was close enough for him to feel the heat of her body, to see the sharp edge of her gaze as it landed on him. Her presence was like a switch being flipped – impossible to ignore. She was all business now. No hint of warmth, no trace of the vulnerability he had caught glimpses of earlier. It was work mode. Her only mode.

"We need to talk," she said, her voice low, hard. No softness.

He didn't say anything, just gave a sharp nod. There was no avoiding it. He followed her down the hallway, his footsteps heavy on the polished floor. She moved with purpose, the click of her heels almost drowned by the sound of his heart pounding. They reached a small coat room at the end of the hall and, without a word, Grace closed the door behind them.

The room felt suffocating, the tension sharp enough to cut. Caleb leaned against the wall, arms crossed, eyes locked on Grace like he couldn't believe what he was hearing.

"He's doing it," Grace said, voice brisk. "Halftime. Tailgaters. Marisol's already set it up."

Caleb's jaw tightened. "Why are you telling me this?"

Her eyes narrowed. "You're security —"

"I don't take orders from you," he snapped.

Her shoulders squared. "This isn't a debate. The president's made up his mind."

"You mean Marisol made it for him," Caleb shot back. "This is reckless, Grace — for the president, for my guys, and even for me."

"It's necessary."

"It's suicide."

Her voice dropped, icy. "Then do your job. Keep him safe."

He pushed off the desk, stepping closer. "You don't get it, do you? You're putting him in the crosshairs for a PR stunt."

Grace bristled. "You think I don't know the risks? This is bigger than you, Caleb. Bigger than me."

"It's not bigger than keeping him alive."

Her glare hardened. "You don't have to agree. Just make it happen."

Caleb stared at her, his frustration boiling. "You keep playing with fire, Grace. Don't be surprised when someone gets burned."

She held his gaze, unflinching. "We're done here." She turned to leave, dismissing him.

Without thinking, Caleb moved. He closed the distance between them in two quick strides, reaching out and grabbing her arm, pulling her back toward him. Her surprised gasp was barely audible before he had her pressed against the cold, unforgiving wall of the coat room. His hand was firm around her wrist, the heat of his body a stark contrast to the chill of the room.

"Don't walk away from me, girl," he growled, his voice low, dangerous with the emotions he was struggling to keep in check. The words came out in a rush, almost as if he couldn't stop them, as if she was the one thing in this damn mess that he couldn't control. His body was flush against hers, his breath coming in short, sharp bursts.

Grace's eyes flashed with something — anger, defiance — but there was a flicker of something else, something more vulnerable. She opened her mouth to speak, but Caleb silenced her with a hard look, his body pressing hers into the wall with enough force to send a jolt through both of them.

She tried to turn in his arms again, toward the door.

"I said — don't fucking walk away from me," he repeated, his voice low, strained. He could feel the heat, the wild pulse of their emotions, and for a moment, he thought maybe — just maybe — she felt it too.

The room seemed to shrink around them, the world outside completely forgotten. All that mattered was the distance between them, the tension in the air, and the fact that no matter how much he fought it, he couldn't seem to let go of this pull.

Grace didn't fight him. Not at first. She just stared up at him, her chest rising and falling with the same ragged breath. But then, slowly, her lips parted, her voice steady, though there was an edge to it.

"Let me go," she snapped, but it only fueled him.

"Make me," he said, his voice a low rasp. He was done with the words, done with the fighting, with all of it.

He cupped her jaw, the roughness of his touch silencing her. She stiffened, but didn't pull away, and that was all the permission he needed. Without hesitation, he kissed her.

God, he'd missed her.

The kiss was raw, desperate, a collision of emotions he couldn't contain any longer. He felt her gasp against his mouth, her body momentarily stiff, but then — finally — she softened into him. Her arms slid around his neck, pulling him closer, her lips moving against his with an intensity that made his pulse spike even more. Every ounce of frustration, every ounce of desire that had been simmering between them exploded in that single kiss.

He could feel the heat of her, her body pressed against his, and for a moment, he thought maybe he could have the one thing he wanted. His tongue found hers. He missed that taste.

At first, she froze under his kiss — maybe shocked by the rawness of it. But she gave in. Her mouth widened beneath his, and suddenly, it wasn't about holding back anymore. It was all urgency, all the anger, frustration, and confusion they'd both been trying to suppress exploding in an instant.

Caleb's hands moved to the back of her neck, tangling his fingers in her silky dark hair as he deepened the kiss, pulling her even closer, if that was even possible. The taste of her, the soft sweetness of her lips against his, made his pulse race. Every part of him, every nerve, was awake, consumed by her. Her body pressed against his, and he could feel the heat between them, the undeniable pull of attraction that had been building for weeks.

Grace's hands shot up to his chest, at first pushing him away, but then as the kiss deepened, her fingers clawed into the fabric of his shirt, pulling him closer. She kissed him back with just as much fervor, her mouth moving against his in perfect rhythm, as if she'd been waiting for this moment too.

"Come back to me again," she whispered, "tonight."

He groaned in response. Hardening.

His lips trailed down to her jawline, his breath ragged against her skin, but the taste of her was too intoxicating. He needed more, wanted to feel her completely, the desperation of their connection making his heart race faster. Her breathing grew erratic as he kissed down her neck, his teeth grazing her skin just enough to make her shudder.

"Grace," he muttered, his voice rough. His hands roamed down her back, pulling her even tighter against him, feeling the curve of her body, the fire between them intensifying with every touch.

She responded, her breath coming in quick gasps, her hands tugging at the hem of his shirt, as if she couldn't get enough of him. He pulled away just long enough to catch her eyes — dark, heavy with need — and his hands slipped to the back of her thighs, lifting her up slightly as if nothing mattered but this moment.

It was messy and desperate, two people who had fought so hard to keep distance between them now giving in to what they'd both wanted from the start. Their kiss was slow and fevered, exploring, tasting. Everything else — the campaign, the tension, the unspoken emotions — vanished.

And in that kiss, it was just Caleb and Grace, no walls left standing.

When they finally pulled away, they were both breathless, their faces inches apart. Caleb's chest was heaving, his heart pounding so loudly in his ears that it almost drowned out the sound of Grace's labored breathing.

"Don't fight me," he muttered, his voice hoarse, his hands still on her, holding her steady. "Not like that."

Grace didn't answer right away. Her gaze dropped to his lips, then back up to his eyes, and for a moment, there was nothing but a world of unspoken words between them. It had been weeks since the hotel night.

"You fight me all—" she started but he interrupted with another crushing kiss. This time it was deeper. Needier. As if he were done with fighting and this was the only way to stop it.

He pulled her into him, his broad shoulders brushing against the hanging coats, arms crossed in a posture that practically screamed discomfort. He angled her pelvis on his hardening cock, hidden in his pants, muttering orders to her. It made her mouth water.

She bit his lip playfully and kissed down his jaw, down his neck, and down his chest. Balancing on her heels, she hiked up her skirt, knelt before him and worked at his fly. Terrible timing, but she had no choice. She needed to be closer to him. Gazing up, she saw his jaw was tight, his gaze fixed resolutely on her like she held the answers to the universe.

Grace bit back a smirk as she unwrapped his gift, the shiny pulsing head of his cock catching the faint light.

"Mmm," she moaned, drawing out the sound as she slowly ran her tongue along the side of cock. The salty sweetness melted against her lips, and she let out a faint hum of approval, just loud enough to draw his attention.

"Fuck." He shifted, his shoulders tensing. "Could you not?"

"Not what?" she asked innocently, massaging his manhood in her hand.

His eyes flicked to her despite himself, narrowing slightly as he caught the mischievous glint in hers. "You know exactly what you're doing. Not here. Not now."

She shrugged, deliberately taking another slow, deliberate lick. She couldn't help but enjoy the added thrill of watching Caleb twitch.

His jaw clenched, the muscle ticking under his skin as he exhaled sharply through his nose. "I'm here to protect you, not...whatever this is."

"But I've been waiting for this," she teased, her voice light and sweet as she slid her mouth over his cock. "I need you right now."

Caleb groaned, weaving his hands into her hair, pulling on her. "Damn, you're a fucking bad little thing."

Grace tilted her head, letting his head linger at her lips for a moment before taking him all back. She sucked up and down, determined to give him the best blow job of his life. Slurping noises echoed softly in the confined space, and she gave him a sly grin. "Release to me. Let me taste you."

"Fuck, girl," he said gruffly, his voice low. "You'll get us both fired."

The tension crackled between them, electric and undeniable. Caleb's eyes darkened, his composure fraying at the edges as he stared down at her working her magic. She could see the war waging inside him —

duty versus desire, control versus chaos — and it thrilled her more than she cared to admit.

Finally, she drove him to the edge.

The hot sweetness hit Grace's tongue in an unexpected rush, his cream filling her mouth almost too fast for her to process. Her lips parted instinctively as Caleb exploded in her, releasing his cum, a smug expression on his face that she both wanted to slap away and savor.

She swallowed quickly, trying to keep up with the flood of airy, creamy sweetness. The texture melted against her tongue, and for a brief moment, the taste of him overpowered every thought in her head.

She worked to contain it, determined not to waste a single drop. Caleb's gaze stayed locked on her, his eyes filled with an amused challenge. She couldn't let him win.

Finally, she managed to swallow the last of it, licking a stray bit of cream from the corner of her lips as she stood and straightened her skirt. Her eyes met his, sharp and defiant, even as his taste lingered in her mouth.

"More than you could handle?" Caleb teased.

"You're impossible," she muttered, her voice rough. "But I kinda like it."

For a moment, the air between them grew heavier, filled with words unsaid and emotions too tangled to name. Caleb's hand flexed at his side, his restraint almost palpable. He reached out and touched the side of her face, playing with her lip.

She finally broke the silence, her voice barely above a whisper. "Where have you been?"

His thumb traced the line of her jaw, his eyes never leaving hers. "I don't know. I've been here."

"No, you haven't really been here." She brought his hand to her heart.

He held her closer and seemed to pray silently. She did too. They had to figure it out. Soon.

"We have to get back," she said. "Before someone comes in."

He nodded, releasing her. "Don't be a bad girl again...unless it's with me."

"You know I will. And I'm going through with the plan."

And just like that, the moment was over. He opened the door, letting the noise of the rally flood into the tiny closet, and gestured for her to step out.

Grace smiled to herself as she walked past him, the faintest hint of a redness creeping up his neck. She'd won this round, and she knew it. But as she glanced back at him, his expression a mix of frustration and something deeper, she couldn't help but wonder how long he could hold his resolve.

And how much she wanted to be the one to break it.

* * * *

Outside, tailgaters were everywhere—loud, drunk, and oblivious to the simmering danger beneath the surface. Thanks to Marisol, the president had insisted on making an impromptu appearance, and despite Caleb's protests, here they were, in the middle of the chaos, with the polls sinking and TVC's threats growing stronger by the day.

The crowd was a sea of crimson and black, with fans celebrating the big game and others barely aware of the political storm brewing in their midst. The president, unfazed by the growing tension, was mingling with supporters and taking photos. His charisma, as always, drew people in — making him seem like a man who had the whole country in the palm of his hand. But Caleb didn't feel that way. Not anymore.

Wyatt moved beside him, scanning the crowd with the precision of someone who'd lived through more than his fair share of danger. "This is a mistake," Wyatt muttered, voice low as he watched the president shake hands with a group of tailgaters. "He shouldn't be out here."

"I know," Caleb said, voice tense. His eyes never stopped moving, assessing the crowd, watching for any sign of trouble. His instincts told him that this was all wrong. The president had pushed for this, but it felt like a ticking time bomb. "But we don't exactly have a choice, do we?"

"No," Wyatt grumbled. "But if this doesn't go sideways, I'll eat my gun."

Caleb didn't respond. He was too busy assessing the faces around them — tailgaters, students, families — none of them were the real threat. Not until they started pushing too close, or until someone had a bad idea. The chants of protest outside the stadium had grown louder, and Caleb couldn't ignore the fact that they had supporters who weren't here for a photo op — they were here to make a statement. And those people didn't care who got in the way.

"Move him back," Caleb muttered, stepping forward toward the president. His voice was sharp as he motioned to the security team to form a tighter perimeter. "We're too exposed."

The president smiled and waved, oblivious to the rising pressure around him. But the moment Caleb took another step forward, he felt it — a shift in the air.

Something had changed. He turned just in time to see a man — drunk, a little too eager — getting far too close to the president.

The man, wearing a University of Alabama jersey and a backward cap, wasn't making any attempt to stop. His eyes were locked on the president, and he was closing the distance with each step. Caleb's hand instinctively moved to his holster.

"Hey!" Caleb barked, stepping in front of the man. "Back up."

The man didn't stop. He was grinning, a bit too wide, too confident. "It's just a handshake, man," he slurred. "What's the big deal?"

"Back. The. Fuck. Up," Caleb snapped, taking another step forward, his tone turning deadly. This wasn't the time for games, and he wasn't going to let this idiot jeopardize the president's safety for a damn selfie.

But the man wasn't listening. Instead, he pushed forward, shoulders square, trying to force his way through the security perimeter.

Caleb's patience snapped. With one swift motion, he grabbed the man by the collar, jerking him back hard. "I said back off, now!" he shouted, his voice cold, his grip tightening.

The man's face contorted in confusion, but the alcohol had dulled his reaction time. He tried to shove back, but Caleb was already moving, pushing the man away with authority. It wasn't just about the physical confrontation — it was about sending a message. *Stay the hell away from the president.*

"Get him out of here!" Caleb growled to the nearby Secret Service agents, his jaw clenched. His eyes flicked to Wyatt, who was already positioning himself to intercept anyone else who might get any ideas.

But the man wasn't done. He shoved Caleb with both hands, his breath reeking of cheap beer. "Who the hell do you think you are?" the guy shouted, not realizing how much worse he was making things.

Without thinking, Caleb shoved him back, hard enough that the man stumbled, almost crashing into a nearby grill where a group of fans had been cooking out. The sizzling heat from the grill rose in the air, but it wasn't enough to mask the growing tension. Caleb's heart was pounding, and he was seconds away from losing control. But before he could do anything more, Wyatt had already closed the distance, gripping the man by the shoulder and pulling him away from Caleb.

"Let's go, asshole," Wyatt barked, his voice lethal. He yanked the man back, away from the crowd, directing him toward the security team, who swiftly moved in to handle the situation.

But, it was too late. The guy's friend appeared at Caleb's side, angry as hell. The man jumped Caleb, and he clutched the guy's jersey. The drunken fool had pushed too far, and now there was no turning back. Caleb's instincts as a former special forces operative kicked in like muscle memory. His body moved before his mind even had time to process, every motion calculated and efficient.

With one swift motion, Caleb twisted the man's arm, leveraging his body weight and pulling him into a painful wrist lock. The man yelped in surprise, his face flushing red as Caleb jerked his arm back, forcing him down.

"Stay down!" Caleb barked, using his knee to pin the man's torso to the ground. The crowd around them was starting to disperse, people sensing the tension but too nervous to intervene.

But the guy wasn't done yet. His other fist swung up, hitting Caleb's cheek with a solid thud.

Caleb wasn't focused. It shouldn't have landed. But he was slow and sloppy.

The impact stung like a slap from a baseball bat, and Caleb's head snapped to the side, his vision briefly blurry. His body flared with adrenaline, and his teeth ground together in irritation. The pain in his cheek was secondary to the fact that this man, this reckless idiot, had just caused him a distraction. Caleb tightened his grip around the man's wrist as he pushed off his knee, flipping him over onto his back with expert precision.

Caleb's movements were smooth, fluid, as if he was born to be in moments like these. He used the man's own momentum against him, pushing his shoulder down with a calculated move that forced the man's body to twist and collapse to the ground. The crowd had cleared, but there was still a line of tailgaters watching with curiosity as Caleb kept the man pinned. His breath was coming fast, his cheek burning, but his focus was absolute.

"You don't want to do this," Caleb said, his voice low and dangerous. He'd learned a long time ago that a fight wasn't just about physical strength. It was about control. And he had control of this situation now.

The man, still struggling, swung his knee upward, aiming for Caleb's stomach. Caleb sidestepped the move with a smooth duck, then immediately pressed his palm to the back of the man's head and shoved it into the grass. The blow didn't knock him out, but it rattled him enough to disorient him.

Caleb didn't waste time. He used his knee to pin the guy's torso while his left arm grabbed his shoulder and twisted, pinning him down with an almost surgical grip. The guy gasped, his breath shallow and quick, his body starting to sag under the weight of Caleb's control.

The moment stretched on, but Caleb was already preparing for the worst. He wasn't taking any chances, not after what had just happened. One hit to the cheek was too close, too personal, and he wasn't going to let this idiot get another swing in.

"Fuck, man," Caleb growled, his voice firm and low, almost a warning.

The man, now winded and realizing he wasn't going to win this fight, finally stopped resisting. His body went limp beneath Caleb's grip, and with a sharp twist, Caleb managed to pin both his arms behind his back, the move leaving him vulnerable but secure.

Behind them, Wyatt stepped in, his hand already on the guy's collar as he helped Caleb drag him up to his feet, keeping him steady and well-controlled.

"You good?" Wyatt asked, his voice still rough, though there was an underlying amusement in his tone.

Caleb wiped the blood from his lip, a trickle from where his cheek had taken the hit. The sting was there, but it was nothing compared to the adrenaline still coursing through his veins. His jaw throbbed, but it wasn't enough to slow him down.

"I'm fine," Caleb grunted, turning his head toward the crowd. He scanned the area quickly. They needed to finish this quickly before anyone else got any ideas.

The president, blissfully unaware of the scene that had unfolded just yards away from him, was still talking to a group of tailgaters, waving and smiling as if the whole damn world wasn't about to come crashing down.

Caleb turned back to the subdued man on the ground, meeting a glare that was equal parts defiance and grudging acknowledgment. Without waiting for any excuses, he jerked his head at the security team.

"Get him the hell out," Caleb growled. Wyatt, still catching his breath, dragged the guy toward the waiting guards.

The man shot one last toxic look before they hauled him off, but he kept his mouth shut this time. No nerve left.

Caleb let out a slow breath, adrenaline still humming in his veins. He touched his cheek, wincing at the raw sting where the punch had landed.

Wyatt raised an eyebrow, smirking. "Nice work. You look like a truck used you for batting practice, though."

Caleb grunted. "Completely unnecessary." He was already dreading the hospital lights, stitches in his face, and the fact that he'd be stuck in the ER instead of with Grace tonight, despite her invitation. It made him mad as hell — but that was the way it was going to be.

Chapter Twelve

Washington, DC
2 days to the election

The Oval Office felt colder than usual, though Grace knew that was just her. The pressure had been unrelenting for weeks, but today, it seemed to cut deeper. President Norman Armstrong sat behind the Resolute Desk, his gaze sharp, his presence commanding as ever.

"You look like hell, Grace," Armstrong said, leaning back in his chair. His tone was lighter than she expected, but there was no mistaking the weight behind it. "You should rest."

She shook her head, forcing a smile that didn't reach her eyes. "I'll sleep when you've won."

Armstrong chuckled, a low, gravelly sound. "You're relentless. I like that." He leaned forward, resting his hands on the desk. "But let's not kid ourselves. This race isn't over. You've seen the numbers. Marisol's been a game-changer."

Grace stiffened, the name alone enough to twist her stomach. "Her numbers are solid," she admitted cautiously. "But her methods —"

"Are exactly what we need," Armstrong interrupted. His voice carried the weight of finality, the tone of a man who wouldn't be swayed. "Marisol knows how to win. She doesn't play safe, and neither can we."

Grace swallowed the knot in her throat. "She's taking risks that could blow up in our faces."

Armstrong tilted his head, studying her. "Or they could give us the edge we need. Look at the last rally. The narrative shifted. She's right about the tailgate, and she'll be right about this too."

Grace shifted her weight, her arms crossed tightly. "I'll handle it."

"She wants you to meet her," Armstrong said. "Tonight."

Grace blinked. "Tonight? Where?"

"Upstate," he said simply. "Her lodge. She's putting the final pieces together for election day."

Her gut twisted. She hated the thought of leaving now, with so much in flux. "I'm not sure it's the best use of my time, sir. There's too much here —"

"Grace." Armstrong's voice softened, but his words held firm. "This isn't a request. She's proven herself, and I need you to make this work. Marisol doesn't wait, and right now, we can't afford to, either."

Grace clenched her jaw, every instinct screaming against this, but she knew better than to argue. He was right — Marisol had been right more often than not. Even when Grace didn't like it.

"I'll go," she said finally. Her voice was steady, but inside, she felt like she was stepping into quicksand.

Armstrong nodded, a faint smile tugging at his lips. "I knew I could count on you."

Grace forced herself to stand tall, her mind already spinning with logistics. "I'll handle it. And I'll make sure it works."

"That's what I like to hear." Armstrong's eyes gleamed with something that looked like pride. "We're close, Grace. Don't let up now."

As she walked out of the Oval Office, the air outside felt just as heavy as inside. Her pulse quickened. This wasn't just about winning anymore. It was about survival—for the president, for the country, and, maybe, for her own conscience.

She hated Marisol. She hated needing her. But she couldn't shake the growing realization that Marisol wasn't just shaping the narrative. She was shaping everything.

And it might cost Grace more than she was ready to give.

* * * *

Upstate New York

The rain pounded on the windshield like it was trying to drown out the tension in the SUV. Grace, his passenger, stared out at the gray, blurred landscape, as if trying to find some sense of calm.

Caleb's grip on the wheel was tight, his knuckles white, his jaw locked. He hadn't said much since they left DC, but the storm inside the car wasn't just from the weather. It was between them—thick, unspoken, and impossible to ignore.

Grace broke the silence first. "Does it hurt?" She nodded at the bruising around his eye and cheek.

Caleb gripped the wheel harder, the tension in his shoulders making his muscles ache. He knew what she was doing, trying to make him talk, trying to ease whatever guilt she was feeling. She couldn't help herself.

"No." His voice came out flat, cold. He wasn't in the mood to discuss it, especially not with her. Not after everything. "It's fine."

Grace didn't let up. He could feel her eyes on him, her blue gaze as sharp as ever, even if she wasn't looking directly at him. She had this way of seeing right through him, like she knew the storm inside his chest.

"I didn't think you'd get hit," she said, her voice softer now, almost tentative. But there was that same stubborn edge in it that always made him clench his jaw. "Those tailgaters were wild."

"They were drunk. I was distracted." He threw her a glance, the kind of look that could either melt a woman's heart or freeze it solid.

"I'm sorry."

"I didn't ask for your apology, Grace."

She flinched, her lips tightening, but she didn't back down. "I'm just asking if you're okay."

He laughed darkly, the sound bitter. "I'm fine. Just—drop it."

She stared at him for a moment, then sighed, her breath fogging up the window. "Good lord, you are stubborn."

Caleb's gaze flicked to the road ahead, the rain blurring the lines of the world outside. He could feel his pulse hammering in his ears, and a knot formed in his stomach. Her persistence was both infuriating and…something else. Something dangerous.

"I told you, I'm fine," he repeated, his voice hard now. He didn't want to get into this. Not with her. Not when every time she looked at him, his chest felt like it might explode.

Grace didn't reply immediately, and for a moment, the car was filled only with the sound of rain, steady and relentless. Caleb tried to focus on the road, but the tension in the air between them was impossible to ignore. It was thick, like smoke that clung to his lungs.

Finally, she spoke again, her tone more careful, but still there—her damn stubbornness. "You're mad at me."

Caleb didn't look at her. "I'm not mad."

She raised an eyebrow, clearly not believing him. "Right. You're just pissed at me."

He shot her a quick, sharp look. "No. I'm pissed at the situation. At this entire goddamn mess."

Her eyes softened for a second, and Caleb could feel her frustration mingling with something else — something she probably wouldn't admit, even if he asked.

She reached over and lightly touched his arm, and Caleb felt the heat of her fingers through his jacket. His skin prickled, but he didn't pull away. She knew exactly how to press his buttons — how to make him feel things he didn't want to feel.

"Caleb," she whispered, voice lower now. "I didn't mean for you to get hurt."

He stared straight ahead, his chest tight. "You never do."

* * * *

When the car finally pulled into the gravel driveway of Marisol's retreat, Grace's eyes couldn't help but widen. The sprawling estate was tucked away in a forest of tall, imposing trees, the grand wooden house barely visible behind them. It looked like something out of a magazine — too perfect to be real. Grace felt the contrast immediately. The buzzing intensity of her work in the city, now replaced by the quiet isolation of the wilderness.

She stepped out of the car, inhaling the crisp air, trying to ground herself. The world outside felt so different from the one she was about to walk into. This wasn't about policy or politics — it was about power.

And she had no choice but to play along.

Before she could even reach the door, Marisol was there — graceful and poised, her presence magnetic. She was everything Grace had expected and more. Marisol was dressed in a tailored white jacket and pants that didn't look remotely practical for the outdoors but somehow made her look even more untouchable.

"Grace, welcome," Marisol said, her voice smooth, sweet, and far too calculated. The smile she wore was warm but not genuine — one that made Grace's skin prickle with the awareness that she was never in control here.

Marisol extended her arms for a hug. Grace took it, but only briefly. The last thing she needed was to get cozy with the woman who could tear their entire campaign apart with a single word.

"Thanks for asking us to join you," Grace replied, her voice steady, professional, though she was anything but. "I assume you have a plan?"

"Always," Marisol replied smoothly, the hint of a challenge in her eyes. "But first, go ahead and get settled in."

Grace nodded, not willing to let her guard down. She followed Marisol inside, the scent of wood and expensive perfume heavy in the air. The interior of the lodge was all sleek lines, minimalist luxury, and floor-to-ceiling windows that overlooked miles of untouched land. There was wealth here, but it was quiet—controlled. Grace could see why Marisol was the one pulling strings behind the scenes. Power wasn't something she had to flaunt. It was something that just...was.

The fire crackled softly in the lounge, casting flickering shadows that danced across Grace's skin. The silence in the room felt almost oppressive. Caleb followed behind her, his presence an undeniable weight.

Grace didn't need to look at him to feel him. She could sense him there, the air charged between them, tight and thick. His eyes were on her, but his body was all business. His shoulders were wound tight, his jaw clenched, like he was waiting for something to explode.

The room seemed to shrink, the firelight flickering in sync with the pounding of her heart. She could feel the pull of him, the unspoken tension, and damn it, she couldn't ignore it. His presence made everything else fade away, leaving just the two of them in that space.

Grace met his stare, unflinching. Her breath caught in her chest. He was too close, and yet, it felt like a world away.

"We aren't staying long." Caleb's voice cut through the thick silence, low, hard, and rough. His words were like a warning, but the look in his eyes told another story.

She didn't know why, but his words unsettled her. She forced herself to smile, her lips curling just enough to show she wasn't rattled. "Just the night."

He didn't respond right away. His eyes flicked down to her lips—lingering just long enough for the tension to coil tighter between them. Grace could almost taste the air, thick and heavy, and for a split second, she swore she saw something flash in his eyes—a flicker of heat.

"One night," he said finally, his voice clipped. But even his brief response had the air between them sparking. It was like he couldn't fight it either, even if he tried.

For a heartbeat, she considered closing the gap between them, pushing past the professional walls they'd built around themselves. But no. Not here. Not now. They had a job to do.

Still, she couldn't shake the feeling that something was unraveling beneath the surface. Something she couldn't put a name to.

But then, the moment was gone. Marisol had returned, sliding into the room with an ease that suggested she'd been watching them the whole time.

"Grace," she said smoothly, breaking the bubble. "I'm so glad you could make it." Her eyes flicked between them, a knowing smile playing at her lips. "Shall we get down to business?"

Grace didn't miss the subtle shift in Marisol's tone. It was calculated, predatory, like a wolf toying with its prey.

She steeled herself, ready to get this over with. "Let's talk," she said. It wasn't time for games, not now. The stakes were too high.

Marisol's eyes sparkled with amusement. "Of course," she said, her voice a smooth purr. "Follow me."

And just like that, the moment was gone, replaced by the looming presence of Marisol's plans — the ones Grace would have to play along with, no matter how much it cost her.

Marisol joined them in the seating area by the fire, where coffee and tea had already been set out. "I'm sure you are exhausted from the campaign," she said as she settled into a chair, eyes glinting with something unreadable. "But we have work to do."

Grace glanced at Caleb before answering. "I am here to listen."

"I hope you brought an overnight bag. We have a lot to work through," Marisol said, her gaze moving to Caleb. "Why is he here? This is private."

Grace didn't flinch, but inside, her thoughts were racing. Of course, Marisol didn't just want to have a nice chat.

"Her safety," Caleb responded.

"And I assume you have a plan for that, too?" Marisol asked, her voice steady.

Caleb's lips curled into a smile that was anything but friendly. "I always do."

The conversation turned to the finer details of election day strategy, but the air between Grace and Caleb was thick with unspoken tension. Caleb didn't say much, sat behind her, his eyes flickering to Grace every now and then, but Grace couldn't help but notice the way his presence seemed to ground her, even in this foreign world of power and influence.

* * * *

Grace stood on the cabin's balcony, her fingers gripping the railing, staring out over the vast expanse of trees. The peaceful setting, far removed from the campaign chaos, should have felt like a respite. Instead, the silence only made the tension between her and Caleb worse.

She could feel his presence behind her, the weight of his gaze settling on her shoulders like a physical force. The air between them was charged, thick with the unresolved argument from earlier.

Turning to face him, Grace's jaw tightened. "You didn't have to stay in the meeting. You know that, right?" Her voice was clipped, but there was no hiding the frustration creeping in.

Caleb's expression was unreadable, his jaw clenched, but he gave no sign of backing down. "I don't trust her. Not for a minute."

"What's an unarmed seventy-something woman going to do to me?" she shot back, crossing her arms. "Just stay out of the way. This is my job, Caleb. Not yours."

He exhaled sharply, his posture rigid, betraying his anger and confusion. "You don't get it. These people are fucked up."

"Worse than TVC?" She laughed bitterly, turning back to the view of the forest. "I don't think so."

"They still want a piece of you."

"Let them have it."

The moment hung between them — raw, harsh, and painful. He was right about one thing, the stakes were higher now. It wasn't just the campaign or her career — it was their lives.

Grace felt the heat of his body as he stepped closer, his breath warm against her ear. "I said I'd have your back. And I am."

His words triggered something inside her, something fierce and volatile. She spun around, meeting his gaze head-on. "For real, this time?"

The words sliced through the air like a blade, but Caleb wasn't backing down. His voice was low, dangerous. "I'm here. I'm not going anywhere." His fingers grazed the side of her face, catching a loose strand of hair, his touch sending an electric current down her spine.

Grace didn't pull away. She couldn't. The heat between them was undeniable, raw, dangerous. "Tell me what's going on with us," she whispered, stepping even closer, her breath mingling with his.

"It's been...complicated."

"What do you want?"

"I want you."

And then, without warning, Caleb closed the distance, grabbing her by the wrist and pulling her toward him. His mouth crashed against hers — hard, needy, desperate. She gasped, stunned at the intensity of it, the urgency in his kiss. His hands found the back of her neck, holding her in place, his lips moving over hers with a possessive force.

Grace's pulse raced as she kissed him back, her fingers digging into his chest, pulling him closer. This — this reckless kiss, the way his body pressed against hers—was something she couldn't control. Something she didn't want to control.

It was everything she'd been trying to deny, everything she'd been fighting against.

But as quickly as it had begun, the kiss stopped. Caleb pulled back just enough to meet her eyes, his chest heaving. "Fuck," he muttered, his voice hoarse.

She reached for him but he stepped back.

"I'm on the job," he said. "Damn, I'm sorry."

"I don't mind."

"I took an oath to do my job right."

"That didn't stop you last time."

He shot her a fierce look, as if to say, *don't fuck with me this time.*

"This push and pull—it needs to stop," she said. "Just decide where you're at and stop throwing me around. I can't take it anymore."

They stood there for a moment, the air between them thick with unresolved desire and tension. And then, without another word, Caleb turned and walked back toward the cabin, leaving Grace standing in the cold, her heart pounding.

Chapter Thirteen

Dinner stretched on, heavy and suffocating. The rain outside pounded against the windows, a steady rhythm that only seemed to underscore the tension in the room. Marisol sat across from Grace and Caleb, her posture perfect, her every movement deliberate. The wine poured freely, the amber liquid swirling in her glass as her eyes flicked from one to the other — sharp, calculating.

"So," Marisol began, her voice light, almost teasing, "Grace, tell me — where does Armstrong go tomorrow? And then on Election Day?"

Grace set her fork down, her tone steady but laced with the faintest edge. "Back to Pennsylvania. The president needs a solid push there. Raleigh, Grand Rapids, the usual stops — rallies, base support. No room for error."

Marisol's lips curled at the edges, just enough to show interest but not enough to call it warmth. She leaned forward slightly, her gaze flicking to Caleb, before returning to Grace. "How very practical," she mused. "But surely there's more to it than just playing safe. A few rallies won't turn the tide, will they? The president needs something more…dramatic."

The subtle jab was clear. Caleb's jaw tightened, the muscles in his neck flexing as he pushed his plate aside, clearly not enjoying the turn the conversation had taken. Grace felt the tension in his silence, the restraint just beneath the surface. She knew he couldn't object to being there, but he clearly didn't have time for Marisol's condensation.

"Son," Marisol continued, "sometimes the best plans need a…fresh perspective. A bold move, perhaps?"

Grace caught the sharpness in Marisol's eyes — this wasn't a casual suggestion. Marisol was always angling, always looking for leverage. And Caleb, well, Grace knew damn well that Caleb didn't appreciate being the target.

"Some people think playing it safe will win this," she said, "and I think it's time to change the game, don't you?"

Caleb's voice snapped the tension, his words clipped, his patience worn thin. "And what exactly would you suggest?"

Grace could see the slight curl at the corner of Marisol's lips. The smile of a predator who knew she'd cornered her prey. Marisol turned her focus on Grace. "Oh, I have ideas." Her tone slipped into something smoother, almost conspiratorial. "Grace, perhaps we should break away from the crowd and speak as professionals, just us two."

Professionals. Grace knew what that meant — Marisol wanted to isolate her, to pitch a strategy that wouldn't fly if Caleb was breathing down her neck. "I don't think that's necessary," Grace said coolly, refusing to look away. "What have you told the president? What does he expect from you?"

Marisol's eyes gleamed, satisfaction dancing there as if this was all going according to plan. Grace's stomach tightened. Whatever came next would not be pretty—it would be the kind of morally ambiguous maneuver Marisol specialized in.

Marisol folded her arms, leaning in slightly. "He expects what he knows I can deliver. Influence over the final headlines, strategic placement of advertising—nothing outright illegal, mind you, but...not exactly squeaky clean either." She paused, and Grace could feel Caleb shifting beside her, bristling at every word.

Marisol continued, voice dropping a notch, her words for Grace as much as for anyone else. "We have star power waiting in the wings—some beloved cultural icons who haven't officially endorsed. They can make last-minute social media posts, hinting at their support. It'll look spontaneous, authentic. Meanwhile, certain media outlets—ones that owe me favors—can tweak their election night narratives. A subtle tilt in tone, a headline framed more favorably. Nothing anyone can point to as manipulation, but enough to sway those final undecided voters."

Grace's throat went dry. This was exactly what she'd worried about—the line between legitimate strategy and outright moral compromise blurred to the point of invisibility. Armstrong had given Marisol leeway, and now she was pushing it. Hard.

"And the cost?" Grace asked, her voice steady but her heart pounding. "What do you want in return?"

"I just want to win." Marisol's smile was almost kind—like a teacher proud of a particularly clever student. "Just a nod in my direction after the victory. Influence on certain policy talks, a seat at the table when immigration reforms are discussed, maybe a quiet say in the next appointments. Nothing dramatic. Just...acknowledgment that without my finesse, this win wouldn't be so certain."

Grace clenched her jaw. This was the game. Armstrong might get his win, but it would come wrapped in Marisol's invisible strings. Caleb shifted again, and Grace didn't need to look at him to know he was simmering, his anger barely contained.

"Grace," Marisol said softly, too softly, "this election is hanging by a thread. We're dealing with voters who make decisions in the last hours. Isn't it worth a few nudges, a few whispered suggestions, to ensure we don't wake up to defeat?"

Grace's mind raced. She thought of the president, so close to victory, and the upheaval that a loss would bring. She thought of the policies on the line—some of which she believed in, others she questioned. And then she thought of the price—handing Marisol more leverage, more power. As for Caleb—she could almost sense his muscles tensing, ready to object, to put a stop to this charade.

Before Grace could respond, Marisol pressed on, "All I'm offering is a strategic push. Nothing public, nothing that would leave a paper trail. Just people playing their parts at the right moment. The president expects me to do what I do best. Are you really going to stand in the way of that, with so much at stake?"

Grace's pulse hammered, enough of this back-and-forth. She stood abruptly, cutting Marisol off before any more insults could fly. "Look," she said sharply. "I need to speak with Jordan about this. And it is late."

"Understood," Marisol said. "Just remember — tomorrow is about results. I will see you first thing in the morning and we can start making this happen."

As Marisol turned and swept from the room, Grace felt the weight of the evening settle into her bones. Tomorrow would be a tipping point — she could feel it in her gut.

* * * *

When the conversation with Marisol ended, Caleb slipped away without a word. Grace felt the tension thick in the air as he disappeared down the hall. The knot in her stomach twisted tighter with every passing minute. She could feel it — the storm was coming.

She found him in his room, the door cracked open, his figure silhouetted against the dim light. His movements were sharp, frantic, as he packed with a cold, mechanical precision. Grace's breath caught in her throat.

"Caleb," she said, her voice tight, but he didn't even glance her way.

"Caleb," she repeated, stepping inside, voice more urgent now. "What the hell are you doing?"

His back stiffened, and he turned, his eyes burning with something she couldn't ignore — something raw, something dangerous. "We're leaving," he said flatly, his voice low, laced with a venom she hadn't heard before.

She blinked, heart stuttering. "What do you mean, 'leaving'?"

"I mean, get your shit together. We're out of here." His jaw clenched as he threw a few more items into his bag. "I'm done. I can't sit here and watch you ruin everything you've worked for just to keep playing Marisol's game. This shit isn't right."

The words hit like a slap, sharp and unforgiving. Her chest tightened. She hadn't realized how close to the edge they were, but now it was all crashing down, every unspoken truth in the air between them.

"Don't do this," Grace said, her voice shaking now. "You know Marisol. You know what she's like. You can't—"

"You think I'm just gonna sit here and watch you let her walk all over you?" Caleb's voice was a shout now, each word sharp as a blade. He took a step toward her, fists clenched, anger radiating off him like heat. "You're just letting her drag you into her shit, Grace! I'm done being your backup, your fucking safety net!"

His words sliced through her, harder than anything he'd said before. She opened her mouth to argue, to fight back, but the truth of it was too much. It stung.

"I'm trying to make this work," she bit back, crossing her arms defensively. "Don't give up."

"No, you don't get it!" Caleb snapped, his voice rising with every word. "This isn't about giving up, Grace. This is about our country. Our freedom. Doing things right. And she's made you into her damn puppet, and I'm done watching you destroy yourself just for the win!"

The heat between them flared, and for the first time, Grace saw the crack in his facade—this wasn't just about Marisol. It was about them—everything they had fought for, everything they had built. The room felt small, the air thick with the weight of everything left unsaid.

He stepped closer, his voice dangerously low. "You're too damn important for this. But you don't get it. You're already making your choice." His eyes were dark, burning with a fierce kind of sorrow. "And I won't stand here and watch you lose yourself."

Grace felt something break inside her. The words hovered on the edge of her lips, but she couldn't say them. She wanted to make him understand, wanted to say please, but the moment was slipping away, and with it, any chance they had left.

He threw his bag down, the thud echoing in the stillness, then he turned away, his back to her. The storm outside battered against the windows, mirroring the chaos in her chest.

"Caleb, please," she said as she reached for him. "Don't leave me. Not now. Not like this."

But he didn't turn around. He just kept packing, each movement colder than the last. The storm outside shook the room, but the silence between them was even more deafening.

"I'm not sticking around for this, Grace," he said, his voice flat, final. "I'll call Wyatt to come deal with this. You'll be fine for a few hours until he gets here."

"No!" She almost shouted, panic rising in her chest. "You can't just walk away from me! Not now, not after everything."

He spun on his heel, his eyes colder than ever. "I can—and I will." His words sliced through her like a knife. "You don't need me. You've said it a million times. All you need is to win."

"No!" she shouted, her heart pounding, desperate. "That's not it! I need you. I—" She choked on the words, trying to steady herself. "I can't do this without you."

His eyes didn't soften. "You already are."

Her throat tightened. "Please...don't leave me. Not now, Caleb. Please."

The silence hung between them like a noose, suffocating, unbearable. His face was unreadable, stone-cold, his back to her once more as he grabbed the last of his things.

"I'm sorry, Grace," he said, his voice low but final. "But you made your choice. Now I'm making mine."

Grace stepped forward, her voice breaking, but it was too late. "Caleb!" she cried out, her heart in her throat.

But he didn't turn. The door slammed shut behind him, cutting her off from everything they had been. From everything she thought they could still be.

Grace collapsed against the wall, her breath ragged, her heart a broken mess of raw emotion. The storm outside howled, relentless. Inside, everything she had known was gone.

And she was left in the silence.

Grace's heart pounded in her chest as she ran through the dark hallways of the lodge, her footsteps echoing against the polished floors. The wind howled outside, shaking the windows and rattling the wooden beams of the mansion. Her breath came in sharp, jagged bursts, the adrenaline of the argument still coursing through her veins.

She had to stop him. She couldn't let him leave like this.

She reached the front door just as Caleb's silhouette appeared through the glass, his figure framed by the dim glow of the exterior lights. He was walking away, his shoulders set in that rigid, determined stance that always made her heart clench.

"No," she whispered to herself. She couldn't lose him, not after everything.

Panic gripped her chest as she threw open the door, the cold night air slapping her face. The rain poured down in sheets, soaking her through in an instant. She didn't care. She just couldn't let him go.

"Caleb, stop!" Her voice was raw as it carried across the yard, cutting through the sound of the rain. She didn't know if he could hear her over the noise of the rain and wind, but she kept shouting anyway, her voice rising with each step she took. "Stop! Please!"

He didn't turn around. He just kept walking toward the car, his movements mechanical, as though he couldn't hear her at all. He reached for the car door handle, and Grace's breath hitched. The weight of it all—his anger, her desperation—settled deep into her bones.

She was running now, her feet slipping on the wet ground, her heart hammering in her chest.

But he didn't stop. Didn't even flinch. He got into the car, slammed the door shut, and turned the engine over. The headlights blazed to life and for a split second, she thought he might just drive off into the night, leaving her here, alone and broken.

And then, something inside her snapped.

With a desperate cry, Grace turned and ran. She found her way down the trail that led to the lake, her feet slipping against the wet earth as the storm raged harder. The trees swayed, groaning under the pressure of the wind. Her lungs burned, her legs ached, but she couldn't stop.

The sound of the car's engine faded behind her as she reached the water. She stood at the lake's edge, her chest heaving, her mind a blur of confusion and anger. The rain beat down on her like a thousand tiny fists, but it was nothing compared to the emptiness in her chest.

The storm around her matched the one inside her — emotions she couldn't control, couldn't even begin to process.

And in that moment, as the cold rain soaked through to her skin, Grace broke. She collapsed onto her knees on the dock, leaning against the wall of a small lakeside bunkie, sobbing, her body wracked with each breath. Her tears mixed with the rain, and she couldn't tell where one ended and the other began.

Why did it have to be like this?

Lightning shot through the sky over the dock. Gasping, Grace stumbled into the bunkie, its creaking wooden frame barely audible over the sound of thunder. The rain lashed against the windows, the wind howling as it tugged at the trees. She slammed the door shut behind her, the sudden silence of the room pressing in on her as her body shook from the cold and the adrenaline of the night.

The small room was sparsely furnished — just a bed, a dresser, and a few chairs — but it felt like a sanctuary. Or maybe a tomb. She wasn't sure. She set her soaked sweater down by the door and glanced around, the darkened corners of the room a reminder of how small and isolated she really was.

Her hand instinctively reached for her phone. Maybe Jordan could help. Maybe he could talk some sense into this situation. She needed to hear a familiar voice, someone who might ground her in the chaos she'd created.

She tapped his name on the screen and raised the phone to her ear, but after a few seconds, the call failed.

"Come on," she muttered under her breath, her fingers frantically pressing the buttons to try again. Her heart thudded in her chest as the call went straight to voicemail. Again.

One bar of reception went to zero. *No signal.*

She walked over to the window, peering through the rain-streaked glass out at the dark lake, the water churning as the storm intensified. The wind gusted through the trees, rattling the frame of the bunkie. Grace's breath fogged up the glass as she pressed her forehead against it. The isolation was suffocating. The realization that she was truly alone, miles from anyone, with nothing but her thoughts and regrets, started to sink in.

She hadn't meant to push Caleb away like this. She'd never meant for things to spiral out of control. But the way they had argued, the way she had let her pride and her desperation cloud everything — it was all her fault.

She had pushed him too far, said too many things that couldn't be taken back. She'd been so caught up in trying to control the campaign, trying to keep everything from falling apart, that she hadn't seen what was really happening — what she was doing to the only person who had been there for her when it all went to hell.

She let the phone fall to the bed, feeling the weight of it like a stone. Her chest tightened as a wave of guilt rolled over her. She'd been so determined to be right, so sure that her way was the only way. But now, in the crushing silence of this small, lonely room, she could see the truth.

She had lost him.

Her eyes stung, and she swiped at her face, wiping away the tears that had started to well up. Her reflection in the window, pale and smeared by the rain, stared back at her.

What have I done?

She had to admit it—without Caleb, she was truly alone.

No one understood her like he did, no one had stood by her through everything. She had pushed him away in her need to control, and now, the silence was what she deserved.

"Damn it," she muttered, her voice breaking. She wanted to fix it, to take it all back, but how? How could she undo what she'd done?

She'd betrayed his trust.

A shudder ran through her as she wiped her face, rain and tears mixing. It was time to face this, face herself—and face the fact that she might be doing it alone from now on.

The door creaked. Heavy boots on the floorboards.

"I found you."

Her heart leaped into her throat. Caleb stood in the doorway, drenched, his eyes fierce and wild. The storm outside had nothing on the storm in his gaze.

"I—I didn't think... I thought you were gone."

"I couldn't leave," he said, his voice hard, but there was a softness in it now, something raw and real. His jaw was tight, fists clenched, struggling with everything he hadn't said.

The rain hammered outside, but the air between them burned with every unspoken word. She could feel it, the heat of the moment, the pull between them.

"I didn't mean for it to go like this," Grace whispered, stepping toward him, her voice barely a breath. "I'm sorry, Caleb. I — "

"Stop," he interrupted. He stepped closer, his presence overwhelming. "That's not why I'm here."

Her chest tightened, the words stuck in her throat. "Then why?" she barely managed, her voice shaky with everything she wanted to say, everything she'd never said.

Caleb swallowed, his eyes intense as he struggled with something inside him. Finally, he spoke, his voice barely above a whisper, yet it carried more weight than anything before.

"You," he said, the word soft but unwavering, like a vow.

For the first time in ages, Grace believed him.

Caleb didn't say anything else. His arms, so strong and familiar, gripped her, pulling her close. His arms slid around her waist, and before she could even process what was happening, he lifted her off her feet effortlessly and kissed her hard.

Grace gasped, her hands instinctively finding purchase around his neck as her body was pulled into his. Her heart was pounding in her chest, so loud it drowned out everything else — the storm, the confusion, the guilt that still weighed on her. All of it disappeared the moment he kissed her.

Her legs wrapped around his waist as he pressed her against the wall. His lips danced with hers in a fierce, desperate urgency that mirrored the storm outside. There was nothing tentative in the way he kissed her. It was raw, as if he'd wanted her for too long, and now, he couldn't stop. His tongue was wet and warm and searching inside her mouth. She melted against him, her fingers digging into his shoulders as the sensation of his kiss flooded her senses.

Caleb grasped the back of her head, holding her close as if to keep her anchored to him, like they were two pieces of a puzzle finally clicking into place. Her breath hitched in her throat, her pulse thundering as his kiss deepened, hungry and searching. She could feel the tension in his muscles, the heat of his body radiating into hers.

For a moment, Grace thought she might lose herself completely, consumed by the storm of desire that raged between them. But then, as if the world had shifted, Caleb pulled back just enough to look into her eyes. His breath was as ragged as hers, his chest rising and falling beneath her, and she could see the raw emotion in his gaze.

"I can't stay away from you," he murmured, his voice rough, almost like a confession. "I'm addicted."

"This is the worst place to do this."

"I don't want to follow the rules anymore."

"For once, we agree."

He kicked off his boots, tearing clothes off her and him — piece by piece.

His eyes were dark, intense, half closed, looking down at her with an expression she couldn't read. She could feel the tension in his body — muscles taut with restraint, though she knew that it wouldn't last. All that was left between them was her bra and panties — and his boxers. He was fighting something, and she wasn't sure whether it was his own desire or something more complicated.

He pulled back and played with her bra straps. His gaze moved from her eyes to her lips, and she felt it deep inside her — the need to be closer, skin on skin, but she couldn't move.

"You feel that?" he asked, his voice low, almost a growl. "Yeah, you know what that is." She was angled just right against his hardness, pulsing at her core. Her breath hitched, heart pounding in her chest as she nodded. God, she wanted him.

He groaned, his body leaning in ever so slightly, his breath warm on her face. His hands moved gently, slowly, running down her back to her hips, the touch both possessive and tender. "I won't let you go," he said, the words a promise, but also a warning.

Grace's pulse quickened, her chest tight with the weight of the moment. She wanted to respond, to say something, but the words stuck in her throat. She wanted to say so many things — to tell him how much she needed him, how much she wanted him to never let go — but somehow, everything felt too raw. Too real.

Instead, she tilted her head up slightly, meeting his gaze. "I fell for you hard, Caleb. I didn't have a chance."

He grinned and her lips parted just enough to invite him closer again, and that was all Caleb needed. His hands gripped her tighter, and without a moment's hesitation, he pulled her flush against him, his lips crashing down on hers in another kiss that was as fierce as it was desperate.

For a moment, there was nothing but the feeling of his body on hers, his heat, his strength, the roughness of his touch and the smoothness of his lips and his cock between her thighs.

She melted into him, her hands sliding up to his neck, pulling him closer as she gave herself completely to the kiss. There was no thinking, no reasoning — just the electricity between them, crackling and consuming them whole.

He broke the kiss only long enough to draw in a deep breath, his forehead resting on hers. "God, Grace," he muttered, his voice hoarse. His grip on her tightened, his arms locked around her as if he couldn't let her go, as if he couldn't bear to. "I've never felt it like this before."

"I want to be yours tonight."

Caleb's gaze was intense, his breath steady but heavy, as he held her up. His hands roamed, finding the entrance to her core. He did that thing he did — fingers in and thumb massaging her clit. She moaned, her head rolling back. Damn, he knew her spots. His scent, a mix of leather and musk, filled her senses. Everything else faded — the world outside, the chaos, the uncertainty. It was just them, locked in this moment, connected in a way that felt undeniable.

"Lie down with me," she said.

"Damn right."

He moved them toward the bed, his steps sure, never faltering as he carried her with ease. Reaching the soft sheets, he lowered her slowly, as if savoring it, placing her gently onto the blanket. The coolness of the fabric contrasted with the heat of her skin, sending a shiver down her spine.

For a second, he stood over her, his eyes dark and intense, studying her. Grace's chest rose and fell with a quickened breath, her heart racing in the quiet stillness between them. Caleb's hands hovered just above her, as though unsure whether to touch or hold back.

Caleb settled next to her, his chest rising and falling in time with her own. The room was quiet now, save for the sound of their breathing and the distant hum of the storm outside. The chaotic energy between them had softened, leaving behind an undeniable warmth and a sense of peace that neither had expected.

Grace lay on her back, her head resting on the pillow as she turned her face toward him. His eyes were still dark with desire, but now there was a tenderness that made her heart flutter unexpectedly. He propped himself up on one elbow, his other hand reaching to gently brush a strand of hair from her face.

"I'm so wild about you, did you know?" she said quietly, her voice almost a whisper. The words were more of a statement than a question, as if she couldn't quite believe it herself. After everything that had happened, after the tension and the chaos, here they were — together, in a way she hadn't allowed herself to imagine.

He gave her a small, almost imperceptible smile. "I knew."

Her heart gave a little skip. She wanted to respond, but the words felt too heavy, too loaded with meaning. Instead, she turned toward him, shifting closer until their bodies were just inches apart. Her fingers traced the lines of his jaw, the rough stubble there scratching gently against her skin.

Caleb let out a groan, his eyes closing as if he was savoring the moment, enjoying the connection. She could feel the tension in him, the years of discipline, of holding things together. But here, in the dark, there was no expectation, no mission, no responsibility. It was just them, raw and real.

"Kiss me again."

"If I do, I'm not holding back."

"I know. I want all of you right now."

"You want our first time to be on the enemy's territory?"

"Yes, because I choose you. I choose you a thousand times over... Fuck Marisol, fuck her plans."

She felt something change in the way he looked at her. His eyes told her everything — pupils widened, green intensified.

"Are you sure?" he asked, his voice a low rumble. His hand slid under the blanket, fingers grazing over the small of her back, drawing her a little closer. "You choose me — there's no turning back. I don't do things in half measures."

"Yeah," she murmured, her voice catching slightly. "I have been waiting so long for this. My heart always was with you."

Lying beside her, he let out a breath, as though some invisible weight had been lifted. He shifted his position and held her close. His fingers brushed over her skin with an almost absent touch, a small caress that made her heart race. She closed her eyes for a moment, just feeling the rise and fall of his chest beneath her hand, the steady rhythm of his breathing.

The soft glow of the bedside lamp bathed the room in a warm, golden light. Grace lay on the bed, her hair splayed out like dark silk against the pillows. Her breathing was steady but shallow, each inhale lifting her chest slightly as she stretched her arms above her head, wrists loosely crossed.

The world outside the door seemed a million miles away — the campaign, the pressures, the constant noise of expectations. Here, for once, there was silence, broken only by the faint hum of her own thoughts.

"Relax," Caleb said, rough and steady, grounding her in the moment. "I'm in control now."

Her lips curved into a faint smile. "You don't get it. Relaxing isn't exactly in my vocabulary."

He chuckled low in his throat, the sound warm and rich. "You don't say."

But for once, she let herself stop — stop thinking, stop planning, stop bracing for the next fight. She closed her eyes, her fingers curling slightly against the pillow.

"Feels weird, doesn't it?" he teased, though there was a tenderness in his tone.

Her smile widened, but she didn't open her eyes. "You have no idea."

She could feel that pull, and it made her breath catch. A spark of something she couldn't name flickered inside her.

Then, without warning, Caleb was over her, his motion deliberate, but not rushed. Grace's breath caught in her throat as he cupped her face with one hand, the heat of his palm sending a shiver down her spine.

For a moment, neither of them moved. Their eyes locked — his dark, intent, and hers searching, almost wary.

"Do you ever let go?" he murmured, his lips hovering just inches from hers.

Grace's heart pounded in her chest, but she didn't back away. Instead, she tilted her head slightly, her lips parting, and whispered, "Not that easy."

"We will see about that."

His response was a swift, almost urgent kiss, his lips pressing firmly against hers, claiming her in a way that was as thrilling as it was unexpected.

The kiss deepened, the heat between them building like a slow, simmering fire. Caleb's lips parted, and Grace didn't hesitate to follow, her tongue gently meeting his, tasting him, needing him closer. And, like he promised, she let go, giving herself up to the moment.

Caleb's breath hitched as he pulled away, their breaths mingling in the small space between them. "Grace..." he whispered, his voice rougher now, more desperate.

She gripped him tighter, unwilling to let go of the electric connection. She met his eyes, her voice barely a whisper. "Don't stop."

And for the first time in what felt like forever, she let herself feel it—all of him. The need, the passion, the desire that had been building between them for what felt like forever.

This time, neither of them held back.

Caleb ripped off her bra and panties in one skilled motion, worshipping her naked body illuminated in the moonlight beneath him. He slid off his boxers and angled himself right at her core.

The first touch of Caleb's cock between her thighs, rubbing against her pussy, was electric, a mix of warmth and pressure that sent a shiver down Grace's spine. His shaft pumped in, strong and deliberate, pressed into her fruit, teasing a need she hadn't realized was there. The tension in her body began to unravel under him, replaced by a simmering awareness that spread like fire.

The way he fucked her, it wasn't just skilled—it was intentional, as though he knew exactly what she needed before she did. It was maddening, this vulnerability she felt under his hands, and yet she couldn't bring herself to do anything either than take it. Rough. Hard.

When he doubled his pace, with the right amount of pressure, Grace felt herself melt, her breathing shallow. Fuck, he was damn good. A too-loud moan escaped her lips and she bit the inside of her cheek, annoyed at how easily he'd unraveled her composure.

The room felt like their own world in that moment, a space where the world noise faded, leaving only the sound of their breath and his rhythmic movement. Caleb was holding her thigh up so he could hit her in the right angle. Every pump was building a deeper sense of connection between them. There was no spoken challenge, no competition, just two people finding pleasure — together.

Caleb's grip on her hair was firm, his fingers threading through the strands with practiced precision as he angled her head back, exposing the delicate curve of her neck. Grace's breath hitched, the sudden rush of sensation making her pulse race.

He pulled her around him, pumping his cock into her.

"Get these legs up here." Caleb's voice was low, commanding, yet laced with something she couldn't quite name. "Wrap around me."

He fucked her harder. The bed was shaking. He grabbed the headboard for leverage, holding her ass in his hand as he slid into her. Faster. And faster.

Her eyes fluttered shut, her body responding instinctively to the tension he was creating inside her. "Damn, that feels intense," she whispered, heart pounding against her chest. "I can feel you everywhere inside me."

"Come for me."

She moaned and screamed out his name as he turned her slightly, positioning her just the way he wanted. It was like he knew exactly the right way to make her lose her mind. The feeling of his hands controlling her movements was intoxicating, thrilling. For a moment, everything else disappeared — just the heat of his touch and the magnetic pull between them remained.

He grinned and gave her more of what she wanted. He reached down and played with her clit as he fucked her, the sensation climbing higher inside her, her pulse quickening as she focused on nothing but the rhythm of his movement. Over her, Caleb matched her effortlessly, his body a perfect blend of strength and control.

She could feel the intensity in his presence, his power syncing with hers in a way that felt almost too natural. Their breaths quickened, but there was something intimate in it — the shared exertion, the way their hearts beat in unison. Grace's eyes flickered up to him, catching the smile on his lips as he glanced at her.

"Feels good?" he asked, his voice slightly breathless but still steady. His gaze held hers, a silent promise that they were in this together. "Like my cock?"

"Mmm — I love it."

"Come."

Grace shot him a determined look, not willing to show any weakness, even though the orgasm was beginning to build. She was going to lose it soon. "Hold on," she teased, nudging the speed just a little higher, pushing him to match her. "Wait for me."

Caleb didn't hesitate, his eyes lighting up. "I'm right there," he said with a grin, effortlessly adjusting his pumping to bring her to the edge.

The sweat started to bead on her forehead, and the sensation of her muscles working hard sent a satisfying rush through her veins.

It was just them, this moment, and the way their bodies were moving in sync. Caleb's focus was unwavering, but his smile was soft, knowing. There was something about this time with him, something about this partnership that felt different from everything else.

"Don't slow down," she said, her voice breathless but laced with a playful spark, knowing he wouldn't back down either. "Harder."

"You like it rough," he replied, his gaze never leaving hers. "I'm your daddy in the sheets."

She rocked harder against him, demanding he go faster. Rougher.

"Good girl," Caleb said. His breath was hot, sending a shiver down her spine. "Stay like that. Take my cock."

"Yes," she screamed. "Fuck yes. Faster, Caleb."

"Tell me you love me."

"I— I..."

"Say it. Tell me."

Grace felt the coiling pleasure in her core, the ache that reminded her of why she loved this. She was there.

"Caleb, I am in love with you."

As they both hit their peak, their breath ragged but steady, Grace felt the familiar warmth of liquid escaping her. He exploded inside her, collapsing on top of her. It wasn't just about finishing—it was about coming with Caleb, feeling how his energy matched hers, how the connection between them felt almost effortless.

They slowed their breathing together, and the smile that passed between them was warm and content.

Grace wiped the sweat from her brow, feeling a rush of affection for the man over her.

"You're incredible," he said, his admiration clear in his eyes.

Grace felt a flush spread across her cheeks, but she met his gaze, smiling in return. "You're not so bad yourself," she said, the teasing tone soft but filled with sincerity.

And in that moment, Grace realized just how much she had come to care about Caleb — not just as a partner in this campaign, but as someone who truly understood her, who was there with her every step of the way.

Grace found herself resting her head against his chest, her body curling toward him as his warmth surrounded her. It was so simple. And yet, it felt like the most real thing she had ever known.

In that moment, the world outside didn't matter. The storm. The chaos. The elections. The threats. It all faded into the background. All that mattered was here, in the dark, with him. The storm outside raged on, but inside the warmth of the blanket, the shelter of his arms, everything felt…right.

Chapter Fourteen

.

The day before the election

Caleb's eyes snapped open, dawn stirring his senses. He woke up the same time every day like clockwork — just before the sun made an appearance. The storm had quieted, its fierce howling replaced by a stillness that felt almost unnatural. The silence was too thick, too heavy, and for a moment, he couldn't place where he was, what time it was, or how he had gotten there.

His phone buzzed from the nightstand next to him, jarring him back to reality. Reaching over, he saw the single bar of reception flicker before a flood of missed calls and messages poured in. He cursed under his breath, the weight of the notifications hitting him like a ton of bricks.

Election day was tomorrow. The TVC, the very group he had been working tirelessly to keep the president safe from, had just pulled an assassination attempt on Armstrong.

He rubbed his face, groaning in frustration as he swiped through the messages. Texts from Wyatt. From guys back at headquarters.

The last text from Wyatt was just one line— *Where the fuck are you?*

Caleb exhaled sharply, his heart rate spiking. His mind scrambled as he tried to piece together the last few hours. He hadn't been thinking about anything other than Grace, that damn kiss, the mess of emotions they were both trying to work through. He hadn't paid attention to the world outside, not when it mattered.

How the hell did we miss this?

The first message from Jordan flashed through his phone— *Caleb, get the hell up. The TVC made an attempt. President's in a secure location. Where is Grace? We need her at HQ. NOW.*

Another message, this time from Duke— *The President's safety was compromised. We've already reassigned to a contingency location. Where the hell are you?*

His hand trembled as he scrolled, the realization hitting him in waves. This wasn't just another chaotic night. This wasn't just some side issue. This was life and death.

He looked to his side, where Grace was still asleep, her back facing him, her breathing slow and steady. He stared at her for a long moment, the weight of everything pressing against his chest, a gnawing pit in his stomach.

The president had nearly been killed while they were…in bed. He'd let his guard down. He'd left everything behind, and now, everything was about to fall apart.

His mind reeled as he processed everything. He couldn't let Grace wake up to this. He couldn't let her see him in a panic. But the truth was, everything had just gone from bad to worse in the span of hours.

There was no time to sit back and absorb this. The people were furious, the campaign was spiraling, and no one had a clue where he and Grace were.

His pulse raced, the adrenaline flooding his veins as he shoved the phone back into his pocket and stood, his muscles stiff, his head heavy. He wasn't sure what he'd expected—hell, he didn't know what he was expecting.

The pale light of early morning barely filtered through the windows as Caleb's hand rain over Grace's shoulder. She was still asleep, her breath steady, her face soft, unguarded, and for the first time in a long while, he let himself breathe deeply, his eyes tracing her features. But the fleeting peace was shattered by the harsh buzz of his phone vibrating in his pocket.

The chaos from the night. He didn't have time for this.

"Grace," Caleb whispered urgently, his voice low but firm as he leaned in and kissed her forehead, running his hand down her hair. "Wake up, babe."

She stirred, a soft groan escaping her lips, her eyes blinking open in confusion.

"Caleb?" she murmured, her voice thick with sleep. She was groggy, her eyes struggling to focus, but the urgency in his tone was unmistakable.

"We need to go," he said, more sharply this time, the reality setting in. The weight of the situation pressed on him like a boulder.

Grace sat up slowly, her expression shifting as she took in his demeanor. The sense of dread hanging in the air was palpable.

"What's happening?" she asked, her voice cracking slightly. She was already scrambling out of bed, pulling on clothes, instinctively reacting to his anxiety.

"Assassination attempt on the president," Caleb muttered, his voice clipped. He grabbed his phone, swiping through the messages, but the lack of a strong signal only made the gnawing worry in his gut grow. "There's more. Inside threat, chaos."

He turned to her, his gaze hard. "I need to make a call. You stay here. Lock the door behind me."

Grace opened her mouth to protest, but he leaned in for a quick kiss and was already on his way out of the door.

Caleb made his way back outside, the cool air of the morning hitting his skin with a sharp bite. The rain had stopped, but the ground was still slick, the atmosphere heavy with tension. His mind raced as he climbed into the car, slamming the door shut behind him, the engine roaring to life as he sped off.

His phone buzzed again, but the spotty reception wouldn't allow him to make the call he needed to Wyatt. He cursed under his breath and swerved the car onto the main road. A few miles out, there was a high point, a spot where cell service sometimes had a connection. He gunned the engine harder, driving with the same precision that had kept him alive in countless high-pressure situations.

The roads were empty, the early morning fog thickening as he approached the rise. He pulled the car off to the side, the tires kicking up mud as he slammed the gear into park. Caleb's hands shook as he grabbed his phone, finally getting the connection he needed.

"Wyatt," Caleb growled into the phone, his voice tight. "What the hell's going on?"

There was a crackling pause before Wyatt's voice came through, tense and urgent. "Caleb... it's bad. They pulled the assassination attempt. Armstrong's in a secure location, but we're dealing with an inside threat. We think there's a mole in the campaign. A few of the team members are unaccounted for, and there's word of some major leaks that could turn everything upside down."

Caleb's blood ran cold. He didn't need to hear any more to know the gravity of the situation. The entire operation was on the verge of collapsing. Everything they had fought for, every sleepless night, every tense moment leading up to this, was now on the brink of unraveling.

He took a long breath, pushing the panic down deep, trying to focus on what needed to be done. "What are the next steps?"

"We're isolating Armstrong. We need to track down these leaks and keep the campaign from going public with this mess. You need to get back here, Caleb. We've got a lot of clean-up to do."

Caleb's heart raced. "Fuck. I'm coming back."

Without a second thought, he threw the car back into gear, speeding back down the winding road. He had to get Grace and get the fuck out. As the weight of the situation pressed down on him, his mind raced. Inside threats, leaks, the president's life in danger, and Grace still in the dark about everything. Caleb cursed again.

Caleb's boots pounded the gravel as he sprinted toward the bunkie, heart hammering in his chest. The rain had stopped, but his skin was still damp, his mind racing with every possible scenario. His pulse quickened with every step.

He reached the small lakeside guest house, throwing open the door and scanning the dark, empty room. There was no sign of Grace. No trace of where she had gone. His chest tightened, a cold knot of panic starting to form as he moved quickly through the bunkie, calling her name.

"Grace!" His voice was raw with desperation, but the silence that followed was deafening.

She wasn't here.

He turned on his heel and ran back toward the lodge, his breath coming faster now, the storm still lingering in the air like a bad omen. The lights in the lodge were out, the dark windows staring back at him like vacant eyes. The whole damn place was silent. Dead.

"Grace!" His voice cracked as he pushed through the front door, his hand slamming it against the wall behind him in frustration. The foyer was dark.

He moved swiftly, checking every room — Marisol's, the study, the kitchen. Nothing. Not a soul. The silence pressed down on him, thick and suffocating. There were no signs of struggle, no indication of where anyone had gone. No note, no messages. It was as if everyone had simply vanished.

His mind spun with the possibilities, each one darker than the last. What the hell happened here?

He charged through the hallways, the tension in his chest growing tighter with each empty room he found. His heart was racing now. Every instinct screamed that something was wrong. He could feel it deep in his bones.

"Grace!"

He shouted again, his voice hoarse and desperate, but the silence swallowed him whole. There was no answer.

Caleb's legs moved without thinking as he sprinted out of the back door, the wet ground slick beneath his boots. He didn't even pause to think about the cold wind cutting through his clothes. His only focus was finding her. She had to be out here.

His breath came in harsh bursts as he ran down the path that led into the surrounding forest, calling her name over and over.

"Grace!"

The trees seemed to bend under the weight of the silence. No footsteps, no rustling leaves, no sound at all. The forest around him was still, eerie, and endless. He couldn't shake the feeling that he was alone in the world.

His feet slipped on the damp ground as he pushed deeper into the woods, searching the dark outlines of trees, the distant echoes of his own voice bouncing back at him.

His heart was in his throat now, his thoughts wild. She had to be here somewhere.

He yelled again.

"Grace!"

Nothing. Not a whisper, not a rustle.

He stopped. He was breathing heavily now, chest heaving with the weight of the fear that was starting to claw at him.

No. He couldn't be too late. She couldn't have just disappeared.

He spun on his heel, looking frantically behind him, his mind racing for any hint, any clue, that she was near.

But the forest stood still. The lodge loomed in the distance, a dark, silent silhouette against the backdrop of the fading storm.

There was no one. Only the hollow sound of his breath in the air, and the emptiness that stretched out before him.

"Grace!" he yelled one last time, his voice breaking on the name. But the silence that followed was louder than anything.

Caleb stood there for a moment, rooted to the spot, his heart pounding in his chest. No response. No movement.

He felt the cold settle deep into his bones as the realization hit him.

She was gone.

And he was alone.

Caleb's pulse raced as he stormed through Marisol's office, throwing open drawers and rifling through files. The silence of the empty lodge had nearly driven him mad, but now his mind was sharp with panic. He knew something was wrong. He could feel it in his gut.

He slammed open another drawer, papers flying out, spilling across the desk. Nothing of significance. *Where are you, Grace?* The thought looped through his mind, frantic and relentless. He needed answers.

His hand froze over a stack of folders. His heart skipped. One file had a distinct red stamp on it. *CONFIDENTIAL.*

Without thinking, he grabbed it, yanked it open, and began skimming through the documents inside. His brow furrowed as he flipped the pages. Notes, briefings, names. At first, it didn't make sense. He scanned through more papers, hoping for something concrete. And then he found it.

A name. *TVC.*

His heart hammered as he read the next line — *TVC operatives have secured Stewart's cooperation. Ensure full compliance with their agenda for the President's capture.*

His hands shook as the weight of the words hit him like a blow to the chest. Caleb cursed under his breath, running his fingers through his hair. There it was, the confirmation he hadn't wanted. Marisol was working with the very people they'd been trying to stop. The Vanguard Coalition. Social justice warriors.

He skimmed through the rest of the document, his eyes scanning frantically. The lines blurred in his vision. More names. More plans. *Grace. Where is she?* His throat tightened as he reached the bottom of the page.

Marisol has been compromised. Grace is in imminent danger. Eliminate any further contact.

Eliminate?

His stomach churned. His hands felt cold as he dropped the papers back onto the desk, his mind racing. Marisol. She'd played them, manipulated them. And Grace... Grace was in danger.

He slammed his fist onto the desk, the sound echoing through the empty lodge. The gravity of the situation hit him like a freight train. Marisol hadn't been helping them. She had been using them. And now, the very people they'd feared — TVC — had Grace in their hands.

No. He couldn't let that happen. Not on his watch.

Caleb spun on his heel, storming toward the door. His mind was racing, thoughts a blur. *Where the hell are they? Why are they still not here?* He had to find Grace. He had to get to her before it was too late.

He grabbed his jacket from the back of the chair and yanked it on, heading straight for the front door. His fingers were cold as they wrapped around the handle, but something stopped him. His eyes scanned the room one last time.

The lodge was still silent.

He bolted outside into the morning light, scanning the grounds around him. No cars. No people. No sign of anyone.

"Grace," he whispered to himself.

And in that moment, he knew — he was running out of time.

Caleb gripped the steering wheel as his car tore down the winding road. The tires squealed on the slick pavement. His heart was pounding in his chest, and his mind was a blur of rage and fear. He had no idea where Grace was, but every second he spent not finding her was a second too long.

He dialed Wyatt's number again. He could barely see through the windshield, the storm blurring everything ahead of him, but he was too focused on the sound of Wyatt's voice when it finally picked up.

"Caleb, you need to get your ass back to HQ. That's an order." Wyatt's voice crackled through the speaker, distorted by the poor reception.

Caleb's grip tightened on the wheel. "Wyatt, Grace's gone! She's been kidnapped. Marisol — she's working with TVC. You don't understand — "

"Kidnapped?" Wyatt interrupted, his voice incredulous but fading. "What the hell are you talking about, Caleb? This is bigger than you! We need you back here now. The president's life is at risk! Get to HQ, or I'll have no choice but to send people after you."

The phone cut out for a second, static filling the car, and Caleb cursed, jamming his finger against the screen, trying to reconnect. But the damn signal was weak, and the call dropped completely. He slammed the phone against the dashboard in frustration, his eyes flickering to the road and then back to the phone screen, but it was dead.

"Fuck!" he spat, slamming his fist against the wheel. His mind raced. The storm was picking up again, the wind howling through the trees, making the road even more treacherous. But he didn't care. He had to find Grace. He had to make sure she was safe. There was no choice. He could already feel the weight of the decision settling on him.

TVC. They had her. They could be anywhere.

But the president... If he didn't go back to HQ, the country would be in chaos. The entire operation would come apart. He could hear Wyatt's voice in his head. The orders were clear—the president needed protection, and Caleb needed to be there.

"Shit!" he muttered, his foot slamming the gas pedal down harder, making the car swerve slightly as he pushed it faster.

His eyes darted to the side of the road as he passed thick forest and dense trees. He could feel the road pulling him in two directions—one to safety, the other to hell. He had no idea where to even begin looking for Grace in this mess.

But the pull toward her was undeniable. She needed him. She was alone out there. And the fear, the gut-wrenching panic that had taken over him since he learned she was gone only worsened with every mile he put between them. He could feel the ache in his chest as if his own heart was telling him to keep going.

His phone was dead, but he could still hear Wyatt's voice ringing in his ears. *The president, Caleb. The president's life is on the line.*

But so was Grace's. He couldn't leave her in the hands of TVC. Not now. Not ever.

I have to choose, Caleb thought, his breath ragged, his heart racing faster than the car could take him.

He slammed his foot on the brake, bringing the car to a screeching halt on the side of the road. The engine rattled to a stop as he stared out into the storm.

The forest loomed ahead of him, thick and impenetrable, but he could handle it. He had tracked through worse.

He glanced at the empty, dying phone screen one last time. The choice was made.

Without another thought, he threw the car into park and dialed Adrienne's number, the familiar beep of the call connecting ringing in his ear. His eyes were bloodshot from lack of sleep, his mind a whirlwind of thoughts, guilt and anger.

Grace was gone. Kidnapped.

His heart thudded heavily in his chest as he heard the phone ring, then the sharp click of the line connecting. In this moment, she was the only person he could think of who might know how to get information fast.

"Caleb?" Adrienne's voice broke through the haze of his thoughts.

"Look," he rasped, his throat tight, the weight of the situation crashing down on him again. "I need your help."

There was a brief pause on the other end. "What's going on?" she asked, her tone turning serious. Caleb could hear the underlying concern in her voice, but it did little to calm the storm inside him.

"It's Grace," he said. "She's been kidnapped. TVC has her, and I think Marisol is to blame." Caleb fell into a quick briefing, recalling all salient details of the event. The lodge. The dinner and morally gray strategies. The morning when he left to make calls — and came back to find her gone, along with everyone else at the lodge.

"It was Marisol," he repeated. "I'm sure she's behind it."

"Caleb, you're...you're sure about this?" Adrienne asked, her voice soft but edged with disbelief. "This is a big allegation. What if they just left for a meeting? You saw no signs of distress at the scene."

"I'm sure. Grace wouldn't have just left like that — not after..." he cut himself off and recalibrated. "Adrienne, I failed her. I was supposed to protect her, and I...I didn't. Now she's gone, and I don't know where to look. She was taken from me." His breath came in shallow, rapid bursts as his thoughts scrambled. He could still see the look on Grace's face when she'd looked at him with that mixture of defiance and vulnerability. The thought of her out there, alone, scared, made his stomach twist in knots.

Adrienne didn't respond immediately, but he could hear her moving, as though she were pacing. "Okay, I get it. But I don't know what I can do, Caleb," she said finally, her voice thoughtful. "I can try to get some people to move. Let me make some calls. TVC has been known to use a lot of underground safe houses, mostly in remote locations. They'll keep her hidden — most likely somewhere where they can't be tracked easily."

Caleb felt the sharp sting of frustration digging into his chest. Underground safe houses. Of course. That was their play—keep her out of sight, hidden from the world. He'd be damn lucky to find her in time.

"Where? Give me locations." His voice was gruff, desperate for any piece of information, any clue that could point him in the right direction. "I'll kick every goddamn door down until I find her."

"Caleb, listen to me. You need to stay calm. There are people I can contact, people who know about these kinds of operations," Adrienne said, her voice now laced with urgency. "But you need to be strategic. TVC doesn't just grab someone and leave them at a random spot—they'll have a plan, a location they've already mapped out. I'll get you a list of likely places, but you need to be prepared. It won't be easy."

Caleb nodded, though she couldn't see him. He didn't feel calm, but he knew she was right. He had to focus. He had to think clearly if he was going to get Grace back.

"Get me that list," he said, his voice firm despite the storm of emotions crashing through him. "I'll go wherever I need to. I won't stop until I find her."

He could hear the familiar sound of Adrienne typing on her end of the line. She was working, trying to get him what he needed. He hated this. He hated that he had to involve her. But he had no other choice.

"Okay, sending now," she said, her voice sharper now. "But, Caleb—"

"What?" he asked, his pulse quickening.

"Don't do anything reckless. You're on your own now," she warned. "And if you go off half-cocked, you'll make it worse for both of you."

His jaw tightened. "I'm not asking for advice, Adrienne."

"Caleb, I can tell you really love her."

"I'm at five percent battery. I've got to go."

"Okay," she said quickly. "Just… I'm sorry — for everything I did to you." She choked up on the line. "I'm just fucking happy to see you happy."

Before he could say anything else, the line cut off, and his phone beeped with an incoming email. He saw the list of possible safehouses and locations flash across the screen. He scanned the text, already mapping out the closest locations — and memorizing them.

His stomach twisted at the thought of Grace trapped in one of those places, at the mercy of TVC, with Marisol playing her role behind the scenes. He would move heaven and earth to find her.

Caleb's jaw clenched as he punched in the numbers for Wyatt's phone. The dial tone rang twice before his friend answered with that gruff voice he knew all too well.

"Wyatt."

"I need a favor," Caleb said, his voice tight with urgency.

"Talk to me."

"I've got coordinates. Slide Mountain. Warehouse. TVC's operation. They've got Grace. I need your help. I'm going in."

There was a beat of silence on the other end. Caleb knew Wyatt well enough to hear the low rumble of contemplation on the other end. Then came the sound of a grunt.

"Are you out of your mind? The president's — " Wyatt started.

"Wyatt," Caleb cut in, his voice sharp. "I don't give a damn about the president right now. Grace is in danger. I'm going to get her."

"Fine. You want to get yourself killed, that's your call. But if you think I'm letting you go in alone, you've got another thing coming."

Caleb breathed out through his nose. "Good. I need you and Duke. I am sending you a location. Meet me there in twenty."

There was a faint rustling noise, and then Wyatt's low voice again. "You better be serious, Caleb. Don't make me regret this."

Caleb hung up the phone without another word. He turned his phone off to preserve battery and fired the car back on. There was no more hesitation. No more doubt.

It was time to get her back.

And nothing — nothing — was going to stop him.

Chapter Fifteen

Twenty minutes later, Caleb's SUV tore down the dirt road off Slide Mountain like it was on fire. No time to spare. He spotted a familiar black SUV parked just off the shoulder and braked hard, gravel spitting beneath the tires. He was out the door before the engine's rumble died.

Wyatt leaned against his rig, arms folded, eyes grim. Duke stood a few steps away, broad-shouldered and silent, scanning the tree line. The tension was electric, crackling in the cold night air.

"You sure about this?" Duke asked.

"Let's go, boys," Caleb said, his jaw set. "It's now or never."

Wyatt pushed off the vehicle, glancing toward the distant safe house. "You're playing with fire, Caleb. The president's barely protected, and if Marisol catches wind—"

"I'll handle her," Caleb snapped, voice razor-sharp. "We're not leaving Grace behind. That's the mission. You in or out?"

Wyatt met Caleb's gaze for a heartbeat, then nodded. "I'm in. Let's go."

No more talk. They climbed into the SUV, Wyatt behind the wheel. Headlights pierced the mist as they charged deeper into the woods, the clock ticking in Caleb's head. Every second counted. Get in, grab Grace, get out. No room for error.

The trees thinned, revealing a lone warehouse crouched in the shadows. Perfect. Too perfect. Vans parked outside, lights on — this had to be the place. Caleb's pulse hammered, but he kept it steady. No panic. No doubt. Just action.

Wyatt killed the engine. Silence pressed in. No time to dwell on the danger now. Caleb double-checked his weapon, loaded a spare clip, and signaled to the others.

"Move fast," he said. "No mistakes."

Wyatt and Duke nodded, their faces set. They slipped into the underbrush, footsteps drowned by damp earth. The warehouse loomed ahead, secrets within its walls. Caleb's nerves sang with urgency, every second dripping away.

They approached the back of the warehouse, sticking to the shadows. Caleb motioned for them to stop and crouched low. The building was eerily quiet, but he could sense the presence of movement inside. Through the small gaps in the walls, he saw men with radios — TVC agents. Caleb's grip tightened on his weapon.

"Time to go in," he whispered to Wyatt and Duke. They nodded, and Caleb led the charge, moving quickly and silently toward the back entrance.

This was it. They were close. He could almost feel Grace's presence on the other side of that steel door. All he had to do was make it count.

The door creaked slightly as he pushed it open, the sound too loud in the tense stillness of the moment. But no one inside seemed to hear them. They were in.

Caleb's heart pounded in his chest as he crept through the darkened corridors of the warehouse. His eyes scanned every corner, every shadow. His mind raced with the thought of Grace — where she was, what they were doing to her.

"Left," Wyatt whispered, nodding toward a narrow hallway.

Caleb signaled and they moved, fast, quiet. Duke was a shadow beside him, his massive form more of a presence than a distraction. They moved with the precision of a well-oiled machine. But Caleb's thoughts were consumed with Grace.

He wouldn't stop. Not until she was safe.

* * * *

The cold, damp air of the warehouse bit at Grace's skin as she sat against the concrete wall, her wrists bound to the chair with tight, unyielding rope. The dim, flickering overhead lights cast long shadows across the room, making everything feel more like a nightmare than a reality. She was alone for the moment, but she knew that wouldn't last. The TVC would be back soon, and they would have questions — dangerous ones.

But Grace's mind was far from the present danger. Instead, her thoughts drifted to everything that had led her here. To Caleb. To the fear she had fought so long to bury.

The memories of last night flooded her mind — the argument at the lodge, the storm, the fear in his eyes when she bolted. She'd been so afraid of how much she'd grown to depend on him, afraid of how much he meant to her. But now, sitting here in the silence, with nothing but her thoughts and the pounding of her heart to keep her company, Grace knew the truth.

She had never been stronger than when she had let herself fall for him.

She squeezed her eyes shut, a painful wave of regret washing over her. She had fought it for so long — pushing him away, pretending that she didn't need anyone. But now, in the harshest moments of her life, it was clear that she did need him. And not just for his protection. Not just because he was a force of nature that could take on the world.

She needed him because he made her feel like she wasn't alone anymore. His strength wasn't just physical — it was in the way he loved, the way he fought for what mattered. She felt the weight of that love even now, even when she was trapped in a dark, cold warehouse, unsure of what would come next.

He was right. I've been so damn reckless.

I screwed up.

And now I'm going to lose him.

The thought hit her like a punch to the gut, and her heart thudded painfully against her chest. It had only taken this one moment — this feeling of helplessness, of being completely and utterly lost — for Grace to realize how deep her feelings for Caleb truly ran. It wasn't just the fear of what might happen if she never saw him again. It was the understanding that she had built a future with him in her mind, a future she couldn't imagine without him.

Her mind began to replay the memories of their time together—the quiet moments, the conversations that had made her feel like she was truly seen. The way he'd held her close that night by the fire, his eyes soft, his touch steady. The way he had kissed her, not like a duty, but like a promise. He had opened her heart when she had tried to lock it away. And she couldn't ignore that anymore.

Caleb had taught her that love wasn't weakness. It wasn't something to be feared or avoided. It was strength. It was the fire that kept you going when everything else threatened to fall apart. And for the first time in her life, Grace understood that completely.

She closed her eyes tightly, imagining Caleb's face. *I will get back to him.* The thought was a quiet promise to herself. She wasn't going to let this be the end. She couldn't. Because she knew, without a doubt, that Caleb was the man she wanted to face the rest of her life with. And nothing, not even the people who had taken her, would stop her from making that a reality.

Her heart steadied as the determination within her grew stronger. She could feel the shift inside of her, the sense of clarity she hadn't had before. She wasn't the same woman who had run away from him in fear. She was stronger now, more aware of her own heart, and the power it held.

Suddenly, the door to the warehouse creaked open. Grace didn't flinch. She was ready now. She wasn't afraid anymore. Not of them. Not of anything.

* * * *

The warehouse was a cacophony of shouts and gunfire, each explosion of sound pushing Caleb forward like a wave crashing against a rocky shore. His heart was pounding in his ears, the adrenaline coursing through his veins as he moved swiftly, fluidly, a machine honed by years of training. The sharp tang of blood and metal filled the air, the smell of destruction he had become far too familiar with.

But none of it mattered.

Not anymore.

His eyes locked on Grace the moment he saw her — leaning against the wall, her head hanging, her body slumped. She looked battered, bruised, and exhausted, but she was alive. Alive. That was all that mattered.

His breath caught in his chest. He wasn't sure if it was from the violence or the overwhelming wave of relief that hit him all at once. His entire body felt like it was on fire, a mix of anger, fear, and a fierce determination to get her out. He was a blur of motion — fast, precise, unstoppable.

"Grace!" His voice was hoarse as he shouted her name, the word full of desperation and promise.

Her head snapped up, her eyes wide with shock and then relief. She blinked, as if she couldn't believe he was really there. The bonds around her wrists were tight, her body shaking as she straightened.

"Caleb?" she whispered, barely more than a rasp.

"I'm getting you out of here," he gritted. His hands shook as he cut through the ropes binding her.

The moment the ropes fell away, she stood, unsteady on her feet, her knees buckling as she collapsed into his arms. Caleb's heart nearly stopped as he caught her, his hands steadying her body, but he wasn't sure if it was from the relief of having her in his arms or the sheer weight of what he'd just faced.

"Babe, I..." His words faltered as he pulled her closer, burying his face in her hair, his breath ragged.

She was trembling in his arms, but she looked up at him, her eyes filled with a mixture of shock and raw emotion. She opened her mouth to say something, but Caleb didn't give her a chance. He kissed her. Fiercely.

She responded in kind, her hands clutching at his shirt, pulling him closer as if she was afraid he would disappear if she let go.

When they pulled away, both of them were breathless, their foreheads resting together as they tried to catch their breath.

Tears welled in her eyes. "You found me."

"Of course I did." He cut the ropes around her wrists with a knife, his hands trembling as he worked. "I would tear apart the whole goddamn world to find you."

She took a shaky breath, standing as he pulled her into his arms, not caring about the danger still looming in the air. "I overheard them. The guards," she whispered urgently, her voice hoarse. "Marisol...she's planning something. She wants to take out the president — put herself in his spot."

Caleb stiffened. "What the hell are you talking about?"

"She's trying to kill him — and everything around him," Grace continued, her eyes meeting his with the same fierce determination he knew so well. "She is not on our side. She wants him gone."

A cold rage surged through him. "I knew it. I fucking knew it." His jaw clenched. "She's a traitor. This is treason."

Grace's hands found his, gripping them tightly. "You were right. All of it. I should've listened."

He looked at her then, his voice rough with something more than just anger. "I'm not losing you to a fucking traitor."

She shook her head, a tear escaping down her cheek. "You won't. You won't lose me, Caleb. Not to anything."

He didn't say anything, but his grip on her tightened, as if to reassure himself as much as her. The weight of everything hung heavy between them. She loved him, and somehow, that was enough.

"Let's get the hell out of here." He held her hand and led her out of the room.

"Is this going to be a shootout?" she asked, following behind him.

He laughed. "No, Wyatt and Duke took care of things."

As he guided Grace out of the warehouse's dim corridor, her hand still trembling in his, Caleb's senses stayed razor-sharp. The air outside was damp and cold against his flushed face. He could smell the wet earth, the lingering scent of danger. But Wyatt and Duke had done their job—no gunfire, no chaos, just the quiet aftermath of a job well-handled.

Grace pressed close behind him, and he tightened his grip. Her presence steadied him in a way nothing else could.

At the exit, Wyatt stood with his arms folded, a satisfied tilt to his head. Duke hovered nearby, watchful as ever. Their eyes met Caleb's, no words needed. Mission accomplished.

Caleb led Grace to the waiting SUV, Wyatt and Duke flanking them. Grace didn't question him, didn't hesitate. Just trust in every step. They piled in, doors shutting with muted thuds. The engine turned over quietly, and Wyatt steered them off that godforsaken property.

After a few tense minutes on the dark back roads, Caleb spotted his old truck where he'd left it. He nodded to Wyatt, who eased the SUV to a stop. Quiet efficiency—no wasted motions, no unnecessary noise.

"Go be with her," Wyatt said. "We will cover the president."

Caleb hopped out, helping Grace onto solid ground. She looked at him, eyes still bright, relief etched in every line of her face. Wyatt gave a brief salute, Duke a curt nod, as they all switched vehicles. Caleb's truck was rougher, less polished than any presidential convoy, but it was his—and right now, it felt like home.

He settled Grace into the passenger seat, gave a final glance to Wyatt and Duke. "Thanks," he said simply. That was all that needed saying. They understood.

Chapter Sixteen

Caleb drove the truck down the narrow, winding road, his hands steady on the wheel, his adrenaline high. The sun was dipping low, casting a warm amber hue over the trees that lined the path. It was a familiar route, one he hadn't taken in a while. But the moment he found her, he'd known exactly where to bring set up camp until they could sort things out.

The lake house.

As they neared the clearing where the house stood, Caleb slowed, his gaze momentarily drawn to the tranquil water shimmering through the trees. The sight of it always had a calming effect on him, even after all these years.

Grace was sitting beside him, looking out of the window, her curiosity evident. "So, what's this place?" Her voice was soft, as if she was unsure whether to ask.

Caleb didn't answer immediately, just let the silence stretch for a few moments as he guided the truck over the gravel driveway. He could feel her eyes on him, waiting for an explanation.

"It's mine," he finally said, his voice low, though there was no hiding the way his chest tightened with the words. "This place...it's been in my family for a long time."

Grace raised an eyebrow, clearly surprised. "You own this?" she asked, looking at him with genuine interest.

He nodded, pulling the truck up to the weathered wood of the house. "Yeah. It's been in my family for generations. My grandfather built it with my dad when he was young. I spent a lot of summers here as a kid."

He parked the truck, cutting the engine, and the sound of the world outside immediately filled the air — the rustling of leaves, the soft ripples of the lake. Caleb sat for a moment, letting it all wash over him. There was something about this place that brought him peace, something about the way it anchored him to his past.

"Come," he said, getting out of the truck and walking around to open the door for her. He offered her his hand, and she took it without hesitation, following him toward the front porch.

As they walked, he gestured to the surrounding landscape. "That canoe over there, by the dock? I used to take it out with my mom when I was a kid. We'd paddle out at sunrise, just the two of us, before anyone else was awake."

Grace's eyes followed his hand as he pointed. "It's beautiful here," she said quietly, taking in the view of the lake, the trees, the distant shoreline. "It's like a different world."

"It is," Caleb agreed, his voice almost reverent. "This place...it's been my escape. The only place I can really think, you know? Away from everything."

They stood together at the edge of the porch, the soft breeze rustling through the trees. Caleb's gaze softened as he looked down at the wooden bench. It was weathered, faded by time, but he could still see his mother's touch in every curve, every polished corner.

"And that bench there? My mom used to sit there for hours," he said, his voice quieter now. "She'd just sit and watch the lake. Sometimes we'd talk, sometimes she'd just be quiet. But that's where she spent most of her time when we were here. She loved it."

"Does she still come here?"

"No, my mom passed away a few years ago. Cancer."

"It sounds like a place full of memories," she said, her voice softer now, understanding the depth of his connection to this place.

"It is," Caleb murmured. "A lot of memories. Some good, some...not so good. We spent a lot of time here when she was sick." He paused, glancing at Grace, seeing the curiosity in her eyes. "But it's always been home. Even when everything else felt like it was falling apart, this place stayed the same."

They stood in silence for a moment, the peacefulness of the lake house seeping into their bones. Caleb could feel the weight of everything had happened those past weeks—the campaign, the pressure, the looming election tomorrow—but here, with Grace by his side, he was reminded of something simpler, something that grounded him.

He turned to her then, his hand sliding into hers, and gave her a small, genuine smile. "I've always come here when I needed to clear my head. I thought maybe…you could use this place right now, too."

Grace squeezed his hand, her eyes soft with understanding. "I can see why you come here," she said, her voice filled with quiet admiration. "It's perfect."

Caleb didn't respond right away, just stood there with her, the weight of everything else lifting for a brief moment. There was something about being here with her that felt right, something about the way she fit into this space, into his world, so seamlessly.

"Come on," he said after a moment, his hand still holding hers. "Let me show you the inside."

As they walked inside the lake house, the scent of wood and fresh air filled Caleb's lungs, reminding him of childhood summers spent with his family. It wasn't just a house — it was a piece of his history, a place where everything felt like it had meaning.

Grace glanced around, seeming to take it all in. He knew what she saw — the rustic charm, the worn leather chairs by the fireplace, the photos of his family hanging on the walls.

And Caleb felt something shift inside of him as he watched her, seeing how she absorbed the space, how she seemed to understand without needing to ask. There was a certain comfort in it. A quiet connection.

"This is incredible," Grace said, her voice filled with awe. "I can see why it means so much to you."

"It's always been a part of me," Caleb replied, his tone steady, but something in his chest tightened as he realized how much he wanted her to understand. "And now, it's a part of you too."

Grace looked up at him, her eyes soft, her expression thoughtful. "I'm glad you brought me here."

He smiled, his gaze steady on hers. "I'm glad you're here. Rest — and I'll get this place warmed up."

Inside the lake house, firelight finally danced in warm patterns across the walls, bathing everything in a comforting glow that he hoped would calm her trembling. After adding another log to the fire, he turned and saw Grace at the window, her arms hugging herself, shoulders tense, eyes distant as she watched the water. The sight of her trembling sent a spike of worry straight to his heart. He took a breath, trying to keep his voice gentle but firm.

"Hey," he said softly, stepping closer. Her head snapped around, startled, but she didn't pull away. Instead, her eyes found his, uncertain yet trusting.

"Did they hurt you?" he asked, voice low. He watched her carefully, looking for any sign of pain or fear.

"Not really," she managed.

Caleb closed the distance between them, holding out a hand, palm up. "Come here," he said, more invitation than order, but still leaving no room for refusal. He needed to check her, to feel that she was whole. Grace hesitated only a fraction of a second before stepping forward, letting him guide her into the circle of his arms.

He placed his hands on her shoulders, gently spinning her so he could see every angle, every inch that might hide a bruise or cut. She let him turn her in a slow circle, her body yielding to his guidance. His fingers slid down her arms, feather-light, checking for tenderness. He ran his hand along her spine, pressing gently, his touch firm but comforting. She winced slightly when he reached a spot on her shoulder, and he saw the small bruise blooming beneath the fabric of her shirt.

A surge of protectiveness flared in his chest. Without thinking, he leaned in and pressed a soft kiss there, a silent vow that he wouldn't let this happen again. Her breath caught, and she glanced over her shoulder at him, eyes damp but steady.

"Are you okay?" he asked, his voice husky with concern. He moved around to face her again, placing one warm palm against her cheek. "I mean it — tell me if something's wrong."

She swallowed, tears threatening to spill. "It's been a lot," she whispered, shaking. "I just... need some time, Caleb."

He nodded, his thumb brushing a stray tear from her cheek. "I'll be here," he murmured. "As long as you need." He gathered her into his arms, holding her close so she could feel the heat of the fire on her back and the steady thrum of his heartbeat against her chest. Outside, the lake whispered, and inside these walls, just the two of them existed.

"I'm going to take care of you," he said quietly, leaning down so his lips were near her ear. "Tonight, tomorrow — whatever it takes. You're safe with me, Grace."

She let out a trembling laugh, a small, wavering sound that felt like hope. "You sound so sure," she said, eyes searching his face. "I'm yours tonight? Is that what you're saying?"

Caleb's gaze didn't waver. He wanted her to feel how serious he was, how real this moment was. "If that's all we have," he said softly, "then I'll make it count. But we both know we deserve more than just tonight."

Her eyes shone, and she nodded, understanding the promise beneath his words. In that quiet, firelit space, with danger still lurking somewhere outside, he would be her shield — and she would be the reason he fought.

"All right," she said, voice steadier now. "Show me."

He smiled, just a hint of it, and bent his head so their foreheads touched. "Then let's get comfortable," he said, guiding her toward the couch. "And figure this out."

And in the warmth of the firelight, he held her, making sure she knew that whatever had happened, whatever lay ahead, he wouldn't let her face it alone.

* * * *

Grace stood inside the bathroom of Caleb's cottage, enveloped by the gentle hush of rainfall against the windows. The cottage smelled faintly of cedar and clean linens, and the muted glow of a single lamp beyond the half-closed door gave the space a warm, intimate feel. She was shivering slightly from an unshakable chill, one hand curled around a warm cup of soup that he had made for her. The steam from the cup rose to meet the already humid air as Caleb turned on the shower, testing the water until it ran smoothly and warmly over his hand.

She watched him, heart beating a bit faster, as he turned back to her, his gaze reassuring. There was a quiet determination in his eyes that eased her nerves. Without a word, he stepped closer, helping her shed her clothes with gentle, patient movements. Fabric fell away layer by layer until she stood before him, vulnerable and yet safe, the heat of the bathroom air and the rising steam coiling around her bare skin.

Grace felt the tension in her shoulders loosen as he guided her under the spray, the warm water cascading over her back and neck. Caleb stepped in behind her, pressing close enough that she felt the heat radiating from his body. She could sense his solidity, his broad chest at her back, the light press of his arm as he supported her. She let out a breath as the water enveloped her, washing away the lingering chill from outside. In her hand, she still held the cup of soup, and she took a careful swig — savory warmth gliding down her throat, a comforting presence in this surreal yet soothing moment. She repeated a few times until she drained it.

When he finally took the empty cup from her hand, placing it on a small shelf within reach, she allowed herself to lean back into him, trusting him to hold her steady.

He took a bar of soap, working it into a creamy lather between his palms. Then his hands came to rest on her shoulders, thumbs pressing gently into the tight muscles there. She felt a wave of relief flood through her as he massaged the soap along her collarbones, the slippery warmth of the lather a tactile comfort. His fingertips journeyed along her arms and over her back, the circular motions coaxing out the tension knotted deep beneath her skin. Each firm yet tender press soothed her further, igniting a pleasant, tingling warmth that spread outward from wherever he touched.

Her pulse raced, but there was a wariness in her eyes, a hesitation she didn't often allow herself. "I don't want to let go," she whispered. "Of us."

Caleb's hand slid to her lower back, pulling her toward him with a force that left no room for argument. The heat of his body against hers sent a shiver through her.

"Tonight, you are going to let go of everything."

She chewed her lip. The anxiety strummed through her. It had been a big day.

His voice dropped lower. "You don't get to decide tonight. I do."

His words reverberated in her chest. He wasn't asking for her surrender. He was claiming it.

"You've been fighting, haven't you?" Caleb's breath brushed against her ear as he spoke, each word deliberate, every syllable cutting through the air like a promise. "Fighting to do it all on your own. To prove you don't need anyone. But I'm telling you, Grace..." He pulled her even closer. "You need me. And I'm going to show you how much."

She opened her mouth to speak, but no words came out. What could she say? He was right. She had fought. Fought to keep control, to protect herself from needing anyone. But here he was, claiming her in a way that shattered all her defenses. And he felt it, that flicker of vulnerability—of need—she'd been hiding.

As he worked lower, her breath hitched slightly when he found a sore spot. She winced and felt his lips brush against that tender bruise—a soft kiss of apology and care. The gentle press of his mouth to her damp skin sent a subtle shiver through her, not of cold, but of heightened awareness. Her body began to relax completely, limbs loosening under his attentive care.

He reached for a bottle of shampoo next, and she let her head tip back into his hand, trusting him to support the weight. The shampoo's scent—something herbal and fresh — mingled with the steamy air. His fingertips worked carefully at her scalp, massaging in slow, deliberate circles. The sensation was exquisite — the light scrape of his nails, the pressure of his fingers, the warm water trickling down her temples. She closed her eyes, surrendering to the moment, feeling as though all the day's worries were sliding away with the soapy rivulets running down her neck.

When he tilted her head forward to rinse, she felt the water sheet down her hair, over her face, and he gently smoothed stray strands behind her ear. Then, with the same careful attention, he soaped his hands again and cupped her chin, guiding her face upward. He ran his thumbs lightly over her cheeks, across the bridge of her nose, and along her jawline. The delicate pass of his hands felt almost reverent, a tender exploration rather than a mere cleansing. She could feel his steady breath, sensed the intent in his motions — he was pouring quiet care into every touch.

Tears pricked at her eyes, not from sadness but from overwhelming gratitude. She could feel love in the way he touched her, in the careful measure of his strength, in the warmth that radiated from his body through her own. Her heart swelled with appreciation. There had been no words needed to declare what was happening here. Each soapy caress, each gentle press of his fingertips, said it all.

Caleb's arms came around her waist from behind, holding her close as water ran over their skin. He pressed a gentle kiss to her damp shoulder, and she leaned into him, letting his presence ground her completely. Outside, the rain continued to whisper against the glass, and she basked in the sensation of being thoroughly cared for—cherished—by a man who knew exactly how to soothe every ache, inside and out.

His cock twitched, hardening, as she pressed her hips back into him. He spun her around so fast she barely had time to gasp, her back hitting the shower wall with a thud. His body crowded hers, his heat searing into her, his jaw tight with restraint that was hanging by a thread.

"You," he said. "I hope you've learned your lesson. You're not walking through this world by yourself anymore. Not if I have anything to say about it."

Grace gasped, the intensity of his words, his touch, leaving her breathless. She felt the flood of emotion rising in her chest—gratitude, relief, yearning. "God, Caleb," she whispered, thick with emotion. "What would I have done without you?"

"I'll protect you from everything, Grace," he promised, his voice hot and low against her skin. "From anything."

And then he kissed her.

The kiss was everything—soft and rough, slow and frenzied, a paradox that left her mind spinning. His lips moved over hers with purpose, demanding and giving in equal measure, drawing out a flood of sensations that washed over her in waves. Each touch was electric, like tiny sparks igniting beneath her skin, leaving her breathless and trembling.

Her heart thundered in her chest as his tongue slid against hers, teasing and coaxing in a rhythm that felt impossibly intimate. The taste of him was warm and addictive, a mix of heat and something uniquely his that made her want more, need more. His hands framed her face, his thumbs brushing over her cheeks, grounding her even as her body felt weightless, as though the world had disappeared beneath her feet.

The pleasure spread, soft and insistent, like a rising tide. The warmth that started in her chest flowed outward, filling her with a delicious ache that made her arch closer to him, her hands fisting in his shirt. The slight scrape of his teeth against her lower lip sent a jolt of heat straight through her, and she gasped into his mouth, her body betraying her with a shiver of pure need.

Every nerve felt alive, heightened, as though his touch carried a current she couldn't escape — and didn't want to. His fingers brushed along the curve of her waist, trailing fire wherever they went. Each caress felt purposeful, like he was memorizing her, mapping every inch of her in a way that made her pulse quicken and her breath falter.

Time lost meaning. There was no past, no future — only this moment, the press of his body against hers, the intoxicating mix of pressure and heat and tension that left her clinging to him, desperate for more.

The world blurred, her senses narrowing until all she knew was him — his scent, his taste, the strength of his hands and the way his voice rasped against her ear when he murmured her name. "Grace."

His tongue found hers again while his hands explored down her waist and toward her pussy. He opened her thighs to him, finding her hot core. He played with her clit, having a better sense of what she needed. Pleasure built inside her, a slow and steady flame that threatened to consume her. It wasn't just physical — it was emotional, raw and unfiltered, connecting them in a way that made her heart ache and her body tremble. It was overwhelming and beautiful, a symphony of sensation and desire that left her breathless and undone.

And in that moment, with his lips against hers and his hands holding her close, she didn't care about anything else. She was lost in him, in the pleasure he gave her, and she wanted more of him.

The shower's spray tapered off with a gentle squeak of the handle as Caleb shut off the water. Her skin still glowed with warmth, lingering heat from his careful, thorough washing. She stood there, heart thrumming, steam drifting around them. The air in the small bathroom felt charged, as if every droplet suspended in the air knew what was about to unfold.

Caleb reached for a thick towel and unfolded it slowly, the fabric plush and warm against her shoulders. He dabbed at her face first, a feather-light touch that made her pulse skip. Then, moving with calm deliberation, he dried her neck, her arms, her back, taking his time. Each press of the towel was another reminder that she was safe, cherished. When he knelt to dry her legs and feet, she almost felt faint, the intimacy of the gesture nearly overwhelming. He rose, meeting her eyes, silent and reassuring.

"You're beyond beautiful. Is there a word for that?" he asked.

She laughed in response. His hand found hers, leading her out of the bathroom into the main room of the cottage. The rain outside still sang its quiet lullaby against the windowpanes, and the soft crackle of the fire greeted them. Caleb guided her toward the couch in front of the hearth, his grip gentle but certain.

The heat of the fire embraced her as he laid her down on the couch, throwing away the towel to drink in her firelit nakedness beneath him. Her body was still humming from his hands on her skin, from the press of his chest when he'd held her in the shower. She leaned back, dark eyes searching his face as he climbed on top of her, finding her mouth again in a slow, passionate kiss.

"Now," Caleb said onto her lips. "No work. No election. Just you and me." He paused, the weight of his words sinking in. His gaze was intense, watching her reaction closely. "And you're going to let me handle the rest. Understand?"

A flutter of excitement danced in her stomach as she felt his rock-hard cock bouncing between her thighs. Those words, that tone — it was a promise and a command rolled into one. She swallowed, voice soft as she answered, "Sounds dangerous."

"Do as I say, exactly." Something in his eyes made her breath catch. This was new territory — his confident assertion, the clear lines he was drawing.

Before she could say anything more, before she could voice the fear, the want, that had been stirring in her for so long, Caleb silenced her with a kiss. It was deep and commanding, the kind of kiss that wasn't meant to reassure — it was meant to possess. To claim.

When they finally broke apart, Caleb's gaze locked onto hers, sharp and unwavering. "There's one thing I want to hear." His voice was firm, but there was a softness now, an unspoken promise. "You're mine. Mine."

The world felt like it had stopped moving, and in that suspended moment, Grace could feel her pulse racing in her ears, staring up at this brilliantly sexy man focused only on her. She wasn't sure what had happened. How this all started. What she had agreed to. But in Caleb's arms, she knew one thing with absolute certainty — she was his.

She wasn't fighting it anymore.

"Tell me," he said, gripping her hips, settling her squarely underneath him. "Say it."

"Yours." With a soft sigh, she pressed up into him, her breath mingling with his. "Yes," she whispered, her voice filled with something she couldn't name.

Grace barely had time to catch her breath before Caleb's lips found hers again. It wasn't hesitant or careful — it was raw, full of heat, and utterly consuming. He kissed her like he'd been holding back for too long, like the firelight wasn't the only thing igniting the room. His tongue twisted with hers, slow and exploring, then quick and fierce.

She slid her hands up his chest, curling into the fabric of his shirt as she leaned into him, meeting his intensity with her own. His weight pressed her deeper into the couch, grounding her as his hands framed her face, thumbs brushing along her jawline with surprising tenderness.

She tilted her head, giving him better access, and his mouth moved against hers, coaxing, exploring, claiming. His kiss left no room for doubt about how much he wanted her, but there was something else there — something vulnerable beneath the passion, like he was afraid to let go but couldn't stop himself.

She tangled her fingers in the back of his wet hair, and she pulled him closer, deepening the kiss until the rest of the world disappeared. His lips left hers for a moment, skimming along her cheek, down to her neck, where he nipped at the sensitive skin just below her ear. A gasp escaped her, and she felt his smirk against her skin.

"Caleb," she breathed, her voice barely a whisper but filled with all the feelings she couldn't quite name. "I want you to be mine, too."

Caleb pulled back just enough to look at her, his eyes dark and intense, his breathing still heavy. Grace stared up at him, lips parted, her pulse racing as she tried to process the heat in his gaze. His hand slid down to her hip, holding her firmly in place as if grounding them both.

Caleb's grip on her tightened, his face softening just enough for her to feel the warmth of his affection beneath the commanding strength. His cock thumped at her pussy, demanding an entrance. And one thing was damn clear—he wasn't letting her go. Not now. Not ever.

And neither was she.

"Are you okay... to do this again?" he grumbled, his voice low and rough, sending chills all over. "Just tell me to stop."

"Stop? Are you fucking kidding me?" Grace raised a brow, trying to muster some semblance of control.

Instead of answering, Caleb straightened himself up and parted her thighs in one fluid motion. The firelight danced across the hard planes of his chest, highlighting every defined muscle and scar like a masterpiece painted in shadows and light.

Grace's breath caught in her throat. "Damn," she muttered, her voice softer than she intended.

"Legs up." His smirk was slow and deliberate, his confidence almost infuriating.

She complied, laying one leg on the back of the couch and wrapping the other around his waist as he angled himself squarely at her pussy, testing the entrance with his thick cockhead. She caught the flicker of approval in his eyes, the slight hitch in his breath that made her feel like she'd won some unspoken battle.

"Better," he said as he slid his cock inside her, his voice filled with a reverence that made her pulse race all over again. Then, rocking slowly, he ran his rough hands all over Grace's body, each touch deliberate, grounding, and maddeningly gentle, the fire cast flickering shadows across her skin. He kissed her again and again, deeper and deeper, until her pussy ached from needing him deeper and harder.

It was driving her insane.

"Caleb, I need more."

But he fucked her slow. Methodological. His focus was unwavering, his movements unhurried, as though he had all the time in the world to draw every ounce of tension from her.

"Relax," he said, his voice a low rumble that vibrated through her. "You're always so wound up."

Grace let out a shaky breath, her fingers curling into the fabric of the couch. "Kind of my thing," she said, though her voice was softer than she intended. "It's always a rush with me."

He slid his hands up her arms, massaging each muscle with a precision that made her skin tingle. "Not tonight, it's not," Caleb said, his tone carrying an unyielding authority that sent a wave of heat through her. "I want slow."

She closed her eyes as his cock worked the tension out of her, coaxing her to give into deep and slow. She hadn't realized just how much stress she'd been holding until he started fucking it away, layer by layer. His hands moved down her breasts, teasing her nipples, and tracing the curve of her waist before sliding back up in a slow, hypnotic rhythm. Finally, he found her clit. With one hand, he circled her tender spot and brought her to the edge, all while fucking her deeper.

Grace's breath hitched as he started rocking into her faster. She was so close to coming that she was going to scream. "I can't—"

"Let go," Caleb interrupted gently but firmly. He paused for just a moment. She felt his cock throbbing hard inside her. His gaze locked with hers, intense and unwavering. "Just let go, Grace. I've got you."

"I've never been good at obeying." She grinned.

"Fuck, you need to learn." He didn't blink as he grasped her hips and spun her over. He pulled her ass up to meet his cock. "You want it harder? Rougher?"

"Mmm... please."

"Fuck." He growled. Something in his tone sent a thrill racing through her, one she hated herself for liking. She gripped the armrest of the couch as his cock bobbed between her thighs again, positioning himself.

Grace had no idea how Caleb knew exactly where to touch, but it was like he'd mapped every nerve ending in her body. He slid his cock head into her pussy and worked over her with a precision that left her breathless, the firm pressure alternating teasing pulses that sent sparks shooting through her core. She bit her lip, trying to keep herself grounded, but the sensation was too much—too good.

"You're holding back," he murmured, his voice a velvet rasp that made her stomach flip.

"I'm not," Grace managed, though the words sounded weak even to her own ears.

He chuckled. "You are. But don't worry. We'll fix that."

His cock throbbed as he fucked her deeper and harder, and she arched instinctively, a soft gasp escaping her lips. Caleb let out a low groan, as if her reaction pleased him, and went even faster. The man was a goddamn athlete — pounding her pussy harder, making that little spot inside her cream all over his cock.

She screamed out his name.

He pumped his long, hard ridge deeper into her, and Grace couldn't stop the pained moan that slipped out. Her head fell down against the couch, her hair spilling over as she tried — and failed — to catch her breath.

"Caleb," she whispered, "this is…unfair."

"What's unfair?" he asked, his lips brushing her ear as his hands continued their relentless work.

"That you can make me feel like this," she admitted, her cheeks flushing even as she said it.

He stilled for just a moment, his thumbs brushing circles over her skin. "Good," he said, his breath warm against her cheek. "You should feel like this. You deserve it."

Then he moved again, riding her rougher than before, and Grace felt herself spiraling, her body melting onto his cock. She didn't care anymore about keeping control, about holding back. She let herself go, her mind clouded by the overwhelming pleasure coursing through her.

"Caleb," she breathed, her voice trembling as she spun out. She found herself screaming his name over and over.

"That's it," he grunted, his tone filled with quiet satisfaction. "You're mine. Hear me? This pussy is mine."

Grace's heart pounded as he stilled, leaning forward. She felt his breath against her neck, warm and steady, but now it was her turn. He was still hard. He hadn't come yet. She wasn't about to let him have all the control — not tonight.

She spun around, pushing him down into a seated position on the couch. She straddled him, her muscles tingling with newfound determination. Without a word, she slid his cock back into her. Caleb's brows lifted in mild surprise, his lips curving into a teasing smirk.

"Decided to take charge?" he said.

Grace didn't answer. Instead, she placed her hands on his shoulders and rocked back and forth, finding the sweet spot. He followed her lead, his green eyes never leaving hers, curiosity flickering in their depths.

"You've had your fun," she said, her voice soft but steady. "Now it's my turn."

Caleb leaned back, holding her waist as he watched her with an intensity that sent a shiver down her spine. "I'm watching," he said, his tone rougher now, edged with anticipation.

Grace rode him harder, her breasts bouncing right in his face. She slid her hands over his broad chest, tracing the ridges of muscle she'd admired too many times to count. He was warm beneath her palms, the steady rise and fall of his breathing grounding her.

"I want to watch you come apart," she teased, leaning in until her lips hovered just above his. "Scream my name, now, bitch."

Caleb's hands twitched at his sides, but he didn't move, letting her set the pace. "Try me."

She kissed him then, slow and deliberate, pouring everything she felt into the contact. She slid her hands up his neck, curling her fingers into his hair as she deepened the kiss. Caleb groaned, his restraint faltering as he found her hips, gripping them.

Pulling back slightly, she met his gaze, her lips curling into a mischievous smile. Caleb leaned back against the couch, tilting his head to look at her. His face was flushed, his hair slightly mussed, and she couldn't help but admire how alive he looked in moments like this — fully present, entirely in his element.

Grace pushed herself harder, her body rocking on his. Caleb was underneath her, his grip effortless and steady, the rhythm of him perfectly synchronized. Finally, his head fell back and he let out a masculine roar, the veins popping out of his neck.

He was almost there.

That was all the encouragement she needed. She rode faster, feeling his cock all the way up inside her core. God, he felt good. Her lungs burned, but it wasn't a bad burn. It was the kind of fire that reminded her she was alive, capable, pushing her limits.

"Damn, you are fucking hot," Caleb ground out. "Making me lose my goddamn mind."

Grace surged on, taking her pleasure. Her eyes rolled back, breath came in heavy, rhythmic bursts, matching his as the two of them crested the peak.

Caleb slowed her to a stop, hands on her hips as he buckled forward, spilling hot seed into her pussy. He drew in deep, measured breaths. Grace went limp on him, her hands on his shoulders as she tried to catch her breath. Tears pricked at her eyes, and she couldn't stop it.

The air between them was electric, charged with the shared intensity of orgasm. Their bodies were slick with sweat, their faces flushed, but neither of them seemed to care.

"You're crazy," Grace said, wiping tears from her eyes.

"And you love it," Caleb countered, his grin widening.

She rolled her eyes, but her smile betrayed her. "Debatable."

As their breathing slowed, Caleb glanced at her, his gaze lingering. "I wish I met you ten years ago."

"Me too." She grinned, kissing him softly. Tenderly.

"I'm crazy in love with you."

"I love you too."

The moment stretched, the tension between them palpable but somehow easy, like the rhythm they'd found on the trail. For a second, Grace felt like she could forget the campaign, the threats, and everything else weighing on her.

It was just them. Two people who worked hard, pushed harder, and maybe — just maybe — were fated to be together.

Grace rested against Caleb, her head nestled into his chest as the crackling fire cast flickering shadows across the room. She could feel the warmth of his body, the steady rise and fall of his breath beneath her, and the rhythmic way his fingers traced patterns on her shoulder. The tension she had carried for so long — anxiety, responsibility, the weight of the campaign and her past — was slowly unraveling in the quiet peace of the lake house.

He was quiet now, his large hand moving through her hair, the soft strokes both soothing and possessive. His touch wasn't demanding anymore — it was tender, a contrast to the forcefulness he had shown earlier.

There was something about it, the way his fingers slid through the strands of her hair with such careful precision, that made her feel seen — really seen. Not as the campaign strategist or the public figure, but as her.

She closed her eyes, leaning further into him, allowing herself to just exist. It had been so long since she'd felt like this — safe, cared for, and utterly cherished. He was so different in this quiet space. Outside, in the world, he was the commander, the protector, the steady force that made people feel secure.

"Caleb," she whispered. "What are we?"

His hand paused for a moment, his thumb resting against her skin, and she could feel the weight of his thoughts behind the simple action. He didn't need to ask what she meant. He understood that she wasn't talking about just this — the quiet night, the firelight, the feel of his arms around her. No, she was asking about them. About what they were becoming.

His response was slow, deliberate, the way he always was when he needed to think through his words carefully. "We are everything," he murmured into her hair, his voice low and steady. His hand resumed its movement, playing with the strands, the rhythm almost hypnotic. "We are what I've been wanting. What I've been waiting for."

Grace felt her heart skip a beat. She lifted her head, meeting his eyes, her brow furrowing slightly. He didn't often express himself this openly — this raw — and the vulnerability in his words left her speechless for a moment. Caleb, the man who was always so in control, was here, in this quiet space with her, giving her something more than his strength — he was offering his heart, his trust.

"I've never been good at this," he continued, his fingers grazing the back of her neck. "At letting go. At letting someone in."

She reached up, placing a hand over his where it rested on her shoulder, grounding herself in the moment. "I know," she said, her voice barely above a whisper. "I've always been the same. Keeping everything inside, trying to control it all. But with you…" She trailed off as she searched for the words.

"With me, you don't have to," he finished for her, his gaze never leaving hers. There was a warmth in his eyes, something deeper than she'd ever seen before. The way he looked at her now, there was no mask, no distance. Just him. The real him.

She took a deep breath, exhaling slowly, the weight of his words settling around her like a warm blanket. It was strange, but for the first time in so long, she felt a sense of peace. Not the fleeting kind that came from being alone or burying herself in her work, but the kind that came from knowing she didn't have to carry it all on her own anymore. He was here. And he was with her.

"I can't believe how much I've needed this," she said softly, lifting her hand to rest on his chest. "You." She paused, her thumb tracing the hard planes of his shirt. "I never realized how much I needed you until now."

He let out a breath, as if he was exhaling some unspoken tension he hadn't even known he was holding. His hand slid to her shoulder, massaging gently, his thumb pressing into the soft muscles. "I've been here, Grace," he said, his voice steady but with an undertone of something tender, something true. "Waiting for you to realize it."

She could feel the weight of that statement, the way he had always been there for her in ways she couldn't see — protecting her, guiding her, keeping her grounded when the world felt out of control. And now, in this moment, she could see it clearly. Caleb wasn't just here because of duty or obligation. He was here because, despite everything, he had chosen her. He had chosen this. Chosen them.

She closed her eyes, the overwhelming tenderness of the moment almost too much to bear. "I'm not used to this," she admitted quietly. "Not used to needing anyone. To letting anyone take care of me."

Caleb's lips brushed her temple gently. "You don't have to be used to it," he murmured, his words a promise. "You just have to let me in."

The simplicity of it hit her harder than anything. She didn't have to fight anymore. She didn't have to stand alone. She could just be. With him.

She shifted, lifting her face to his, her gaze soft and searching. "You're in... and you can stay with me as long as you want."

His expression softened, his lips curling into a small, almost imperceptible smile. "Forever sound good?"

Her heart fluttered, and for the first time in so long, she felt herself let go completely. She didn't need to be in charge, didn't need to have it all figured out. With him, she could surrender. She could trust.

Caleb pulled her in closer, wrapping his arm around her as he continued to massage her shoulders, his presence filling the space between them. "I've got you, girl," he said. "Don't forget that."

And as she melted into his embrace, she realized that for the first time in a long time, she had no need to question where she was, or what came next.

* * * *

Election day

The soft light of dawn filtered through the tall windows of the lake house, casting a warm glow across the room. Caleb stirred first, his eyes fluttering open as he shifted slightly, his arm still draped protectively around Grace. He felt the weight of the day settling on his shoulders before he even fully woke — the day they had been working toward for months, the day that would determine the future of their country.

Grace was still asleep, her head resting on his chest, her breathing slow and steady. Caleb allowed himself to simply watch her, the way the morning light danced across her face, highlighting the soft curves of her features. There was a peace about her in this moment, something serene and unburdened by the world outside. And yet, he knew that today would change everything.

He gently brushed a strand of hair away from her forehead, careful not to wake her, but the soft touch was enough to stir her. Grace blinked awake, her eyelids heavy, as she slowly came back to the present. When her gaze met his, she smiled softly, a small, tired curve of her lips.

"Morning," she said.

"Morning," Caleb replied, his voice rougher than usual, weighed down by the gravity of the day. "You ready for today?"

She stretched slightly, pushing herself up to look at him, her eyes still sleepy but focused. "I don't know if 'ready' is the word I'd use," she said, a quiet chuckle in her voice. "But I don't think I have much of a choice."

Caleb smiled, the edges of his mouth twitching upward. He ran his hand over her back, his touch reassuring. "You've got this. You've been preparing for this moment your entire life."

Her eyes softened, and for a moment, she didn't say anything. Just took in the comfort of being close to him, of knowing he was there. But then the reality of what lay ahead took hold, and her expression shifted. "I can't believe it's finally here. Everything we've been working for... It feels like it's all happening so fast."

"I know," Caleb replied, his tone serious, though he didn't break eye contact. "But we're in this together. Whatever happens today...we face it side by side."

Grace exhaled, her gaze softening as she took in his words. She shifted closer to him, laying her head against his chest again. "You make it easier, you know that?"

Caleb's heart quickened at her words, a tight knot forming in his chest. She had always been so strong, so focused, never showing the cracks of vulnerability that threatened to break through. But here, with him, she was more than just the fierce political strategist the world saw. She was someone he could protect, someone who trusted him with parts of her that no one else had seen.

"I mean it, Grace," he murmured, his hand moving to her back once again, rubbing soothing circles. "I'll do whatever it takes to keep you safe, to make sure you're okay."

She lifted her head slightly to look at him, her gaze intense and steady. "I know you will."

For a moment, there was a silence between them, filled only by the sound of the fire crackling in the other room. Caleb's mind raced with the day's enormity — the weight of the election, the stakes of the campaign, the pressure on Grace to win. And yet, here, in this moment, it was just the two of them, connected in a way that no one else could understand.

"You don't have to do this alone," Caleb continued, his voice low and certain. "I'm here. I always will be."

She nodded, leaning into him again, letting her breath even out. "I know. And I'm grateful for that... More than you'll ever know."

He kissed the top of her head, holding her tighter. "No matter what happens today, Grace... I'm proud of you. Proud of everything you've done."

She smiled, her lips pressing against his chest. "And I'm proud of you. For all the ways you've kept me grounded, for always being the steady force I needed, even when I fought against it."

Caleb chuckled softly, the sound rich and deep in the quiet of the morning. "You're hard to keep up with."

Grace grinned and sat up, stretching her arms over her head. "And you love it."

The tension that had settled in his chest eased as he watched her, her strength, her quiet resolve. They weren't just facing the election together today. They were facing the rest of their lives—no matter the outcome.

She turned to look at him, her eyes catching his. "I think it's time, huh?" she asked, the weight of the question evident in her gaze.

Caleb nodded, his jaw tightening with determination. "Yeah. Time to see this through."

They both stood at the same time, the reality of the day hitting them both like a wave. Caleb placed a hand on her back, guiding her toward the door.

"Let's do this," he said, his voice low and commanding.

Grace nodded.

The two of them, united by everything they had faced together, walked out of the bedroom and toward the lake house door.

They were ready.

Together.

Chapter Seventeen

The election had been won — President Armstrong had secured a second term — but the cost had been steep. There were still lingering questions about the recent assassination attempt, and the nation was divided.

The air in the Oval Office was thick with tension as Wyatt, Duke and Caleb stood around the president's desk, debating security measures for his victory speech.

Wyatt, ever the pragmatist, cleared his throat. "Sir, I know you're ready to address the nation, but after everything — especially the attack — it might be wise to hold off on a public appearance for a few more days. We haven't even fully identified all the parties involved in the assassination attempt. We need time to contain this."

Duke stood with his arms crossed, his jaw tight. "Wyatt's right, Mr. President. There's no need to rush out there. The press conference can be closed-door only. We can get everyone through security first."

Caleb, leaning casually against the wall, looked over at Grace, who stood near the window, her face pensive but resolute. He glanced back at the president. "Let the man do what he wants. He didn't get to the White House by hiding. You know that."

President Armstrong, standing by his desk, stiffened at the suggestion of hiding. His face, usually so stoic, now burned with that unmistakable fire that had carried him through the campaign. His hand gripped the back of the chair, knuckles white.

"No," Armstrong said, his voice low, simmering with determination. "To hell with that. I'm not hiding."

Wyatt grumbled, but before he could speak out, Armstrong was already striding toward the door. "I've had enough of this," the president muttered, shaking his head. "Enough of letting them control the narrative. They tried to take me out, but I'm still standing. And they'll know it."

Duke didn't even flinch at the president's defiance. He'd seen this side of Armstrong before—unyielding and brash. Caleb exchanged a quick look with Grace, the faintest grin tugging at his lips. Grace's eyes flicked to Caleb, her lips curving upward in agreement.

"He's going out there," Caleb murmured under his breath, his voice filled with a quiet excitement.

"Better get ready, then," Grace replied with a knowing smile, crossing her arms.

The president strode to the door, turning back to face the group. "I'll do it my way." His voice was steel, unbreakable.

Wyatt and Duke followed as Armstrong marched down the hall, his heavy steps echoing in the silence. Caleb remained behind, nodding toward Grace with a mischievous gleam in his eyes. "Let's see how this goes."

The lawn was already buzzing with energy, reporters and cameras set in place as they prepared to hear Armstrong speak. As requested, the lawn was open to members of the public. There were thousands there.

The moment the president walked to the microphone, the lawn fell into a hush.

"Today we stand united," he bellowed into the microphone, his voice cutting through the air like a bolt of lightning. "Today, we are reaffirming our commitment to the principles of freedom, justice, and equality that define our great nation. Together, we will build a future where every citizen has the opportunity to thrive, where human rights are protected, and where our democracy remains a shining beacon of hope for the world."

The words hung in the air, the bluntness of it shaking the press. And then—without warning—the reporters erupted in applause, a standing ovation ringing out in the press pit.

Duke grinned and, unable to resist, stood up and clapped. "Damn right, Mr. President," he shouted over the roar. Grace's laugh was full of admiration as she joined in, clapping harder than anyone else. She looked over at Caleb, her eyes sparkling with approval.

"That's our guy," Caleb said, his grin broadening as the applause continued.

For the first time in days, Armstrong allowed himself to bask in the moment. He stood tall at the podium, watching the press and the country react, letting the wild energy wash over him. This was his fight, and he wasn't going to let anyone forget it.

"My fellow Americans," Armstrong continued, his voice now calm, yet brimming with authority, "Today I address you with a resolute spirit, undeterred by the challenges we face. Some may have attempted to undermine us, but they have failed. Our nation's foundation is rooted in the principles of freedom, principles that we defend relentlessly. We pay homage to the brave souls who have sacrificed everything for our country, and we carry their legacy forward. To those who seek to sow division among us, hear this: you will not break us, you will not defeat us. We are America, a nation of strength and liberty, and we will fight for our values at any cost. I extend my gratitude to you all, and may God bless you and bless the United States of America."

The crowd cheered. The president had spoken. And the nation would hear it loud and clear. This country was about bravery and freedom — even in the face of threat.

In a simple, unspoken gesture, Grace reached for Caleb's hand. It was a small thing, but in that moment, it felt like everything had changed. Her fingers threaded through his, the warmth of her touch grounding him in a way he hadn't realized he needed. The weight of their journey, the struggles, the highs, and the lows — they had endured them all. But now, with her hand in his, it was clear. They were a team, not just in the chaos of politics, but in life.

As the press conference wound down and the crowd began to scatter, Grace stood near the edge of the White House lawn, trying to take it all in. The sky was soft with evening light, the air charged with that lingering hum of excitement after a monumental victory. She could still hear echoes of cheering in the distance. She felt lighter than she had in months.

Caleb stood beside her, a quiet pillar of strength at her shoulder. He didn't say much, just rested a hand near her arm, his presence calm and unwavering. They caught one another's gaze, and in that brief look, Grace felt the weight of everything they had endured — every threat, every doubt — pressing and then releasing, as if the tension had finally broken and drifted away.

Before she could say anything, President Armstrong approached, his usual commanding stride softened by real gratitude. She straightened unconsciously, old habits of respect and duty kicking in, but this time there was genuine warmth in her heart, too. They had forged something more than just a working relationship — there was understanding here, built on shared struggle.

"Mr. President," she greeted him quietly, inclining her head. Caleb nodded at his side, respectful and steady as always.

Armstrong's smile reached his eyes. "Grace, Caleb — I wanted to thank you, personally. I wouldn't be standing here if it weren't for your sacrifices, your dedication."

Grace felt a flutter in her chest at the sincerity in his voice. She knew this was no hollow praise. They had held the line when everything was at stake.

Armstrong's gaze moved between them before settling back on Grace. "You've both been through hell. I owe you. And I promise — I won't let what happened go unpunished. I'm going after the people who tried to tear us apart. Marisol and her allies... they'll face justice."

Her throat tightened at the conviction in his words. She saw Caleb's jaw set, a grim satisfaction there. Grace remembered the terror, the danger they had survived — and now the president was vowing to avenge it, to set things right.

"We'll stop her," Grace said softly, meeting Armstrong's eyes. "We'll all make sure of that."

He nodded, a hard edge to his determination. "No one pulls this kind of stunt under my watch." Then his expression gentled. "You two, get some rest. You've earned it. And don't forget to invite me to the wedding." He winked, leaving them both speechless for a beat, then strode off, blending back into the swirl of staff and supporters.

Grace turned toward Caleb, a flush on her cheeks at the president's last remark. But Caleb didn't tease. Instead, he took her hand and gently guided her away from the lingering crowds, leading her over the damp fall grass until they found a quieter corner of the lawn, half-hidden by foliage. It was peaceful there, away from the bright lights and the buzzing victory celebration.

The silence between them felt warm, charged with a thousand unsaid things. Grace could feel Caleb's heartbeat in the way he held her hand, steady and strong. When they stopped, he turned her so she was facing him. She looked up, meeting those dark, intense eyes that had so often seen her at her worst and never once wavered.

Her heart pounded. The campaign was over. The war they'd fought in secret corridors and dangerous fields was done. And now?

Caleb's hand drifted to her wrist, fingers gentle but sure, and he pulled her close, pressing her back against his chest. She relaxed into him, feeling his warmth and the firmness of his body. The scent of damp leaves and fresh grass surrounded them, and the distant hum of laughter and conversation at the White House gradually faded to background noise.

"Caleb?" she asked softly, her voice barely more than a whisper. She felt the tension in him, that he was on the brink of something big, something that would change everything.

He inhaled, and she could feel the rise and fall of his chest against her shoulders. "I've watched you," he began, voice rough with emotion she'd rarely heard from him. "I've watched how you fight, how you care, how you never back down. You've made me believe in things I never thought I would. You've changed me, Grace."

Her breath caught, tears pricking at the corners of her eyes. No one had ever said words like these to her, no one had ever valued her beyond her performance, her intellect, her resolve. Yet here he was, baring himself in the quiet darkness.

She turned slightly in his arms to see his face, and he didn't pull away. She saw sincerity in every line, every soft breath he took.

"Caleb," she managed, voice trembling. "I've never let myself depend on anyone. I never thought I needed to. But with you…" Her throat tightened. "With you, I don't have to be strong all the time. I can just… be."

His eyes glistened in the dim light, and he cradled her face in one hand, his thumb brushing gently over her cheek. "Girl, I'm better with you. And I know the world's still a mess, and we've got scores to settle, but right now — I want you to know how I feel."

She swallowed hard, heart thudding. "I love you," she whispered, voice cracking on the admission. "I love you, Caleb, and I—"

"Marry me," he said, cutting gently through her words. His voice was warm, steadfast. "Marry me, Grace. Let's stop waiting for perfect times or perfect circumstances. Let's do this, together."

She froze, the world narrowing down to the man in front of her, the heat of his hand against her skin, the quiet courage in his eyes. He was offering her a future, a promise that went beyond campaigns and crises. He was offering her a home in his heart.

Her lips curved into a teary smile. "Yes," she said, voice steady despite her tears. "Yes, Caleb. Yes, I'll marry you."

He let out a breath, relief and joy flooding his features. She felt him tremble slightly as he leaned in and kissed her—soft, lingering, full of promise. The taste of him, the scent of autumn leaves and the distant hum of celebration, all fused into a perfect moment in time.

They held each other, the chaos of the world at bay. And for once, Grace felt no fear of the future. Only the gentle thrum of love and the certainty that, together, they could face anything.

Sign up for our newsletter and find out about all our romance book releases, eBook sales and promotions, sneak peeks and FREE romance books!

Want to see more from this author?
Here's a taster for you to enjoy!

Secret Service:
The President's Bodyguard
Zoe Normandie

Excerpt

White House, Washington DC.

The East Room felt like a stage where Cassidy Evans was the one person who hadn't memorized her lines. The air buzzed with a polished energy — the clink of glasses, the hum of power, and the subtle sway of people who knew they belonged here. She didn't.

A month into her assignment, Cassidy had thought it would get easier. But it hadn't. In fact, it had only gotten worse. Her colleagues seemed like they were always a step ahead of her, always a step above her. She was the outsider. The one they talked about behind closed doors. The reporter who didn't know how to fit in, how to play the game.

She stumbled through the crowd, clicking of her heels softened by the chatter around her. She needed to get out of here, to disappear into the shadows where she wouldn't be noticed. She found the doorway and slowly backed out of the room. She could feel the night breeze on her back — almost finding freedom.

But fate, it seemed, had other plans.

As she stepped back, and before she could even register the movement, her heel landed right on someone's foot.

"Watch it, Evans." The words were laced with venom, each syllable like a dagger she could feel in her chest.

Duke.

Of course it was Duke.

She barely had time to react before his hand shot out, grabbing her arm with a force that made her skin flare with heat. His fingers tightening around her wrist were like a vice, cold and unyielding. He spun her with effortless force, pulling her just inside the door, out of sight of the others.

"Don't trip," he said, so smooth it made her skin crawl.

"Get off me."

And there she was, cowering in front of Duke Armstrong—tall, broad-shouldered, dark hair, dark eyes, with a crisp black suit that screamed authority, the kind that could only belong to someone in Secret Service. She jerked back instinctively, but it was no use—his grip was steel.

"Still pissed at me?" His tone was mockingly light, almost playful, as if he enjoyed seeing her discomfort. He fed off it, the bastard. His breath was warm against her ear, a whisper of danger that made her pulse race in a way she didn't want to acknowledge.

She stiffened, jaw clenched. "Let go of me."

But Duke only grinned, the same arrogant, knowing smile that made her want to lash out.

Her face flushed as she shook him off her, taking an intentional step away from him. "You think you're winning," she said, her voice hollow. "But I'm done here. I'm done with this whole damn circus."

He raised an eyebrow, amused.

Cassidy didn't let him see her break. She turned but barely made it a few steps before she saw the president marching down the hallway. He was flanked by the usual entourage of assistants, but as he passed by the open doors of the East Room, his eyes flicked over to her. It was a brief glance, but it made her stomach twist.

Before she could look away, the president's gaze lingered, and with a subtle motion, he nodded in Duke's direction. Of course, he was the one the president would call to his side. His loyal servant. *His nephew.*

Duke immediately turned to follow. His smile slipped, his gaze hardening — issuing an unsaid warning. It was there in the way his jaw clenched, the way his eyes narrowed.

Cassidy stood there for a moment, feeling her heart slam against her chest. Duke moved to the president's side, falling in line with the others as they continued their path down the hallway.

The sound of her own breathing was the loudest thing in her ears as she turned on her heel, her mind a blur. She didn't want to make a scene. She didn't want anyone to see the unraveling thread that was her composure.

She couldn't stay here. Not like this. Not anymore.

The lies, the games, the endless humiliation. It had been months of Duke toying with her — giving her fake names, twisting the truth, and then watching her crumble as she tried to keep up with him. Duke was always one step ahead, always the one in control. And she? She was just the joke.

As she moved toward the patio doors, she caught the eye of a young staffer standing nearby. The girl's expression was anxious, a slight tremor in her voice as she said, "You're not supposed to go out there alone."

Cassidy didn't stop. Didn't even slow down. She waved the girl off without a word, her heels clicking sharply on the marble as she slipped through the door and into the evening air.

The cool breeze hit her like a rush of relief, sharp and refreshing after the stifling heat inside. For a moment, she just stood there, inhaling deeply, trying to fill her lungs with something other than the suffocating atmosphere of the East Room. The tension in her chest eased just a little, the air outside tasting almost sweet in comparison to the chaos she'd just escaped.

She didn't look back. She couldn't. She wouldn't.

The gardens lay ahead, a quiet refuge, and beyond that, the side exit where the press buses waited. She had to get there, away from this place, away from Duke and the White House circus.

But as she rounded the corner, her steps faltered.

There, leaning casually against the marble columns, was Congressman Richard West. The faint glow of a cigar dangled from his fingers, the smoke swirling lazily around him. He took a slow drag, exhaling through his nose, eyes half-lidded in a lazy, predatory way. She recognized him immediately — her editor had warned her about him, told her to steer clear at all costs. West was infamous for his reckless behavior, the kind of man who thought he could get away with anything when he had a drink in him. He was a predator in a suit.

She froze, debating whether to turn and go back inside. But it was too late.

"Look who it is," West slurred, his voice dripping with a mix of condescension and amusement. "Little lost lamb wandering out here all alone." He took another drag of the cigar and flicked the ash onto the gravel at his feet. "Shouldn't be finding you out here."

Her pulse spiked, but she kept her posture straight, her voice even. "I'm just getting some air, sir," she said, standing her ground, though the pit in her stomach was growing. She had heard enough stories to know what kind of man he was, and she'd seen how he treated people he thought were beneath him.

West's lazy grin spread wider. "I read your article. Got it all wrong, didn't you? You don't know a damn thing about this place or people like me."

Her heart raced, but she forced herself to stay calm. She wouldn't let him bait her. "I think you've had too much to drink," she said, taking a small step back, trying to distance herself. Her heel slipped slightly, but she regained her balance, her grip tightening on the champagne glass still in her hand.

West chuckled low, the sound crawling under her skin like a bad omen. "You think you're so clever, don't you?" His voice oozed disdain as he took a step toward her. "You're just a girl playing dress-up, trying to fit in with all the big boys. But you don't know your place."

Cassidy's gaze hardened. "I'm not here to learn it from you," she shot back.

His grin vanished, replaced with something much darker. His eyes narrowed, and his posture shifted — suddenly more aggressive, unsteady but purposeful. He took another step toward her, his breath heavy with alcohol and cigar smoke. "Don't talk back to me, little girl. You might want to show some respect."

Before she could react, his hand shot out, grabbing her wrist with startling force. The pressure of his grip made her wince, and her heart jolted with fear.

"Let go of me," she said, low but firm, the warning clear.

West's grin returned, wider now, as if he were enjoying the game. "I think it's time you learned a lesson." His fingers tightened around her wrist, pulling her a little closer, his breath rancid against her skin.

The anger inside Cassidy flared, but there was a knot in her chest that told her this wasn't just a game anymore. She had no one to rely on — but herself.

And this man had underestimated her.

With a burst of adrenaline, Cassidy twisted her wrist, using his own forward momentum against him. Her heel dug into the gravel as she slammed her elbow into his ribs with all the force she could muster. West gasped, stumbling back in surprise, giving her the space she needed to break free. He tried grabbing her again — but she kicked him right in the groin. Hard. Heart pounding, she ran, the hem of her dress catching on her knees as she darted down the shadowed path. She didn't dare look back, her only thought to get away.

All she could hear was his angry grunting behind her.

You can't scream, she told herself. *Don't make a scene. Don't prove them right.*

The lights of the East Room flickered faintly in the distance, but Cassidy turned away from them, plunging deeper into the gardens. She didn't stop running until her lungs burned, until the shadows of the towering trees seemed to swallow her whole.

When she finally stopped, she leaned against a cold marble bench. Her chest heaved, her pulse hammering against her ribs.

She was alone in the dark, trembling, and furious. At him. At herself.

This wasn't the story she had come to tell.

Cassidy's breath came in ragged gasps as she leaned against the bench. Her fingers trembled, her pulse thundering in her ears, when she heard the crunch of footsteps on the path again.

"You little—" Congressman West boomed, closer than she expected. "Where the hell are you?"

Cassidy froze, her heart lurching. He was coming after her.

She stumbled forward, her heels sinking into the soft earth. Her hands fumbled to hitch her dress higher, her movements desperate and clumsy. She tripped on a rock and tumbled down, breaking her fall with the palms of her hands. Crying out, she pushed herself up and kept going. The glow of the White House seemed impossibly far away, the faint hum of laughter and music drowned out by the angry curses of the man chasing her.

"You think you can hit me?" he yelled, slurred with rage. "This isn't over."

Cassidy bit back the whimper threatening to escape her throat. She didn't want to give him the satisfaction of hearing her panic. As she ran, she scanned the shadowed gardens, searching for anywhere to hide, when the faint outline of a row of SUVs came into view.

Security detail. They must have been parked on the far edge of the grounds, barely visible in the darkness.

Her shoes slipped as she darted toward the line of vehicles, her breath hitching as the sound of his footsteps grew louder. *Don't stop. Don't think. Just go.*

She dropped low behind the nearest SUV, her knees scraping against the gravel as she crouched in the shadows. Her lungs burned, the cold air cutting into her throat. She tried to quiet her breathing, to shrink herself into the smallest possible space, but she could hear him, his heavy footfalls slowing as he searched.

"You can't hide from me," he called, his voice jagged and raw. "Come out, and maybe I won't make this worse for you."

Cassidy's chest tightened. She peered under the SUV, her stomach twisting as she saw his dark silhouette pacing closer.

Her options dwindled. If he found her crouched here, it would be over.

No, she thought. *Not here. Not like this.*

Before she could talk herself out of it, she reached for the SUV's door handle. It clicked open, quieter than she'd expected, but her stomach dropped at the faint beep that followed. She froze, waiting for him to hear it.

"What the hell was that?" he muttered.

Cassidy swallowed her fear and slipped inside, her hands trembling as she pulled the door shut as silently as possible. The interior of the SUV was dark, the smell of leather strong and oddly comforting. She pressed herself into the far corner of the seat, curling up her legs as she tried to disappear into the shadows.

Outside, Congressman West's footsteps drew nearer. She could see his shape through the tinted windows, his movements erratic as he scanned the area.

He lingered there for a moment, breathing heavily, his anger radiating even through the thick glass. Then, with a frustrated grunt, he moved on, his footsteps fading into the distance.

Cassidy didn't move. She stayed curled in the corner, her breath shallow, her body shaking.

Minutes passed, or maybe it was seconds—she couldn't tell. When the silence stretched long enough to convince her he was gone, she allowed herself to exhale, the sound shaky and raw.

But before she could plan her next move, the click of a car door startled her. Cassidy's head snapped up as the opposite door opened, and a man climbed into the SUV's driver's seat.

He wasn't her pursuer. He was tall and broad-shouldered, dressed in a crisp black suit that marked him as Secret Service. And she knew exactly who he was — his slicked back dark hair unmistakable.

Oh no. Oh no, no, no.

The SUV rumbled to life, the low growl of the engine vibrating through the seat beneath Cassidy. Her head shot up, heart hammering in her chest as she realized they were now driving away from the gardens.

She pressed herself lower in the shadows of the back seat, praying he wouldn't glance in the rearview mirror. The last thing she needed was to be caught here, looking like a wreck, and by him of all people.

Duke.

The name alone made her stomach twist.

And now here she was, crouched in the back of his SUV like an idiot, her dress torn at the hem and her palms still stinging from where she'd scraped them on the gravel during her escape.

If he found her…

She squeezed her eyes shut, already imagining the disdain that would harden his sharp features. He'd probably toss her out without a word, disgusted by the very idea of her being here.

The SUV rolled to a smooth stop, and Cassidy held her breath as he spoke into his radio, his voice low and clipped.

"Unit three, I'm heading back to the northwest entrance. Report any movement in the gardens."

Her heart sank. He must've been sent to patrol the grounds after her little escapade. Of course he had. Of all the agents who could have found her, it had to be Duke Armstrong, the man least likely to cut her a shred of slack.

The vehicle eased forward again, the dark gardens slipping past the windows. Cassidy's mind raced. Should she wait until he stopped and try to sneak out unnoticed? Should she confess now and try to explain herself?

Neither option seemed good.

Then Duke's voice startled her out of her thoughts. "You're awfully quiet back there."

Cassidy froze, her breath catching. Had he seen her reflection in the rearview mirror? She stayed perfectly still, her heart pounding so loudly she was certain he'd hear it.

The SUV rolled to a stop again, and she heard the creak of his seat as he turned. "If you're going to hide, at least be better at it."

Her stomach dropped.

Slowly, she straightened, the shadows peeling away from her as she sat upright. Their eyes met in the rearview mirror, his sharp gaze locking on hers with an intensity that made her shiver.

"Evans," he said flatly, his tone devoid of surprise but dripping with disapproval. "Stowing away in my truck?"

She swallowed hard. "It's not what it looks like."

"Really?" His brow lifted, his expression as unreadable as stone. "Because it looks like you broke protocol, wandered into a restricted area, and snuck into my vehicle...for what? I don't think I want to know."

"This has nothing to do with you." Her cheeks burned. "I wasn't sneaking—I was…escaping."

"Escaping," he repeated, his tone incredulous. "From what?"

She hesitated, torn between telling him the truth and trying to downplay the situation. "I just needed to get away," she said finally, her voice quiet.

His gaze flicked to her torn dress and bloody hands, his lips tightening in a way that made her want to sink into the floor.

He sighed, a heavy sound filled with frustration. "If you were anyone else, you'd already be detained for questioning."

"I didn't mean to cause trouble," she said quickly. "I was just—"

"Trouble seems to follow you, doesn't it?" he cut in sharply.

The words hit harder than she expected, and Cassidy clenched her fists in her lap, hating the way her throat tightened. He didn't even know the half of it, but he didn't have to. He'd already made up his mind about her.

Duke turned back toward the front, his hands gripping the wheel as he muttered something under his breath she couldn't catch. The SUV began moving again, the tense silence thick between them.

Cassidy bit her lip, staring at the back of his head. She wanted to defend herself, to explain everything, but what good would it do? He wouldn't believe her. To him, she'd always be the naive reporter who didn't belong in the big leagues.

But she wasn't going to give him the satisfaction of breaking down. Not tonight.

Not ever.

About the Author

A little snapshot on who is Zoe Normandie…

After ten years working with the police and attending a military university, I weave stories filled with danger, heart, and the grit of those who serve. An army brat, I grew up on military bases across the country, giving me front-row seat to the world of duty and sacrifice. With a veteran husband, my passion for writing military-themed romance, suspense, and mystery is rooted in real-world experience, supporting him through every mission.

Zoe loves to hear from readers. You can find her contact information, website details and author profile page at https://www.firstforromance.com

ENTWINED PUBLISHING